REBORN

THE ROYAL PACK TRILOGY: BOOK 1

ANNE K. WHELAN

LIZ CAIN

CLAN WHELAN
PUBLISHING

Cover design by MiblArt

Who wants to fit in? Normal is overrated anyway.
Liz Cain

Do not overthink, just do it.
Anne K. Whelan

PROLOGUE

Nyko looked down at the woman he carried, her eyes closed; dirt covered her oval-shaped face, her lips were so pale you could barely see them. She wore a thin tank top and canvas shorts, which did nothing to cover the myriad of purple and yellow bruises marring her body.

His development had always been slow. Even now, in his late teens, it still disturbed him. Ridiculed for his youthful appearance and weakness, he felt like an outcast—until his master had taken him under his wing.

He struggled with his precious cargo, putting one foot in front of the other. Darkness still covering his presence as he approached a sleepy town that he'd walked through the night to reach. Exhaustion pulled at him as he carried the still form further from their home. He was used to heavy loads, the manual work in the town he grew up in was challenging and kept him fit, but he had never hauled anything this far before.

The forest around them was thick, but his superior night

vision stopped him from tripping on the roots and rocks dotted on the ground. He could see a light in the distance as the sun tried to break into the sky. He didn't have long to deposit the body and return home. His master instructed him to leave her far from the settlement, but he risked being caught with the approaching daylight and his proximity to this town.

Nyko never dared to defy his master and struggled to hide his shock at the situation, but a swift blow to the side of the head had motivated him to obey. As he walked, her body grew cold, and he felt the life drain from her. She was assumed dead, but Nyko wasn't so sure. He might not always agree with her methods, but he hadn't wanted to hurt her. So, when he was instructed to dispose of the body, Nyko couldn't just leave her alone in the woods.

His arms ached after hours without rest, but it wasn't much further. Finally, the trees started to thin, the smell of pine now overpowered by the foreign stench of the town. As he entered a clearing, Nyko could see the back of a building ahead. The white wall peeked through the trees, and the sound of vehicles hummed from a nearby road as early morning traffic passed by.

Gently, Nyko placed the woman down on a patch of moss and leaves. The smell of a rotten tree trunk nearby flooded his nose. As he crouched, his legs screamed in protest. Her black hair fell across her face, and Nyko lifted a hand to brush it back. Her skin was like ice, and she didn't move.

Nyko swallowed tightly as tears stung his eyes. She looked peacefully asleep. As he straightened, he looked towards the building and hoped someone would find her soon so she could be laid to rest with the respect she deserved. Despite his fatigue, he knew he would have to be quick to get back to his master. He allowed himself one last look at the still form before him.

"I'm sorry," Nyko whispered before he jogged back into the darkness and safety of the trees.

1

___

Her eyes were closed, but she could smell trees and rotting wood nearby. The scents of the forest comforted her at first but were unfamiliar. This was not her home, and that thought caused her heart to stop and her grogginess to disappear. Panic engulfed her as she squeezed her eyes tighter, not daring to look around. The ground beneath her felt cold; moss tickled her arms, and the smell of earth was close to her nose. Pain shot through her head when she started to stir, so she stayed still, not daring to open her eyes. Paralyzed, she lay there and listened. She could feel the soft light of dawn gently caressing her face, then unfamiliar noises broke the silence around her.

She could hear the chirp of birds in the distance and creatures moving in the undergrowth. A noise close to her head shocked her into movement, and she jumped back too quickly. One moment she was laid on the ground; the next, she was crouched near an old tree stump. Leaves scattered as she moved, while the squirrel that startled her ran from where she had been unconscious. The swift way she moved and opened her eyes was a mistake. Nausea and dizziness threatened to overtake her as she swayed in her crouched position. The light hurt her eyes, and her surroundings flooded her senses like a jumble of blurred images, sounds, and smells. Her breath came in short, rapid gulps.

She looked down at herself, she wore a simple tank top and canvas shorts. She didn't feel cold despite moisture beading on her skin from the morning dew. She tried to take a deep breath but failed. Black splotches spread through the edge of her vision, and she tried to steady herself. She didn't recognize where she was; nothing was familiar. Panic seized her, and she sat hard on the ground. Her mind felt like fog—she didn't know who or where she was. Frantic, her head snapped in every direction, desperate for anything she recognized.

Her mind felt blank, with ghosts of memories at the edge but outside her grasp. Pain crept into her senses as she moved her arms. She looked down to faded purple-tinged bruises that lined her limbs. She put her hand over one on her arm and saw it resembled the shape of her fingers but much larger.

Eyes closed, she willed herself to be anywhere but here. When she opened them again, nothing had changed. She could see a building through the trees just beyond the clearing. The loud revving of an engine made her body jolt as she looked through to a path; when the engine stopped, she could hear loud voices. As the sound echoed through her head, there was a sharp pain behind her eyes. She closed her eyes against it and crouched to make herself small.

"Hey, Phil! You're not usually up this early!" A man's voice carried to the forest, followed by a second man's voice. When the voices didn't come closer, she opened her eyes again. Her breath had slowed, but the panic had not gone. They didn't seem to know she was here, but she knew she couldn't stay. Curious, she crept closer, her movements stealthy so as not to make a sound but leaves still ruffled some as she approached the edge of the trees. There was a large, moss-covered tree near the entrance to the path. She ducked to hide behind it and looked to see where the voices came from. Did she know these men? She didn't know and couldn't trust anything right now, not even herself. How could she not remember who she was? She pushed the thought away as she listened.

"Deliveries, and the usual kid's on vacation with his parents," a large man grunted. He was heavily built, wearing blue coveralls that were scruffy, but mostly clean. He had broad shoulders and looked like he could easily lift a person as he leaned over to pick up the large boxes from the back of a truck. The truck was parked in an area around the back of a white building.

"Shit, they sure do pack this heavy," the man grumbled. He set the box on the ground and reached into his pocket to pull out a single key.

The woman watched, frozen, as he entered the building. It appeared old, with huge glass windows that surrounded the front and sides. Her eyes felt less pain as they adjusted to the light, and she caught the words "Phil's Diner" in huge, faded red letters on a white background at the top of the building. She hugged closer to the tree, confused and unsure. The rough bark scraped her bare arms, a dull pain against her bruises reminding her that she wasn't in a particularly good position right now. What should she do? Leave before they saw her? Ask for help?

Her hesitation cost her, as the large man turned back and spotted her looking out behind the tree. He froze and squinted his eyes with his hand raised against the sun to get a better look. Fear gripped the woman as she frantically turned to run. Her legs had other ideas and collapsed beneath her; she hit the ground hard. Whatever she had been through had left her in rough shape; her energy felt drained. When she struck the ground, the pain in her head intensified, and she cried out as it shot through her entire body. Loud footsteps approached from behind, and she scrambled away.

"Jesus Christ! She's barely wearing anything. Stu—go grab my sweater from my office. That'll keep her warm," the man croaked as he stared right at her.

"Are ya alright? What happened to ya?" He started to run briskly forward, his large, rough-looking hands outstretched. The woman rolled over to face him, and pain jolted through her as she scrambled back through the dirt and leaves. She left shallow trenches in the ground from her movements, and a fresh pain in her hand indicated she had scratched herself against something rough and sharp. She threw her arms up to shield her head, and the large man stopped. Through the gaps in her arms, she saw him crouch, failing to make himself look small.

"Easy now, I just want to help. What's ya name?"

She could smell maple syrup, meat, and grease on him. His overalls had worn patches on each knee that she hadn't noticed earlier, and his t-shirt was covered in dark stains. She saw a thick tree branch to her left and flung herself towards it. Weapon in hand, she struggled to her feet and leaned to one side with the weight.

"Back!" she stammered as she swayed. Her legs shook from weakness, and she wasn't sure she could stand for long.

"I'm not gonna hurt ya, lady! Uh-oh." Still crouched, he swore in a thick, southern accent. She winced at the sound of his voice; it reverberated through her head, and he lowered his hand slightly.

"Where is this? Who are you?" she croaked, then coughed to clear her throat, not taking her eyes from him. Still, the man did not stand, even as she waved the branch in front of her.

"I'm Phil. What's your name?" His voice was softer when he spoke this time, almost a whisper.

"Aine," she said reflexively, the word clear and immediate in her mind. Had she known that already? She frowned, distracted. Her free hand shot to her head as another sharp pain lanced through her. With her eyes closed, she realized he could have easily overpowered her by now. Sadness flooded her; she was tired and felt weighed down. The branch felt heavy in her hands, and her whole body trembled with the effort of standing.

"Aine?" she said again, now more of a question.

"That's a beautiful name, Aine. Different, though you don't seem sure of it." Phil chuckled and grinned, which revealed a mouthful of yellowed teeth. One was missing and created a gap in the bottom which Aine found surprisingly endearing. His face was soft and his eyes kind.

"This here is my diner. Only one in town, not that there's much of a town," Phil proudly declared and lowered his hands. He pulled a faded license out of his pocket and extended it out to Aine with a steady hand. "This here is my ID. You're welcome to look, tells you that I'm being truthful."

Aine swayed again as she leaned closer to look at the card in the man's hand. She could see a small picture of the man in front of her; her brows scrunched, and she looked back at his face.

Aine switched back and forth between the ID and the man, her eyes sharpening the blurred edges. The hair in the picture was the same frizzy blond that stopped just below his ear; the eyes were just as big and light grey, the slight smile unsure but expressed kindness. His face was rounder in the picture, and he looked younger.

"Your face," Aine said with a frown. "It's...bigger in the little picture?"

Phil laughed nervously and touched his face awkwardly.

"Yep, I cut back on the beers and beef patties. Marianne, just up the road, makes the best Jamaican cuisine if you're hungry, but it wasn't doing my health much good. Doctor warned me if I carried on, I would have health problems."

The thought of food made Aine's stomach churn as she felt hollow. She swayed, dizziness claiming her again, along with another jolt of pain in her head that made her groan. She used her free hand to push her palm into one of her eyes. The pain eased slightly.

"How about we get you inside? You can barely stand, and we won't hurt ya." Phil had lowered his voice to speak softly again.

Stu chose that moment to appear, Aine tensed. He held what looked to be a worn-out, oversized sweater. He skidded to a halt with a red face, breathing labored after running towards Phil with it. Stu flushed when he looked at her and quickly looked away, then shuffled to Phil with his eyes on the ground, nearly falling over in the process. His face became redder, if it was possible, as he awkwardly gave the sweater to his friend.

"I called Abbie and Caroline. She looks banged up, and I thought they could help?" Stu's voice came out high and tense. He looked at the ground again as he clenched and unclenched his hands.

Aine's stomach growled audibly, and the edges of her

vision started to blur again slightly. She took another step back and looked around.

"I need food," she said weakly, her voice still scratchy. When was the last time she ate? The pain in her stomach was severe. Phil motioned behind him with raised brows, Aine was surprised he had heard her.

"I'm sure I've got something I can put together for ya, though if we ain't quick, the morning rush will be here, and I'm not sure you'll appreciate an audience," he said gently. "Stu, you can go, don't need both of us to look after her...and you're making me nervous, let alone poor Aine," he added.

Aine smiled in appreciation; Phil must have realized she felt uneasy with two strange men. They were both bigger than her, and there was no way she would go with them both. Phil reached for Aine's hand, the one with the branch, but stopped when she stepped back. He looked slightly comical, half-leaned towards her and half-backed away.

"You won't need that, I won't hurt ya. Stu is going...or you can bring it with ya if it makes ya feel better," he added hastily and moved away when Aine gripped the branch harder and raised it like a baseball bat.

Stu had disappeared quickly and started his truck. The engine's rumble was loud, and Aine held her hand to her head as the noise rose, then quieted as Stu drove away. Phil dropped the dark blue sweater in front of her, throwing it slightly so he didn't have to come closer, then took a couple more steps back. It made a soft thud when it hit the ground.

"Put that sweater on. Ya must be freezing."

She poked the sweater with a branch and dragged the material closer.

"What is it?" Aine questioned with a frown.

Phil laughed when she tilted her head to one side and scrunched her face up at the sweater. "It's a sweater. You put it on over ya head, it'll be big on ya, but it'll keep ya warm till I find you something better." He leaned against a tree and kept his distance.

Aine's eyes never left Phil as she stretched forward and snatched the sweater up with her free hand. Leaves fell from the garment as she held it to her chest. It took several minutes for Aine to put the sweater on; she wouldn't let go of the branch and each time she tried, she nearly fell over. Phil tried to hide a smile as he patiently watched. Aine scowled at him each time he dared to laugh, which made him laugh harder while trying to hide it with his hand over his mouth.

Once she was dressed, the soft material felt strange on her skin, like she had never worn anything like it. The warmth surrounded her, and she sighed. The sweater smelled woodsy and sweet like the man who stood before her. Phil started to walk towards the building, eyeing her warily like an animal about to bolt. He glanced back occasionally to make sure she was still there.

"I'm going to make some food for ya. Come down when you're ready." His figure disappeared through the trees, and Aine found herself suddenly alone.

Aine sighed. Should she follow him? The man seemed kind and hadn't been aggressive in any way. There were times he could have overpowered her, and he'd waited patiently for her to put the sweater on. But how could she trust him when she didn't even know who she was or what she was doing here?

Her eyes stung as she tried to remember; a single tear fell down her cheek. Despair swept through her as she lifted her free hand to her face and looked behind her into the depth of the woods. Where had she come from? She took a deep breath; if she was to find out, she needed help. Determination slowly filled her chest. Enough was enough. She held the thick tree branch tight against her; it gave her some measure of comfort though she wasn't sure it would do much good.

Aine hesitantly took a step forward, then another. She craned her neck to see where Phil had gone, but he was nowhere in sight. She stumbled after him with her branch and paused before she entered the building. With nowhere else to go, she took one last look around and opened the door.

AINE LOOKED around the dark interior; the inside was shabby but clean. She then walked into a bright kitchen area with white walls and sizeable shiny steel cooking equipment. A light flicked on ahead of her and she heard Phil's shoes scuff the floor. She walked towards the light and blinked as all the booths and tables lit up in the large room through the doorway.

There were black and white pictures on every wall with men wearing hats, riding horses, or standing next to them. Aine liked horses—or at least she thought she did. They were such elegant creatures with power and grace in every movement. But, in contrast to these gentle creatures, the men held large rifles in their hands or balanced them across shoulders.

The booths lined the right-hand side, and a breakfast bar was positioned opposite, with red stools pulled up. The booths were set next to large glass windows which looked out onto a deserted road and the small town. The atmosphere was cozy, with spotlights dotted around the ceiling. As Aine looked towards the ceiling, she could see that different colored squares covered it in a giant patchwork pattern, each with a distinct symbol and name across it.

"What are those?" Aine exclaimed and pointed upwards, openly staring at the intricate pattern. The branch, still held firmly in her other hand, dragged on the floor. Phil looked up and smiled proudly at his unique decorations. He took a step towards Aine but paused when she flinched back. She walked around the edge of the room and stood next to the main entrance, as far from him as she could get.

"Coasters. Took me years to collect them. I've never traveled, so I mainly found them on the internet. I know it's small, but it's mine, built it up from scratch. My parents said I'd never amount to anything but here I am," he answered in his rough voice, full of emotion as he walked behind the breakfast bar. "Take a seat; I'll be right out – what do ya like?"

"I......I don't know," Aine answered meekly. She sat at the bar and looked inquisitively at the coffee machine on the counter.

Phil watched as she winced with each movement; her body felt heavy, and everything took a lot of effort. The man smiled sympathetically and trudged back into the kitchen. Aine sighed as he left and listened as he clattered around within.

She looked down at herself. The sweater felt warm and covered her bruised and tired body, stopping just above her knees. Aine lifted the sleeve to her nose to inhale deeply. It wasn't dirty, but she felt it had recently been worn. Other smells came to her as she waited, chemical and harsh. Nothing like the woods outside.

She remembered her name—Aine—but that was it. How did she get here? She lowered her head to the bar counter and closed her eyes; a dark, empty feeling threatened to overpower and drag her under. Aine sighed at the feel of the cool surface against her forehead. The pain had dulled, but she still felt weak and exhausted. Hopefully, food would make her feel better.

She breathed deeply, enjoying the wood that was still close. Even over the harsh smells around her, she could make out the faint aromas of pine and leaves. It reminded her of home. But where was home? And why did that make her feel uneasy?

Forehead still on the counter, her eyes closed against the bright diner lights. Slow, deep breaths calmed her turmoil, and the hum of a fan soothed her.

SHE RAN with all her strength but stumbled far more often than she should have. She recognized the woods around her, and the once comforting scene felt menacing. Harsh growls rent the air as the thunder of large, wet paws hit the damp earth close behind her. She could feel her heart try to escape as it hammered in her chest, urging her to go faster, to go further. A strange sensation gripped her, and she tried to draw on the power in her center with expectation and then disappointment when nothing happened. Frustration coursed through her, and she screamed.

She ran on but couldn't push harder; panic threatened to overcome her as she felt the shadows gaining. The trees flashed by faster and blurred as she flew through them. She pulled again on her center to no avail and nearly fell, then saw the edge of something ahead, feeling relief in the knowledge that she was about to escape.

A large shadow suddenly blocked the path, and her abrupt halt nearly landed her on her face. Horror filled her as she stared at the figure before her.

"Nearly ready!" Phil shouted from the kitchen, still clattering loudly.

Aine jolted and nearly fell off her stool. Groggy, she shook her head, which cleared the dream from her mind as she tried to remember. It floated away with the memories she no longer possessed. She slowly relaxed back onto the seat, the empty feeling inside her somehow made her more tired. The fear from the dream—or was it a memory?—lingered; it had felt so real.

A sweet and spicy aroma came from the kitchen, and Aine's stomach grumbled loudly, pain rumbling through the empty feeling.

"I added some honey and cinnamon. Hope ya like it!" Phil called.

"I did wonder how it could be sweet and spicy at the same time. Do I smell blueberries too?" She smiled at him for the first time as he walked through the door. He seemed satisfied when she didn't flinch at his entrance.

"How could you smell that from over there?" Phil puzzled as he slowly came towards her.

She shrugged and put her left hand around the bowl as he set it down to warm it. Aine tensed when Phil didn't step back, and the big man sighed as he walked to the kitchen door. Finally, she let go of the branch and dropped it to the floor with a thud. Both hands now warming against the bowl, she sighed at the smell and glanced towards Phil cautiously. He smiled at her, and she didn't feel any danger from him. She shook her head at herself and reached for the spoon he placed next to the bowl.

"Careful, it's hot!" Phil tried to warn, but Aine shoveled

the porridge into her mouth, obviously ravenous. The man left her to it and walked back into the kitchen.

Aine relaxed again as she continued to eat the porridge and moaned as it warmed her belly. She could feel her strength return the more she ate, and the warm feeling spread through her. Once she finished the bowl, she looked towards the kitchen and hoped there was more. She cocked her head and listened, hearing Phil's voice. Aine concentrated, and the conversation's volume increased, coming to her as clearly as if Phil stood next to her.

"Please—I need ya to get down here. Something isn't right, she was alone, with barely any clothes on, and it looks like she's been beaten..." His voice trailed off.

Aine remembered the bruising on her legs and arms. She looked down and noticed the marks had faded slightly. They were still visible but weren't as dark. Was that normal?

"I don't know what to do if she's...different! You'll be better at this sort of thing, and I have customers arriving soon. I need to open up and cover Lucy's shift. She's still camping with her friends."

Aine slid off the stool and quietly walked towards the kitchen; her bare feet didn't make a sound. She didn't want to burden this kind man.

"I can leave if you want?" Aine's voice came out small and weak. Phil jumped and turned around; the cellphone dropped to the floor with a loud clatter.

"Aine, I'm sorry, I didn't realize you could hear me." He held his hand over his heart and crouched to pick up his phone. He paused, then quickly turned it around to look at the screen, sighing with relief when he saw no damage.

"You'll give me a heart attack sneaking up on me like that," he said.

Aine looked at the floor and shuffled her feet back and

forth. She stopped suddenly and straightened as if reprimanded.

"I'm sorry," she replied softly, looking him in the eye before she returned to her porridge bowl.

As she walked back to her seat, the large glass doors at the front opened, and a tall, muscular man walked in. Aine froze as a quiet growl escaped her throat and her muscles tensed. He moved with a lethal, controlled grace. She dropped into a crouch as she watched his muscular frame push the door closed.

He had rough facial hair along a prominent jaw, his ice-blue eyes were cold with inexplicable anger as he looked at her. His hair was dark chocolate brown, slightly grey around his ears.

Dizziness overtook Aine as he walked forward—not the best moment to be left vulnerable. Her instincts screamed at her to escape. The little energy the food had given her drained away as she faced him, ready to fight.

The man frowned, as he looked her in the eyes, and when her gaze met his, a jolt of recognition shot through her. Confused, she growled a warning. The kitchen door slammed behind her, and Aine quickly turned to keep both entrance and exit in view.

"Lachlan! Thanks for coming, man," Phil said, relief evident in his voice.

Phil's presence calmed her slightly; otherwise, she would have leaped at the stranger. She shook her head to clear the mental image from her mind. Aine glanced at the kitchen door and moved her weight to the balls of her feet, ready to run. The stranger, Lachlan, moved with a slow fluidity contradictory to such a large frame. She didn't know how, but Aine knew he was a warrior of some kind. Her instincts overwhelmed her, and the need to run tried to take control.

Lachlan's gaze shot to Aine as she shifted and his eyes burned into her as he noticed her position. His body moved into a similar crouch, ready to stop her. Aine felt another growl deeper in her chest—was this reaction normal? She needed to get out of there; adrenaline filled her and her whole body vibrated. Her eyes jumped between the door, Phil, and the stranger, unable to see an easy exit. She didn't dare turn her back on Lachlan. Aine's heart pounded in her chest and pumped even more adrenaline through her. She didn't know how long she could continue to stand in her exhausted state once the energy stopped.

"Okaaay. Woah, guys! Chill!" Phil had noticed the tension, arms held out to them both, looking between them. "Do you know each other or something?" He frowned. "Aine, are you okay? You've gone white."

Her breath came fast, and she swayed as blackness crowded her vision; she could feel dizziness start to overcome her again. She tried to fight it, but the blackness took her, the last of her energy spent.

Aine collapsed to the floor and desperately tried to hold on to consciousness.

2

_____

As the woman before him collapsed, Lachlan instinctively leaped to grab her. He then gently lowered her to the floor and jumped back quickly as if burned. When Phil said "girl," he expected another teen who had passed out on drugs or alcohol at the back of the diner. Instead, this woman was in her mid-thirties and utterly beautiful, despite the oversized sweater and dirt. Lachlan shook his head, muscles still tense as he tried to shake himself out of it.

"You okay, Phil?" Lachlan finally relaxed when he realized she was unconscious. "Your phone cut out."

"Yeah, sorry, man, I dropped it." Phil came to stand next to him.

Lachlan stared down at the figure on the floor, toned, muscular, and lethal. It was impossible. How could one be here? He hadn't had to worry about this sort of thing in nearly fifteen years, yet here she was.

Phil and Lachlan were close; it had been a decade since Lachlan first walked into the diner on the edge of town. Phil was easy to be around, and at first, it hadn't been hard to avoid talking about his past. Phil was his best friend; in truth, he'd never had a friend before, and eventually, Lachlan had trusted Phil with the knowledge of his past. Lachlan hated to think of the years he spent with his family and the secrets that haunted him.

When Phil called him, Lachlan had assumed it was another false alarm. He'd told Phil what to look out for, just in case, so the man could avoid danger—not invite it to breakfast. Lachlan took a deep breath and looked his friend over, relieved to see him in one piece. He seemed fine but certainly needed a better sense of self-preservation.

Lachlan shifted uncomfortably. He could feel Phil's eyes on him as he waited for Lachlan to say something. The big guy had really landed him in it this time, though out of everyone in this isolated town, Lachlan was the only one equipped to handle such a situation and his friend knew that. He frowned and sighed. He had moved here to get away from the life his family had forced him into, and here he was, dragged straight back into it. He looked at the beautiful woman before him; she obviously needed help, *and* she hadn't hurt Phil.

"What ya gonna do?" Phil asked, wringing his hands.

Lachlan huffed, then scowled at his friend. He was saved from an answer when the door to the diner opened. Caroline and Abbie walked in, concern on their faces. Caroline, a supposedly retired nurse, and her niece, Abbie, helped around the town. They had become the primary source of medical support, with the hospital being a long drive away and few with health insurance. Those who were too stubborn or poor to go to the clinics or hospitals needed them. Lachlan rolled his eyes and looked towards the unconscious woman.

"Let's see this girl then; Stu was hysterical on the

phone." Caroline approached, all business as usual. Lachlan stood between the women and the unconscious girl.

"Just be careful." His hand was up, reluctant to let them pass.

Abbie smiled at Lachlan just a little too long, making him shift uncomfortably. The town's women often acted this way around him, since he was one of the few available bachelors and an outsider who brought in "new blood." Caroline pushed past him and bent over the girl to examine her.

"Was anything broken, Phil?" Caroline looked up to the diner owner.

"No, she was moving timidly but didn't appear too hurt —just lots of bruises. Huh, they don't look as bad now. Her name's Aine." Phil frowned as he looked at Aine's legs in confusion.

Caroline slowly turned Aine over to continue with her assessment. Abbie held her aunt's bag and continued to stare at Lachlan. He sighed and pinched his nose with his hand.

"POOR THING! She's so bruised. Do you think it was a boyfriend?" a bright voice queried.

"I don't know—I can never understand why a girl would stay with someone who hurts her, but they do. Look at those faded bruises on her legs and arms! That one looks like a hand!" a second woman replied.

Aine slowly opened her eyes to find herself where she had collapsed in the middle of the floor. Phil was next to the dangerous man from earlier; they didn't talk, just stood sentinel over the two women. It was at that moment Aine realized they touched her methodically and were far too close. With an elegance she didn't think possible, considering her state, Aine pushed both women off her and rolled away with a move that landed her on her feet. Her head was dizzy from the movement, but she managed to stay upright. She made sure she positioned herself so she faced everyone in the room and was near the door. The man with Phil moved with lightning speed and was between her and the others instantly.

"Jesus! What was that?" Phil exclaimed. "You okay, Abbie? Caroline?"

Phil moved towards Abbie now sprawled against the bar, her dark hair falling out of her bun.

"Careful, honey." The older of the two women approached Aine cautiously, but Lachlan shifted to block her.

"I think you're just exhausted, and you've obviously been through a lot. Phil says you're called Aine. Who did this to you?" The older woman tried to approach again.

Aine, still crouched, flicked her eyes between everyone; there were too many people. Agitation and panic bubbled up inside her. She tried to slow her breath and think.

"Aine." Phil caught her attention, and she looked at him. "This is Abbie and Caroline; they're here to help ya. You trust me, right? They want to help ya."

Caroline, the older of the two with grey permed hair and a kind face, approached her slowly. Aine felt a booth behind her as she backed up further.

"What happened, lovely girl? We just want to help you." Caroline held out both hands in a placating gesture.

Aine sat down hard on the booth edge as her legs gave out. Frustrated, she wasn't sure how much more of this she could take. She lowered her weary head to her hands, listening for any movement.

"I don't know, I don't remember," she admitted, her voice pained. A sob escaped her, and her throat tightened as she swallowed hard. "I don't even know who I am. I can only remember my name."

Aine looked towards the strangers in the room; the women looked sympathetic, and Phil's eyes were concerned. Her eyes began to sting, but she wouldn't cry. Aine looked to the stranger, Lachlan, who frowned, with his arms crossed and scowled at her. He looked furious.

"Oh, you poor dear, no wonder you're jumpy," Abbie said sweetly, more generous than Lachlan would have been if he'd been the one thrown across the room. She tried to approach the girl again as Aine sat in the booth.

Lachlan moved between Aine and the stupid woman again. She clearly didn't know what she was dealing with.

"She can't stay in the town." His voice came out rough and devoid of emotion. She could not roam free around the locals; he didn't know exactly how dangerous she was.

Phil's mouth fell open, and he pulled at Lachlan, who didn't budge. Phil's face hardened, and he frowned at the man. Caroline walked around Lachlan while he was distracted but stopped a few feet from Aine.

"I was right then?" Phil whispered under his breath.

"Yeah." Lachlan subtly nodded and shifted in place.

As he did so, Aine's eyes shot to him. She knew he was the biggest threat in the room. Her green eyes narrowed at him, and he attempted to assume a less threatening posture. *If she doesn't remember who she is, does she remember what she is?* Lachlan wondered. He heard a faint growl from her; instinctively, she must have known he was dangerous.

The entrancing green eyes which complemented her pale skin didn't look away. Lachlan looked at her shoulder-length black hair; tangled though it was, it softened her otherwise sharp features. Despite her exhausted state, she still moved with a lethal elegance he recognized. He wondered what happened to her and how she had been hurt. When he first looked into her eyes, he felt a connection, which quickly disappeared once she became defensive. He'd been so ingrained from a young age to act a certain way in the face of danger that it was difficult to fight that instinct.

Lachlan softened as he looked at her now, timid, and vulnerable. He took a breath and tried to relax. He couldn't help his reaction; since he was a boy, he only knew one way. But she was a lost woman in pain, and he needed to remember that. No matter what she was, there was no way he would leave her to get hurt further; no one deserved that. He also could not subject the town to the possible danger she represented.

"Who are *you*?" she demanded as she scowled at Lachlan. "And why do you talk funny?"

"My name is Lachlan, and I'm Irish." He watched her for a reaction. "If you're going to hang around, you will stay with me."

Phil's head snapped to Lachlan, and he felt his own surprise as the words left his mouth. Aine's brow scrunched, and she continued to scowl at him. Unsure, Lachlan continued.

"You can have the basement at my house until you figure out what you need to do or who you are. It looks like something has been done to you, and we need to figure out if you're going to bring danger upon us."

Aine bristled at his harsh words.

Phil gaped at Lachlan, his mouth open and eyes wide. Lachlan had just offered to let her stay in his space. Where else could she stay and not be a danger? Either directly or by those who hurt her? He knew he shouldn't care, but he just couldn't help it. He should know better, but how could he not help someone who was obviously hurt and needed help?

"Just promise not to hurt Abbie or Caroline again—they're honestly trying to help." Phil recovered and looked back toward Aine.

She tried to get up, but her legs gave out again. Lachlan knew something must be seriously wrong; he approached her, and Aine scrambled back further into the booth, baring her teeth at him. Lachlan halted but failed not to react to the threat. This would not work if this was how they responded to each other.

"Go away," she exclaimed through gritted teeth.

"I won't hurt you. You trust Phil, right? He can vouch for me. I just want to help. It's not your fault how you're reacting to me. It's instinct. Just let me help," Lachlan pleaded. He crouched, going against everything he knew. He needed to get her out of there and away from Caroline and Abbie. They would grow more suspicious the more they were around her, and he didn't want the town to find out about his past.

Aine tried to stand again as he came closer. She moved with a desperation he could understand. Phil stood next to Lachlan.

"Aine—just calm down and listen to Lachlan. I know he's scary, but he's a good man." Phil tried to appeal to her, and Lachlan snorted. Aine's eyes darted to Lachlan once more.

"He will look after ya, and I swear he won't hurt ya," Phil

went on. "Lachlan? Maybe back off a bit for a minute, man. You're not giving off great vibes right now."

Aine looked at Phil, and her face changed completely; she almost smiled. Phil only knew to be kind; she visibly trusted him. Lachlan laughed. Even in a short space of time, Phil could coax someone dangerous into liking him.

When she wasn't frowning or angry, the girl was stunning. But when she looked back at Lachlan, her scowl returned, and her green eyes burned into him.

"You swear?" Aine asked Phil quietly, her energy to argue depleted.

"Yes, darlin', we all just want to help you. I don't know what happened to you, and neither do you, but we will figure it out. I can't imagine what it felt like wandering around the forest not knowing who you are." Phil put his hand out to help her stand up and looked surprised when she took it. Lachlan watched her, noticing how much effort it took.

"I wasn't wandering. I woke up in the clearing behind here. I heard you talking to the other guy and came to see if I was in danger." Aine staggered slightly as she tried to move forward.

"I'll carry you over to mine." Lachlan walked to her to pick her up, and she turned to him, eyes wide.

"No," she growled, deep in her throat and chest.

Caroline and Abbie took a step back, their faces shocked. He wasn't surprised, as the noise Aine had just made was not human. Lachlan ignored her and put his arms under her legs and upper back. She struck out at him weakly, but he ignored the blow. She would be a force to be reckoned with at full strength, but she was as weak as a puppy right now.

"Lachlan!" Caroline cried. "Put the poor girl down."

"Caroline, Abbie—you should follow me if you still want to look her over. Phil needs to open, and you can take care of her at mine."

"This is absurd! You can't just go around picking up women like that!" Caroline's angry shout followed Lachlan out the door. He didn't really want the two women to come, but they probably would anyway, and Aine did need to be looked over.

She would likely be alright in a day or two, but he would let Caroline look at her on the off chance there were more severe injuries. Lachlan ignored Aine's fists, which continued to beat against his chest, while he strode toward his house, just along the tree line. A short walk from the diner.

"But she needs to go to the hospital," Abbie argued as she followed, obviously recovered from Aine's previous outbursts. She had picked up Caroline's medical bag, and the two women marched after Lachlan, angry looks on their faces. Phil followed, trying to catch up.

"Nope." There was finality in his tone. Hospitals would mean blood tests, and he was quite sure Aine would not only object but react violently if anyone went near her with what she perceived as a weapon. Blood tests would only create questions neither of them would want to be asked.

"She will be fine once you've looked her over," Lachlan said. "Phil said she was moving fine. So you guys just check her for infection and concussion."

Abbie and Caroline looked at each other, both dubious, but Phil gave a reassuring nod that it was the right decision. Still unsure but wanting to help the girl, the two women continued to follow. Phil hesitated before he turned back to the diner.

"Don't tell me how to do my job, Lachlan O'Reilly! I was

working as a nurse before you were even born," Caroline huffed at him, shock evident in her tone. "There's no need to manhandle the girl."

It wasn't a good idea to be on her bad side, but he didn't want her to take too much interest in Aine. Lachlan's house appeared in front of him; it looked more like a British country cottage than the average house one would find in the area. Grey brick made up the exterior, peeking through gaps in the ivy and climbing roses that enveloped the house. The whole place looked a little worse for wear, but it was his and reminded him of home. The overgrown front garden made it look abandoned; Lachlan had meant to sort that out but had never gotten around to it. Various plants and perennials grew wild, tangled in weeds. The house looked deserted to the outsider, it created a wall between him and the rest of the world and gave him a feeling of comfortable safety.

Aine let out an animalistic scream as she slowly recovered from the shock of being carried. This caused Caroline and Abbie to stop and exchange an uneasy glance.

"Put me down, you beast!"

Lachlan laughed at the irony. Animal attacks did happen in the town, and he was always on call to deal with them. It was usually a coyote, which was more of a pest and didn't require much to run off. He had more than enough experience to deal with them.

It had been fifteen years since he left Ireland and the family business, which he did not miss. They started them young in Lachlan's family, and by the time he was twenty, he was spent. He had left for America to escape the expectations and his failures.

For five years, Lachlan had traveled from place to place and explored the incredible world he had never known, before finding this sleepy town ten years ago. Nowhere had quite felt like home until he stumbled upon it. As a boy, he had always loved the woods, feeling like he could connect to nature and be part of something pure. He was used to isolation and didn't make friends easily, and Phil had let him buy the derelict house near the diner on the edge of town.

Not wanting him to be alone, Phil had bugged Lachlan and became part of his life. The man was too kind for his own good and always made sure everyone had their place. It was hard to be near the big guy and not let his guard down. Phil appreciated it when he kept any wilder animals at bay, and Lachlan felt purpose when the town was protected. It was what he was born to do. The townsfolk now somewhat trusted the lone stranger, at least to help when he was needed.

Phil had helped him set up his woodcarving and furniture business; eventually, he had opened his own shop to sell what he made. But he was still the outsider, never entirely fitting in with everyone else.

Lachlan entered the house and carried Aine down to the basement; he easily flipped the light switch while holding her in place with his other hand before he descended the stairs. Aine still struggled in his arms but he could feel her blows to his back weaken.

There was a worn-out couch and a small bed in the corner. Unopened, dust-covered boxes were piled against a wall, and had been since Lachlan had moved in. He wasn't sure what was in them anymore. A bookcase was proudly integrated under the stairs, filled with Lachlan's prized books. Reading had always accompanied his solitude, and Lachlan appreciated any reason to expand his knowledge on any subject.

The room wasn't much, but it would be enough to keep

her comfortable and safer than if he had let Caroline and Abbie take her to the hospital. Unfortunately, there was only one bedroom set up upstairs, and that was his.

Lachlan placed Aine on the couch; the bed felt inappropriate right then. He quickly stepped back as she lashed out at him again—her blow would have been weak, but she might have hurt her hand.

"Alright, I've put you down; now stop fighting. You are safe." Lachlan punctuated the last three words with frustration.

Aine stopped her struggle but quickly lifted herself into a sitting position. Then, she tried to stand and swayed with a hand held to her head.

"Have you checked for a concussion?" Lachlan queried.

"Get out the way, Lachlan, and let me do my job. Now, Aine, let's get a good look at you." Caroline barged past Lachlan, no small feat.

Aine immediately tried to jump up again but had worn herself out and collapsed back onto the couch. She had no choice but to give in to the ministrations of the two women.

Lachlan watched for the sakes of Caroline and Abbie. He didn't think Aine would hurt them now, but he would take no chances. Once it was clear Aine had given up the fight against them and let them check her over, Lachlan backed toward the stairs and sat down.

Aine only flinched once when Caroline took care of a particularly nasty cut on her hand. The rest of her bruises had faded even further and were barely visible, much to the women's surprise. Caroline's calm voice explained that it was disinfectant in her hand and why it was vital as she dabbed the cut. After that, Aine sat almost regally and listened to Caroline's deep timbre as she explained each procedure and how it helped.

Once Caroline had ascertained that none of Aine's injuries were too severe, she suggested rest. Aine looked at Lachlan, a scowl still on her face, but didn't argue. Caroline led Aine to the bed and helped her get ready; Lachlan looked away, uncomfortable, and stood, approaching the stairs.

"I'm within shouting distance," he said abruptly as he climbed upstairs to the kitchen.

3

———

Lachlan stood in the center of his tiny kitchen next to a small wooden table in the corner, he ran his hand through his long hair. Tea. That's what he would do, make tea. That's what his mum used to do in these sorts of situations.

The usual pang of grief threatened to overwhelm him, as it always did when he thought of her. His mother had been an Irish beauty, and he never knew what she'd seen in his father. The guilt when he thought of her never went away.

He maneuvered around the area, built to be practical with plenty of cupboard space. Lachlan filled the stovetop kettle, turned on the stove, and waited for the water to boil.

He stared out the window; his kitchen faced out the back of his house, overlooking the edge of the woods. The trees swayed in a light breeze, and their sounds called to him; dark shadows moved as clouds passed over the sun. Lachlan wondered where Aine had come from and why she was here as he watched them go by. If others follow her, he may have a bigger problem than one woman with no memory.

The shrill whistle of the kettle broke his reverie. Lachlan went through the motions as he prepared the beverages, still distracted when Caroline and Abbie came up the stairs from the basement.

"We've given her a sedative and put her to bed," Caroline stated gently. Her rich, deep voice calmed his nerves.

"She's been beaten," she went on, "and there are cuts and bruises, though the bruises are fading fast. No internal bleeding as far as I can tell, and no concussion, but what-ever happened has clearly traumatized her." Caroline came to stand next to him.

Maybe Aine won't hang around too long if her injuries aren't serious? he thought optimistically.

"Thanks, Caroline. Tea?" Lachlan offered.

Caroline looked at the tea. "Nothing stronger?" she asked, looking hopeful.

"It's not even eight in the morning yet, Caroline! If I didn't know any better, I'd say you were the Irish one between us." Lachlan laughed before he noticed Abbie's not-so-subtle heated glance. He handed each woman a mug of tea and turned to his own.

"My great-granddaddy was Irish if you remember. You spend too much time out here by yourself, Lachlan," Caroline scolded. "You should mingle a bit more, then you wouldn't still be the outsider. Folks will think it strange you are taking this girl in, and I don't understand it myself. She should be in the hospital."

Lachlan frowned and huffed at the change of subject. "She needs help, and I'll be the best person to give it. I might be an outsider, but who else in town will take her in? You won't have time with you looking after everyone, being out and about with Abbie all day. I remember what folks were like with me when I first started living here. A hospital will scare her—you saw how she was with just a few of us. How will she react with lots of people around?" Lachlan looked towards Abbie, who hadn't said a word since coming into the house.

Abbie didn't appear hurt from Aine's earlier attack. Instead, she looked around curiously, then often stared openly at him. Her crush annoyed him, and he had hoped she would have given up by now. Though she was close to his age, in her mid-thirties, and was pretty, he didn't think she would have the strength to cope with his baggage—not that he would ever tell anyone else about his past.

They finished their tea awkwardly, the women obviously reluctant to leave Aine.

Lachlan sighed. "You might be right about the hospital, but I really think it's best she stays here."

Caroline glanced at Abbie.

"You can come back and check on her when you want. I'll let her sleep it off and get her some food. It mostly looked like exhaustion."

The two women reluctantly gathered their things. Lachlan realized that if Phil hadn't given his nod of approval, they wouldn't have considered leaving Aine with him.

"You call if you need help," Caroline told him. She turned to leave.

Abbie hesitated slightly. "Good to see you, Lachlan," she said. "Do you...well, let me know if you fancy doing something in town. It's not good for you here by yourself."

Her concern was sweet, but he preferred to be left alone and didn't want to lead her on.

"Thanks, Abbie, I'll be fine. Tell your brother I have that dresser ready for him—I know he wants to surprise Jeanette next week, and I got it finished early. I'll drop it off tomorrow or the day after, depending on how Aine does."

Lachlan closed the door after them, not giving them another chance to start a conversation. He turned around to lean against the door and breathed a sigh of relief, then realized with a jolt that he was now alone in his house with Aine.

He scowled towards the basement door. Was he crazy? If anyone could deal with her situation in this town, it was him, but he honestly didn't want to be involved. At least this way, he knew the town would be safe. How could Aine not remember who or what she was? Could she be faking it? Lachlan ran both hands through his hair and grunted. He would need to calm down if he didn't want to scare her.

It would be a couple of hours before she woke up, so he headed outside to his shed, where he was working on a project for the church. He took his time and walked along the rough path to his sanctuary at the rear of the yard. The shed was large, custom-built to facilitate his workshop. It became his safety net, a place where he could relax and create in peace; it was another reason why he lived on the edge of town near Phil's diner. The locals were less likely to bug him, and he was more than okay with that.

The townsfolk had slowly come to accept him. Opening the shop on the high street meant he could control how much contact he had with them, and they knew when he was accessible if they needed work. The business had grown incredibly in the last few years; being the only woodworker in town, the demand was immense. In truth, he needed help, but he was firm and took on only what he could cope with.

The shed door creaked as he opened it and walked in. Lachlan strode over to the chest at the back of the shed, one he hadn't opened in over fifteen years; he hadn't needed to before.

He lifted the lid and studied the contents, huffing. That was his old life, one he firmly wanted to keep in his past. But, unfortunately, Aine's appearance meant he would have to deal with it soon, one way or another. So he rummaged at the bottom until he felt the cold impression of what he was looking for.

Lachlan held up the medallion to the light. He was never sure exactly what it was made from, but it looked like bronze. Intricate symbols surrounded the edge, and two swords crossed each other in the center. It was small in the palm of his hand, and the chain was heavy. *I never wanted to use this again,* he thought gravely.

Drawing the chain up, Lachlan put it around his neck. He then slammed the lid of the chest shut and closed off that part of himself.

He turned to survey his workshop and the pew he had worked on yesterday. Looked like it was going to be a full day. Time to get to work.

AINE WOKE from unconsciousness for what seemed like the hundredth time that day. Instinctively, she knew it was early afternoon. The sleep had helped, though she hadn't been too happy with the older lady for giving her something to help her sleep. Aine needed to be on guard with Lachlan upstairs—the warrior. She didn't know how she knew that, but the thought of him made her wary. She pulled her knees to her chest and sniffed the sweater she wore.

Phil had said he was a good man and wouldn't hurt her. She trusted Phil, but could she trust Lachlan? Her head screamed at her to run from him as far as she could. He was dangerous, the way he had stood ready for her. She didn't know if she had met him before; he didn't act as if they had. But she felt like they were enemies—when she first saw him, there had been that spark of recognition.

Aine crinkled her nose. It didn't feel right. He had helped her and hadn't caused her harm... yet. And if anything, he was angry she was there. But she couldn't let her guard down.

She took a deep breath and swung her legs over the side of the bed as she took in her current accommodations and decided she liked the basement. Being underground felt comfortable and cozy. There was a couch near the bed and boxes stacked neatly against one wall. The smell of wood from a bookcase was a comfort that gave her a warm feeling. She looked down at the oversized sweater she wore; it was cozy and smelled like the kind man who had given it to her.

Aine walked to the couch to sit and look out the small window close to the ceiling. She could see the woods clearly and felt drawn to them; an image of running through the trees flashed through her mind.

She cocked her head as she heard Lachlan approach the door up the stairs. Aine groaned. She knew she would have to stay for the time being; he would probably stop her if she tried to leave. Even so, she didn't want to talk to the man right then. Down he came anyway.

Lachlan slowly descended the wooden steps and ducked his head just in time to avoid hitting the ceiling. He was tall and muscular, and Aine snorted at the thought of how ridiculous he would look if he hit his head on the beam.

"I brought you some more clothes, a t-shirt, and some shorts of mine. They will be a bit big, but at least you'll have some modesty while your clothes are in the laundry. I know you probably want to run around naked, but it'll be the scandal of the town if anyone sees you." He attempted a half-smile and gestured in what must have been the town's direction before he laid the clothes on the bed across the room.

"I'll go to town later for some clothes that will fit you." Lachlan stepped back and moved awkwardly to the bottom of the stairs.

As Aine watched, she could see in his movements that he tried to appear less threatening, but his motions were fluid, and she could tell he was ready to act if he needed to. She decided to keep her distance from him but accept his help. What other choice did she have? She walked over to the clothes, pulling the sweater over her head to get changed, and Lachlan quickly turned away. The borrowed garments were excessively baggy but comfortable and wouldn't restrict her movements too much.

"Thank you," Aine softly spoke. "I know you don't have to help me, but you are. Just don't carry me off again." She scowled at him as she said the last bit; he huffed and moved to walk up the stairs.

"You must be hungry. I'm cooking bacon if you'd like to come up," he said.

Aine quickly followed; food was always a good idea.

When they entered the kitchen, he gestured to a chair at the small table that sat in the room's corner. He opened the fridge and started to gather objects around the kitchen before he stood over the hob with a pan and started to cook the bacon.

As Aine watched him, she admired his evident strength and had to catch herself as she imagined what his muscles looked like under his clothes. No doubt she was attracted to him—but she shouldn't be.

The smell of raw, salty meat hit her hard, and her mouth filled with saliva. It smelled incredible. As Lachlan cooked the bacon, she shifted uneasily and swallowed. He turned away from her to cook but kept her in sight, he watched her in his periphery. How could she trust him when he didn't trust her? But then again, she didn't know who she was, so how could she even trust herself?

"Food first, and then I'll let you get cleaned up." Lachlan eyed her. "You will probably get tired of this question, but what do you remember?"

Aine could feel his frustration, but she didn't want to talk. She groaned before she spoke. Lachlan didn't know anything about her and obviously didn't like her, and yet here she was in his home, she felt obligated to tell him something.

"When I woke this morning, I was in the clearing in the woods behind Phil's diner. I heard Phil and the other guy talking, so I went to see what was happening. Phil saw me and helped me. To be honest, I tried to run, but my legs gave out." Why had she said that? It let him know how weak she was. Aine rolled her eyes at herself.

"I had some food before you arrived, and you know the rest."

Aine's face looked sad when he glanced at her.

"Nothing else?" Lachlan's voice was soft with a hint of concern. Aine looked up and shrugged.

"Just my name. Phil asked me what it was, and it just came to me. I don't remember anything else." Her face screwed up, and she banged the table, which shook hard. Shocked, she looked up at Lachlan, who had snickered at her outburst.

"What?!" she snapped.

Lachlan chuckled again. "It was just the look on your

face when you hit the table. I thought you might fall off your chair."

Aine relaxed and smiled timidly. Lachlan scowled at the floor and turned back to the bacon. She again caught herself watching his muscular back as he flipped the food over in the pan. He seemed to try hard to help her feel less tense, but she could tell it was quite an effort for him.

"Yeah, I guess I didn't know my own strength," she said after a moment.

Lachlan seemed a serious person, but she felt less tense when he smiled at her. Maybe he was not used to being around people often.

He walked over and placed a plate with a bacon sandwich in front of her. Aine picked it up and bit into it with a moan as the bacon juices flooded her mouth and dribbled down her chin. She quickly wiped her face; the saltiness and juices from the fat were delicious. Quickly she finished the sandwich and was surprised when Lachlan placed a second in front of her.

"You look like you need it." He turned away to make one for himself.

Aine ate the second more slowly, savoring the flavors until she finally felt satisfied. Maybe she would stop passing out now.

ONCE THEY HAD BOTH EATEN, Lachlan showed Aine to the bathroom. As they climbed the beautifully ornate stairs, Aine stopped to admire the detailed carvings of ivy up the banister, running her hands along the design, her fingertips following the vine as it intricately ascended. Patiently,

Lachlan waited at the top of the stairs until she finished and followed.

"It's beautiful," she breathed.

"Thanks, it took me a while when I first moved in. The old stairs were rotten, so it was the first thing I took out and replaced. Gave me the idea to start carving again, and eventually, I opened the shop in town." Lachlan's voice was soft but reluctant; he cleared his throat. Then, he stepped through a door in the hallway at the top of the stairs. Aine watched curiously as he turned on the shower after he handed Aine a towel out of the cupboard next to it. She just admired him as steam filled the room.

"This is how you make the water hotter or colder, and this is on and off," Lachlan demonstrated.

Aine looked at the towel, her brow creased and her lips twitched.

"Use the towel to dry yourself after. There's shampoo and shower gel in there already to wash with. I'll have to pick up something nicer from town when I get you some more clothes."

Aine stood there and stared at the running water. "It looks hot, but I expected it to be cold."

"Come on, you'll feel better after, I promise. I'll be in the shed out back." He turned and walked out, closing the door. Aine heard him let out a long breath before he moved away.

She held her hand out to the water and felt the heat and steam on her skin. It felt wonderful. Quickly, she undressed then slowly eased into the shower. It felt like heaven as she washed the dirt away; the pain she had been feeling all over lessened. When she finally felt clean, and her skin started to look wrinkled, Aine stepped out of the shower and turned it off as Lachlan had shown her.

She picked up the towel, wrapped it around herself, and

sighed. The towel was soft and felt soothing on her skin as she dried. Dressed again, Aine walked over to the mirror and wiped the condensation off to look at her face, no longer covered in dirt.

She stared. She knew her face, and it looked familiar, which was a relief. Deep black hair fell to her shoulders, dripping with water. Her complexion was pale, her nose straight and lips full. She looked deep into her eyes and hoped to glimpse something of her past. Her frustration grew; everything still felt blank. Finally, when nothing came to her, she glowered and growled at the image in the mirror, then startled back with a gasp.

Her eyes changed. The green morphed into a deep amber color, which burned back at her, anger evident in her face. Coming closer to the mirror to look again, all she saw was emerald-green.

Aine shook her head to clear it and turned to leave the bathroom. It would be a while before she felt the need to look in a mirror again.

The carving on the stairs caught her attention once more. She tried to merge the aggressive, handsome stranger she knew with the man who had fed her and carved this ornate banister. The feature was unbelievable, and only someone with an observant eye for detail could obtain such realism. She closed her eyes and tried to get a feel for the home of the man with such a violent presence but the ability to create such delicate work.

She knew the feelings she could pull from her surroundings was her doing, like she knew she could pull the essence of Lachlan from the house, and she also knew that she'd done this many times before. It felt like muscle memory as she probed her surroundings with her mind. Like Phil said,

Lachlan was a good man, but she also sensed a very dark and violent past.

Aine let the feeling go; it felt too intimate and personal. Like she had spied on him. Feeling ashamed, she carried on down the stairs toward the back of the house.

LACHLAN RAN his hand over the carving as he assessed the frame of the pew. The Reverend asked him to build some new ones to replace the older seating in the church. He finished most of them and would have to ask Phil to drop them off later in the week.

Carving calmed him, another reason he started doing it when he finally settled in the town. He usually managed to forget about his family and his past, but Aine's presence that morning had brought it all to the surface. He could never truly forget who or what he was, even though he'd like to. Lachlan's stomach churned as he thought about Aine, visualizing her as she caressed the ivy carving, her face so expressive. Wonder and admiration had taken over her beautiful features.

Lachlan slammed his tools down and growled, throwing his hands in the air. Aine was stunning; he couldn't shake the image of her face from his mind. If he was being truthful, she needed help, and he didn't want to be involved.

He abandoned the pew and stormed out of the workshop toward the house. Aine was probably finished showering by then, and he needed to figure out what to do with her. As he climbed the few steps up to his back door, Aine appeared on the other side of the screen.

As she walked out, he watched her face. She was wary of him and went to stand at the railing on his porch.

Lachlan kept his face blank and watched her. He heard her breathe in deeply and exhale slowly. The curve of her neck and body was beautiful. She stood with regal elegance in complete contrast to the lethargy she had shown before.

"It's so peaceful and rich out here," she spoke quietly.

Her posturing from the diner had disappeared, which surprised him. Something had changed; maybe she felt better after the shower. He looked at the back of her head, trying to assess whether she was in pain. The bruises on her legs had already disappeared, another sign she was different.

"I'm not in pain, Lachlan."

His head snapped up to look at her. Could she read his mind? It was at that moment he realized he would have to tell her what she was. If she didn't remember anything, then she probably didn't know. Lachlan groaned and shifted, the movement alerting Aine to his unease. Her forehead crinkled, and her eyes narrowed at him.

"Sorry," he quickly said. "I'm just not used to having someone around. I've lived here for ten years, just me...." His voice trailed off.

Aine frowned but stood straight and proud. "I'm sorry I've invaded your space. I don't know where else to go, though." Her mouth turned down before she looked out at the trees again.

Lachlan could almost feel the strength in her, going through what she had and accepting the help of strangers. She didn't know who she was, and yet she faced him and didn't back down. But she could tell he was dangerous to her, of that he was sure. "Come on, let me show you something," he said.

He looked at her feet, realizing they were bare and went

inside. He came back a couple of minutes later with a thick pair of socks.

"No way will my shoes fit you, but here are some socks. Stick them on and follow me." He walked toward the shed and opened the door.

Aine hesitated before she put the socks on and followed him along the path. She waited for him to enter before she came through the door. It went against all his instincts to turn his back on her, but he wanted her to relax more. Woodwork calmed him; maybe it would help her.

Her face lit up as she looked around and inhaled, closing her eyes. Eventually, a contented sigh escaped her lips, and she opened her eyes to look at Lachlan.

"This is familiar." Her face softened as a small smile appeared. Lachlan stared; he knew he shouldn't be distracted by her, but her face was captivating when she was happy. He could almost tell what she was thinking with every expression.

"Here, let me show you." Lachlan picked up his tools and a new piece of wood. He showed Aine how to use them to shape the wood how he wanted. She watched him closely, picking up the tools when Lachlan put them down. He stiffened, realizing he had just handed her a weapon. Muscles tensed, he took a step back, just in case. Aine didn't seem to notice, and he cleared his throat.

"You try," he said. "Don't expect to be able to carve like me straight away, but I find it really calming. The distraction may help your memory return." Lachlan couldn't help but smile as Aine eagerly picked up a fresh piece of wood and started. He watched, stunned, as she carved with a practiced hand. Her work quickly took shape.

"Safe to say, I think you've done this before," he chuckled, some of the tension leaving his body.

"I have, and it feels right." Aine smiled up at him, a real one, not one of the careful smiles she had given him so far.

The effect it had on Lachlan took his breath away. How could she be affecting him so much? He'd been with beautiful women, but the way she held herself and her inner strength made her more attractive. He pushed away the recognition he felt. He needed to get a grip on himself. He didn't know her, and she could be dangerous.

4

The shed didn't have a lot of furniture. Tools neatly hung on the wall, and a large table was placed in the center of the room. Lachlan and Aine were on opposite sides of it. Aine deftly carved the wood in front of her, sitting on a stool she had pulled over from the corner where the large chest sat. Lachlan had gone back to carving the pew he had clearly been working on before she came downstairs.

They worked in comfortable silence for hours. Lachlan kept his distance, but Aine felt him watch her. He looked away when she glanced in his direction.

When Aine thought about it, it should have felt weird being comfortable in his presence, but it felt right. Her carving took careful shape and once she'd finished, a wolf howled at the world in front of her. The wolf looked young but not a new pup. The thought brought a wave of sadness over her, and she didn't know why. She realized Lachlan had stopped what he was doing and looked over.

"I...I don't know why." Aine couldn't explain it, but she

felt like an abyss had opened in her. Something was missing, and it hurt.

"Maybe you're tired?" Lachlan asked kindly. The gruffness he'd displayed earlier had softened. "Or hungry, it's past dinner."

He moved towards the door, and Aine realized the sun had started to set. They had carved together the whole afternoon, and she hadn't noticed the time passing. Her stomach growled at her to complain of its hunger.

As she followed Lachlan in, that hollow feeling inside haunted her. All the joy she experienced when she had carved and done something familiar had drained away, leaving her feeling empty.

"I don't have much—I'll have to pick up some food from town tomorrow as well. Do you want to stay here or come with me?" Lachlan asked. When she didn't answer, he continued to the house and opened the door, turning back to see she hadn't moved. "Come on, it's getting cold!"

Aine could hear the concern in his voice and followed. Once inside, she shuffled towards the table they had eaten at earlier. She couldn't explain the sadness that overwhelmed her as Lachlan cooked pasta and sauce topped with cheese. He didn't speak while he prepared the food, and Aine stared at the table. When he placed the meal in front of her, she finally snapped out of her mood.

"No bacon?" She looked up, hopeful. She couldn't smell it on her plate, so she knew there wasn't any in the meal.

"Sorry, no, I used it all earlier." Lachlan sat down next to her.

She felt safer with his proximity than when she first met him, but Lachlan still seemed wary of her. Aine studied his face as she ate. The pasta was not as satisfying as the bacon from earlier but helped make her complaining belly happy.

She liked how rough around the edges Lachlan was. His face wasn't perfect, and he gave off a violent power that both terrified her and attracted her. Aine shook her head as the thought went through it; she had to admit he was handsome, but she really shouldn't think about him like that. She felt safe with him now, drawn to his strength. Finally, after spending all that time in comfortable silence, she decided that Phil was right. He was a good man, and he only wanted to help her. *Other than the manhandling from the diner to his house* Aine thought. Aine crinkled her nose and scowled at that memory.

She had admired the muscles in his arms as he worked earlier, as they flexed and carved. She took glances when she thought he wasn't looking. It was as much of a distraction from her predicament as the carving. Aine shook her head; there was no doubt she was attracted to him, but they were strangers. Yet the feeling of familiarity washed over her again, it made her shiver.

After they finished their meal, Aine could feel she was tired again. Whatever happened to bring her here had drained her completely. She thanked Lachlan for the meal, and he didn't look surprised when she went down to the basement. The shorts and t-shirt were comfortable, but she took them off and got into the bed in Phil's sweater. It didn't take long for the day to catch up with her, and she drifted to sleep.

Aine could feel the man's hand in her hair; it pulled painfully on her scalp while he dragged her through the quiet village. She slipped in and out of consciousness as they went. She tried to call for help, but the gag in her mouth kept her silent. He continued to

the other side of the village and into the Temple, then threw her across the room. She skidded to a halt at another man's feet.

"Found you, stupid bitch. Did you think you could get away from me?" the second man taunted her. He lifted her up and roughly tied her to a chair next to him.

"What did you do to me?" Aine couldn't move, but she struggled all the same. He pulled her head back by her hair. The man who had dragged her there passed over a rancid-smelling cup.

"I slipped you something in your evening meal—you should be unconscious, but somehow you still managed to run. This should sort you out." A wicked grin spread over his face as Aine was forced to drink or choke, her head still pulled back. The chair was kicked over, and pain lanced through her as both men punched and kicked her. She was slowly worn down until blackness took her away from the beating.

Aine fell out of the bed as she woke and thrashed at the covers that suffocated her. The men were no longer there, and she came to recognize Lachlan's basement. Her breath was ragged and fast, and her heart pounded in her ears. That was no dream; she was sure it was a memory. She looked at the bruises no longer on her arm, particularly at where the one shaped like a hand had been, and felt the back of her head. There wasn't a large lump like she expected, but a bald patch of hair where it had obviously been yanked out.

Aine hugged her knees. What happened? Why had those men done that to her?

AINE'S MOOD changed when Lachlan brought her inside; her curiosity and vibrant personality disappeared. Instead, she seemed a ghost of herself—not that he knew her, really. He wasn't sure why, but it had something to do with the little wolf she carved.

He held the piece in his hands, and admired her workmanship; it was unreal. He could use the help, and he hoped that if she helped him with his work, she could start to recover and figure out her past. Then again, sometimes, not knowing one's past was a blessing. He imagined not knowing his and decided he would be better off.

Lachlan was sitting on his back porch facing the woods in a rocking chair he carved when he first moved there; it was his favorite spot. He sipped a beer and watched as he often did; the peace outside always calmed him. But tonight, he could not relax.

A crash from the basement surprised him. In an instant, Lachlan was on his feet. His heart pounded, and his fists were clenched. He listened for another sound, but all was quiet. Head cocked, he heard the distant sound of the basement's steps creaking and the basement door slowly opening. Muscles still tensed, Lachlan watched as Aine appeared at the screen door; carefully, she pushed it open. She looked out into the shadows with wariness. She quickly crossed her arms over her chest as she stepped onto the porch, and she rubbed her hands up and down her arms. Lachlan eyed the sweater she wore. He hoped Phil didn't want it back.

"You okay?" he asked, catching the look on her face. Her eyes were red and her jaw set; warily, she looked at him, and he tried to relax.

"I had a dream, or maybe a memory, I can't be sure. I fell off the bed." Aine paused as she stared out into the dark trees. "I can feel a presence out here, and it's wrong."

Aine looked out again, and Lachlan felt her body hum

with tension. He quickly turned and picked up his rifle from its spot against the side of the house. The beer he'd held rolled off the porch, and he ignored it.

Aine stiffened when she saw the weapon but didn't say anything. The peace he usually felt in the woods was gone; he could feel Aine's fear but could also feel what she meant. There was malevolence in the shadows. A growl sounded from the woman's throat and chest; Lachlan didn't think she realized she'd done it. He stood and strode down the steps toward the woods. Aine cried out and followed him.

"Don't!" she ordered, the command in her voice palpable. But Lachlan ignored her and carried on.

A large shadow moved quickly and disappeared further into the darkness. The presence vanished with it. Lachlan stood, holding the gun, and waiting for the woods to return to normal. Aine stood by him as he waited and relaxed when he did.

He turned to look at her. "This is not good."

THE FOLLOWING DAY, Lachlan decided it was safer to bring Aine into town with him rather than leave her alone at the house. Neither had slept well, it seemed; both were on alert when they left.

Lachlan marveled at his compulsion to protect her as he gently helped her into his truck. It was strange to think he had been raised to hate her kind; shaking his head, he got behind the wheel. He turned to look at Aine and laughed. Her eyes darted between the radio buttons and the electric windows as he put them down, and she watched in wonder when he put on a local radio station.

The woods disappeared as buildings replaced them. Phil's diner and Lachlan's house sat on the edge of the town. It was only a short drive from his house into the Burntwood Falls town center, but it was far enough away that he could remain secluded.

A circular garden and fountain, Lachlan's favorite spot to sit and have lunch, appeared in the center of the high street. Summer flowers colored the area and complemented the sleepy neighborhood. It felt beautiful and calm in contrast to the menace from the woods the night before. Locals were setting up their shops; it was late in the morning, but everyone opened at this time. A buttery aroma escaped from the small bakery near the local grocery store. There weren't many shops, but enough to keep the town going. Unfortunately, not many tourists visited the town—they usually just drove through.

Lachlan led Aine to the one clothing store in town first, run by Madison, a mom of three teenagers. The locals stopped their work to stare as they passed; Lachlan scowled at them and placed a hand protectively on Aine's back.

Madison, a short woman with long, curly blonde hair tied up in a fancy twist, squealed as they entered the shop. She already knew about Aine from Caroline and Abbie. Gossip spread fast in a small town.

"You're so pretty! Can you really not remember anything? Caroline said you were badly bruised. Oh, my!" Madison exclaimed when she gave Aine the once over. "Let's get you out of those shorts and that hideous shirt!"

Aine's eyes widened, and Lachlan chuckled as Madison took a shocked Aine towards the back of the store. As she looked back with helplessness, Lachlan couldn't help but laugh, tension leaving him—it felt good. Madison was a force to be reckoned with, and Lachlan left them to it. He didn't want to get between women and clothes.

Lachlan sat outside on a bench and sighed. He genuinely loved it here, but his humor soured when he thought about what would happen with Aine around. He took a deep breath through his nose and exhaled. Aine was a problem, and he'd briefly forgotten that she'd invaded his life. With a growl, Lachlan stood and strode down the street. His mind whirled with thoughts of his past. Aine had a way of making him forget what she was and who he was.

When Lachlan had done three laps of the center, he looked back in the store window. Aine now wore jeans and a green blouse; he entered the store and stared at her. The blouse made her eyes stand out, and her skin looked radiant. She was stunning.

"Thanks, Madison. Aine was probably getting fed up with my shorts and t-shirt." Lachlan kept his face blank, and Madison frowned. He looked away and held out some bills, and Madison continued to glower as she rang through the sale. Aine fidgeted behind him and pulled at the clothes she wore.

"Actually, I preferred the shorts; these are very restrictive," Aine said, looking down at herself and twisting slightly to test her movement.

"I've also added a sundress, and there's a jacket here for her." Unfortunately, Madison failed to keep her smile bright.

Lachlan could only imagine how hard it was to try to dress Aine. The thought made him chuckle despite his determination to keep his distance, and Madison looked up sharply. Lachlan realized that she had probably not seen him around town much, let alone seen him smile or chuckle. He guessed he would be making a new impression, adding to the gossip that already surrounded Aine.

"Come on, let's get to the shop." Lachlan didn't want to be there anymore. He put his hand out to Aine as Madison helped her into her jacket and handed her a few bags. He was shocked when Aine took his hand, unsure why he offered it in the first place. He led her out of the store before he let go, then clenched his hand as he continued to walk. It tingled and felt warm—so much for keeping his distance.

Lachlan cleared his throat and led the way to his shop, which was across the street. Aine followed him as he crossed, pulling at the jacket Madison had put on her. They stood at the entrance to his storefront, and he unlocked the door as he hid his face.

AINE YANKED at the jacket again; it felt tight and uncomfortable, as did the jeans. But as Madison said, they did make her butt look good. She looked up and stared at the exterior of the shop. It was plainly decorated with "Wood Shop" in bold letters across the top, typical of Lachlan not to embellish it further. It wasn't massive inside, but the displayed chairs, tables, and large, ornate frames filled the space elegantly. There were animal carvings along one shelf, which sparked Aine's interest, and a small counter at the back with an array of tools lining the wall behind it.

"It's not much, and to be honest, I do most of my work at home, but it helps to have a presence in town a couple of days a week. Folks don't like trekking out to the house even if it is an excuse to go to Phil's diner." Lachlan looked around as if trying to see what she did.

"I love it!" Aine exclaimed. "It feels like the happy part of you."

Lachlan looked at her, bemused, but she ignored him and continued to take in the store. She touched nearly every surface as he went to the back and sat on the chair behind the counter.

"Take a seat." He pointed at one of the rocking chairs in the back corner. "I'll only stay for a couple of hours today, but you may as well make yourself comfortable."

They spent the next few hours taking orders from the locals. At first, Aine sat in the corner, but when she could see Lachlan was busy with an older gentleman, she got up to speak to a young mother who had walked in with her son. The boy was shy and hid behind his mom, so Aine knelt beside him.

"What's your name, youngling?"

"Cory."

"Cory, that's a lovely name. What are you here for today?"

Cory looked up at his mom with uncertainty, and she gave him a reassuring smile.

"I would like a toy chest made. Mama says that I need to be able to tidy up all my toys, and Jeff had Lachlan make a really cool toy chest for him." Cory glanced nervously towards Lachlan.

"I'm sure Lachlan will be happy to make one for you!" Aine smiled and mentally reached out to soothe the boy; he grinned at her from behind his mother's leg. It felt natural to soothe the child. The woman mouthed a thank you at her, her eyes sparkled as she watched Aine with her child.

Lachlan had finished with his previous customer and took the young mother's details while Aine, still crouched, spoke to Cory about giant lizards that used to live on the planet. Cory called them dinosaurs.

Lachlan approached her after they left. "Paige said she'd never seen Cory say more than a few words to anyone. What did you do?" he asked.

"Spoke to him like an equal?" Aine shrugged as another customer walked through the door. Lachlan smiled at her and went to talk to them.

By the time Lachlan decided it was time to go home, he had a list of new orders to work on. Aine looked at him and could see how content he was. Whatever Lachlan's past, he was happy when he made things for people.

LACHLAN TOOK Aine to Phil's diner for some lunch after they had picked up groceries and dropped them with the new clothes back at his house. She held the laminated menu in front of her; she had no idea what any of the food was. He ordered them both burgers when Aine admitted she didn't know what to get.

"Aine!" Phil called out. "Good to see you here."

His evident joy warmed Aine. "Hi, Phil. Thank you so much for all your help. I don't know what I would have done without you."

His face reddened, and he smiled at her. "S'nuthin," he mumbled. "I'll go and sort your burgers."

Aine could see why everyone liked him. She thought of the sweater she still hadn't given back and felt a little guilty. "I should give him his sweater back," she said when he moved to the kitchen.

"I doubt Phil would take it; he seems smitten with you." Lachlan didn't look at her but stared out the window.

Aine watched his face—Lachlan was in a weird mood. He had been a bit gruff with some of his customers, who didn't seem surprised. Lachlan was a puzzle, and she wasn't sure why he had offered to take her in. He seemed a good man but troubled. Aine's mouth watered at the smell of cooking meat coming from the kitchen area and found her train of thought changing from Lachlan to the burger.

"I'll start Cory's chest this afternoon, you can help if you'd like" Lachlan interrupted her, pondering. "The other projects will take a bit longer, but no one is in a rush."

Lachlan took his hands off the table just before Phil put down two plates of burgers and fries. Aine swallowed as she watched Lachlan pick up his burger and take a bite, then she did the same. A groan escaped as she bit into the patty; she didn't think she ever tasted anything like this—not that she would ever remember tasting something like this if she had. The flavor of seasoned meat juices rolled around her mouth. The burger did not last long, and she moved on to her fries, but after a few bites, she lost interest. She liked the potato, but the burger was better.

"Not liking the fries?" Lachlan asked her as he finished his meal.

"They just aren't as nice as the burger." Aine looked to see if Phil was coming back with another one. Lachlan laughed; the sound was deep and rich and caused her face to heat. She felt a warmth flush through her and turned to look at him.

Lachlan's eyes were full of laughter as he looked at her. She let out a breath she hadn't realized she held—he had undoubtedly relaxed around her. At that moment, there was no sign of the warrior she had first seen. As he held her eyes, Lachlan's face flattened, and his lips thinned. He looked out the window again.

"I'll order another if you're that hungry." When Lachlan looked back, his gaze was intense.

She wondered what it would be like to touch his face, and her hand twitched at the thought. When he smiled, he looked younger and more carefree. Aine liked him much better that way, rather than the unapproachable and violent man she had met the last time she was in the diner. Or the gruff persona he used as a shield.

Phil must have heard their conversation because he soon brought out another burger for her, which she promptly devoured. Phil looked astonished, his eyes nearly popping out of his head, and Lachlan laughed again with his friend. Phil looked across at Lachlan, and from his face, Aine could tell he was stunned. Lachlan must not laugh very much. The fact that she could make him laugh warmed Aine again, and she felt a pleasant tightness in her chest.

Once Aine had finished, they walked towards his house together, so close their fingers almost brushed. The air around them felt electric, and Aine couldn't believe how much had changed in just two days. What little she could remember before yesterday morning filled her with dread, but the time she spent with Lachlan had more than made up for it. Even grumpy, his company was pleasant.

Heat shot through her when her fingers accidentally brushed Lachlan's arm; he tensed but didn't move. She still knew he was dangerous, but now it felt like he would use his lethal grace to protect her. He tried to hide it, but Aine could tell how by the position of his body, that instinctively, he did it to protect her. And she realized she would do the same for him if it came to it.

Aine shook her head to clear the thought. After only a day, she felt safe with him, which seemed ludicrous.

AINE WAS ARGUING with the man from her dream, the one who poured the pungent drink down her throat.

"It's not your place to send them out; the more we keep to ourselves, the better," she snarled in his face.

"We should not be cowering in the shadows, Aine. You're weak, and you're making your people weak. Why can't you see that I'm the better leader here? It is my right!"

"Your RIGHT?! Are you crazy? You're not even pure Aoibhan! This is my birthright, I'm of the Royal bloodline, and your resentment is ridiculous!" Aine could barely contain her anger. "What is wrong with you?"

She could feel her power surge through her; her fingertips started to tingle, and a growl, begun at her core, released in a violent snarl. The muscles on the man before her tightened, and his eyes burned into hers. Aine felt her hands hit the floor, but her face was still level with his. She could feel saliva drip from her mouth. She growled again and stared intensely at the man until he bowed his head and backed up to cower in a corner.

Aine woke with a start, breathing hard while staring at her hands—a sharp pain shot through them and up her arms. Her fingers were elongated, and sharp claws protruded from her fingertips. Pure white fur covered her up to her forearms, and she released a scream, which came out as a deep growl. Her face tingled, and her head felt heavy. She closed her eyes and attempted to slow her ragged breaths. An image of a beautiful woman with Aine's eyes and raven hair appeared in her mind; she followed the woman's lead and counted as she took deep breaths to regain control.

A few minutes later, she opened her eyes, and her hands

were hers again. First her eyes, and now her hands. Was she going crazy?

The sun crowned the horizon and streaked the sky red and purple outside the basement window. She couldn't hear Lachlan upstairs but decided to head up anyway.

She grabbed some coffee, grateful Lachlan had shown her how to use the coffee machine. He rarely used it, preferring tea, but it had been a present from Phil. Aine loved coffee; it was incredible and gave her the kickstart she really needed in the morning. When Lachlan came downstairs an hour later, she was on her second cup and had watched the sunrise while sitting in his rocking chair on the porch, her legs folded underneath her. Aine had felt safe with his scent on the chair surrounding her.

"You're up early." His voice was warm and didn't hold any of the roughness it had when they first met, though he still seemed wary of her.

"I couldn't sleep."

"Nightmares?" His eyes met hers as he crouched to her level.

Aine stared into his ice-blue eyes; they were anything but cold. The look of concern in them caught her breath, and she didn't dare break the moment. A warm tingle started in her chest, and a strange butterfly sensation in her stomach caused her to lean closer to him. They were inches apart; his scent was a comfort that drew her closer. Lachlan's gaze dropped to her lips, and Aine finally let out the breath she had been holding. She felt like the air crackled between them, and if he leaned closer, their lips would touch.

"Lachlan, you back there?"

Phil's deep voice broke the tension, and Lachlan quickly stood up. The moment was shattered, and Aine felt a cold shock at Lachlan's absence; heat flooded her face.

"Yeah, Phil, around the back with Aine." Lachlan coughed to clear his throat; his voice sounded weird to Aine's ears, and she watched as his hand brushed through his hair. He looked anywhere but at Aine.

Her cheeks felt warm as she sipped her coffee and looked toward the forest. She couldn't help but smile and stifle a laugh as she stared out into the distance.

5

As Lachlan left the house and walked toward his shed, he rubbed his face and groaned. Aine and Lachlan had fallen into a routine. They ate breakfast together before they worked in Lachlan's shed, and he had kept his distance since their near kiss that Phil interrupted, but he would often forget himself. Aine was so beautiful, and her strength shone through. He could tell she struggled with her nightmares over the last week and often heard her shouts while she slept. He awoke every time he heard her in the basement, but she went on as if nothing had happened during the day. Lachlan had tried to talk to her about it, but Aine made it clear she didn't want to.

Lachlan couldn't help but touch her; he felt at peace when she was near. Each innocent brush of their hands caused heat to crawl up his arm. He would feel her watch him when she didn't think he was looking. He was frustrated with himself—when they had been in town together, he had decided to stay away from her, but he couldn't help himself. He knew what she was, but his attraction to her still grew. He was inexplicably drawn to her.

The first project they worked on together was Cory's toy chest. Lachlan built it as Aine carved. Lachlan was impressed with her skills; she obviously had experience, and the muscle memory meant she could produce beautiful and intricate carvings with no training. Aine carved an elaborate jungle scene on the chest, depicting all of Cory's favorite dinosaurs.

"I thought you told Cory you didn't know what a dinosaur looked like. Did you look up the images for him?" Lachlan watched in wonder, a hint of amusement in his voice as he ran his hands over the finished piece.

"No, I just saw them in my head as Cory described them. He has posters in his room and on his bedspread. So this will match his bedroom." Aine grinned at him as she answered and ran her finger over the horns of a triceratops.

"How do you know what's in his bedroom?" Lachlan's brow creased when he looked at her, wearing the sundress Madison had picked out and tried to keep his face blank. She looked feminine and beautiful in it. He had warred with himself as to whether he should tell her what she was, especially in moments like these. Sometimes it was like she read others' minds when she described seeing images.

"I could see it in his head when I talked to him." Aine's mouth twitched as she watched Lachlan.

He could feel her amusement when she said things like that to him. He'd never heard of such skills, though, so maybe he was wrong, and she was something else. At times it was like she was a psychic; he'd never believed in them, but what if they were real? He didn't want to burden her more than she already was or scare her if he was wrong. Of course, he wouldn't know for sure until the full moon, and that was tonight.

They lived comfortably together, despite Lachlan's

conflict. He taught Aine to cook, and they shared house-work. He'd never had a partnership like theirs; he had always chosen to be alone. He had attempted a relationship once when he lived in Seattle but hated living in a city, and it was the longest he spent in one. Lachlan had missed the woods too much and ended up leaving the woman when the relationship turned toxic. She had married a trust fund douche who gave her everything she wanted and didn't have to lift a finger. He preferred honest work and living with Aine. She made him realize what a real partner could be—but of course, he couldn't let it go further.

"This is incredible, Aine!" he exclaimed as he ran his hand over the pattern again. She didn't notice him lost in thought. Her attention to detail was unparalleled, and even he couldn't have done a better job. Her hands were small enough for more detailed and delicate work. Aine leaned over to watch him admire it, and as she brushed against him, electricity seemed to shoot through his body. He grew heated at her closeness and found it hard to breathe.

"Do you really think so?" Her face looked up into his, and as their eyes met, a jolt shot through him again. He'd resisted touching her face, but as she stared up, the heat in her eyes was unmistakable, and he couldn't help but bring his hand up to cup her jaw. She gasped as his thumb gently brushed her cheek.

When Aine leaned into Lachlan's hand to nuzzle it and closed her eyes, he glanced towards her lips, which parted to let out a soft breath. Lachlan let out the one he had been holding. He ached for her but held himself back before now. His resistance crumbled as he looked at her.

Aine opened her eyes to meet his intense gaze; they were so close. Lachlan stared down into her emerald eyes and bent towards her slowly. When she didn't back away, his lips met hers, and he kissed her slow and deep. A yearning he'd forgotten existed blossomed in his chest, and he lifted his other hand to stroke up her arm.

Aine's hands lifted to rest on his chest, and he moaned as she deepened the kiss. Lachlan brushed his hand through her hair, which felt like silk and pushed her against the worktable. A gasp left Aine as her butt hit the bench, but she didn't seem in pain. As her arms circled his back and caressed, he moved his hands to her waist and held her up, her legs quivering. When he broke the kiss, he looked down into her face, which gazed up at him in awe.

She now sat on the table in the center of the shed; the sundress she wore had ridden up and revealed the creamy skin of her thigh. Lachlan couldn't help running his hands up her soft skin and kissing her again feverishly as her fingers dug in his back.

Lachlan realized if he didn't stop himself, he might take this further than she was ready. She couldn't remember anything before last week, and it wasn't fair to her. He tried to push the thought away, but as he broke the kiss and looked into Aine's glazed eyes, he froze. It felt like a bucket of cold water had been thrown over him. He couldn't get involved with her—they were already too close.

"That was…" Aine's voice trailed off as she breathed deeply.

Electricity still crackled between them, and Lachlan stiffened. He knew she was strong, but there was an immense amount she still didn't know about herself. He cupped her cheek once more and leaned his forehead against hers. How could something so wrong feel so right?

She smiled as their breath mingled, and they rested against each other.

THAT AFTERNOON, they delivered the chest to Cory. Lachlan held Aine's hand as he navigated the truck through the town streets. He tried not to touch her but craved her contact. Aine was quiet, and her face blushed every time she looked at him. He chuckled, amazed that he could affect her like that.

Cory's face lit up like a Christmas tree when Lachlan unloaded the chest and brought it into the house. The boy's eyes were wide as Lachlan pulled aside the blanket he'd used to protect it on the drive. He was enamored by Aine as she explained what she'd carved and why. Lachlan didn't blame him; he was infatuated with her himself and listened just as intently as he stood next to Cory's mom, Paige. Finally, he turned to the woman to see her reaction, and the look in her eyes showed shock, her mouth open.

"He never talks to anyone, Lachlan," she said. "Where did you find her?"

"Phil found her out the back of his diner; she doesn't remember anything before that." Lachlan sighed; he had hoped she would have remembered something by now. He scratched his beard as Paige stared at him.

"Seems she's good with more than just my son." Paige winked at him, and Lachlan could feel his face heat, realizing his feelings were written there.

He shouldn't feel like this for her, but she captivated him. Aine didn't even know who she was, and he felt like he'd known her forever; the draw had become too much. He looked at the ground and then up at Aine, who still chattered away animatedly with Cory. The young boy made dinosaur noises and ran around the chest to look at the other side. She was great with the kid, and it made Lachlan think she would be a wonderful mom. He frowned thoughtfully.

Aine was quiet in the truck on the drive back.

"You okay?" Lachlan asked as he steered towards home. Aine stared out the window, withdrawn once more and watching the trees thicken on the side of the road.

"Do you ever feel like you've lost something—forgotten what it is, but know something is missing? I realize that sounds stupid, considering I can't remember more than a week ago, but I have this pull, this feeling, I need to go back. But back to where?" Aine huffed; she was frustrated and fidgeted in the passenger seat, rubbing her hands up her arms. Lachlan continued to watch the road but was aware of her discomfort and stayed silent.

"Lachlan, I need to go back to the clearing. I need to know where I came from," Aine said quietly.

"I know." Lachlan sighed and felt his hands grip the steering wheel; his knuckles whitened. They did need to go back to the clearing but should wait until after tonight. The tension in his body caused Aine to react; her whole demeanor became defensive in contrast to her reaction to him when they kissed. The thought of the kiss made Lachlan smile, then frown. His stomach churned. He hadn't felt in control of his actions, and that thought worried him.

Lachlan's house came into view, and Phil was sitting on the front steps.

"What's up, Phil?" Lachlan parked and stepped out of the truck. He tried for nonchalance but could hear the tension in his voice as he headed over to the big man. Aine followed and gave Phil a big smile.

"Hi, Phil!" The girl threw her arms around him and squeezed. Phil's shock made Lachlan laugh as the big man put his arms around Aine. He gently rubbed her back before letting her go, then shuffled his feet to stammer out a reply to Lachlan.

"Er...well...I...." Phil coughed. "There's been some coyotes spotted across town. The Jones boys was hoping ya would look."

"Sure, but I can't be too long." Lachlan glanced towards Aine. "Do you want to come or stay here?"

She shrugged and walked towards the house without a word. She was too quiet; he would have felt better if she came but sensed Aine wanted time alone.

"She okay?" Phil looked after Aine, concern on his face.

"Yeah, just frustrated, I think." Lachlan gestured for Phil to hop into the truck with him. He glanced back after Aine, his jaw tight. "I'll be back before nightfall."

She turned back and smiled wanly while he kept his face blank. He silently promised himself and Aine that he would be back in time.

AINE WATCHED the truck pull away before she looked to the back door. She should really wait until Lachlan got back, but she needed to be out. Her skin tingled; she was drawn to the woods and the need to go back to the clearing.

The last week with Lachlan had been incredible. They were both comfortable around each other, a clear contrast from how they had met. Yet, every time she was near him, she couldn't help but stare. His quiet demeanor and thoughtfulness touched her. She yearned for closeness when he was around, and this afternoon she would have given herself to him. The memory of the way he'd touched her face and the kiss, oh that kiss, had left her shaky and breathless. Aine sighed. She couldn't move forward with him as half a woman. She didn't know her past, and when she had been around Cory, she had felt a pang. Like she'd forgotten someone important—it brought her back to reality with a nasty jolt.

Her nightmares had been getting worse. They haunted her and blemished her time with Lachlan. From what she could piece together, they centered around the man who had poisoned her. Aine either argued with him in her dreams about the same thing or replayed him feeding her poison. If it was poison she had drunk, the taste lingered still, and she felt sick to her stomach every time she thought about it.

It was time to go and find some answers. Aine changed into shorts and a shirt before she determinedly walked out the door.

Lachlan had bought her some sneakers when they were at Madison's, but she preferred bare feet most of the time. As she entered the woods, she closed her eyes and tried to feel her way, just like in Lachlan's house; the same calming power she'd felt then returned. Finally, it seemed ready for her to make her move.

The woods felt calm on the edge, but she could sense there was something more profound, a hum of tumultuous life. Aine slowly walked through the trees, and the rough ground didn't bother her calloused feet. She opened her eyes, looked in the direction of the clearing she woke in the week before behind the diner. It didn't take long to reach, and Lachlan would be a while if he tracked the coyotes.

As Aine approached where Phil had found her, she could feel tension through her body. A sick feeling started in her stomach, and she could smell a familiar, rancid odor, causing bile to rise in her throat; her legs to tremble. Her hands shook violently as the sickness began to overwhelm her, and her vision blurred.

Aine now stood where she had woken; she fell to her knees and heaved as her stomach burned. Tears leaked down her face, and she nearly choked on bile. Then, after several more painful retches, a thick black liquid expelled from her mouth and nose. The smell caused Aine to gag again and brought up more of the disgusting vomit. Once she was sure there was nothing left, her head came up. Her mind felt sharper than it had been.

Adrenaline had started to course through her, and her vision sharpened—she felt she could zoom in on objects in the distance. At this point, she would bet anything her eyes were doing the weird color change she'd seen in the mirror. Her senses honed further, and she looked around. Over the putrid smell, she caught a familiar scent towards the edge of the woods furthest from Phil's diner.

There was no trail, but the woods weren't thick there or overgrown. Aine took a deep breath and spat. She wiped her mouth. For the first time, Aine felt she was where she was supposed to be and more like herself.

The evening wore on as Aine walked; she started slow, but as the scent got stronger and gained power, she strode faster. She tried to remain calm, but the further she walked into the woods, the more weighed down she felt. There was an ominous presence that pressed in on her. It didn't help that the light had started to disappear as time passed, and Aine started to worry that Lachlan would be back soon and she had walked several miles.

Before too long, it was fully dark, and the woods were now only illuminated by a full moon crowning the horizon. As the light touched Aine, she felt a strange but natural power build inside her. It was more than the connections she felt with others. She felt strong, more herself than she had since she woke up. Aine wanted to look up to the moon, wanted to shout her joy.

She turned to look back the way she had come but wouldn't return until she had some answers. When she focused back in the direction she traveled towards, her entire body locked up.

A man stood in front of her. He wasn't one of the men from her dreams, but she knew him. Instinctively, her body crouched slightly, and she coiled, ready to spring at him if needed. His mental feel was vile and toxic as it came to her.

"Well, well, well. Nyko said you were dead when he left you out here. Guess he was wrong." The man paused as a sneer crossed his face. "Or he was lying."

He was slightly up an incline, and Aine was aware he had the higher ground. She stayed silent as she assessed the danger. He was well-muscled, with long hair tied back in a ponytail. His face was angular, his mouth thin and shaped into a cruel smile as he looked down on her.

"Han," Aine shocked herself by saying. By the look on his face, he was more surprised.

"Why are you here?" She bluffed, able to remember his name but not who he was. Every time she had woken from a nightmare, she felt the residue of power running through her. Now that she was faced with a dangerous adversary, she could feel that power building more strongly inside her. Aine needed to stall; she wasn't sure how much longer she could contain it, but it wasn't ready yet. The light from the full moon caressed her skin; she could almost feel it pulse energy into her.

"So, you remember as well. Rolan will be upset that after everything, it didn't even work."

"Didn't work?" Aine growled, her voice deeper than it had been. Her skin felt hot and too tight.

"Maybe you don't remember after all—shame, really. Such a waste, but how pleased will Rolan be when I tell him that I disposed of you." Han looked her up and down, and Aine felt revulsion run through her as he leered.

"After I've had some fun, that is. You always thought you were better than us, but you won't feel that way when I've had my taste of you. Rolan won't mind if I have a go before I kill you."

Han's growl was the only warning before he launched at her. Aine felt her body move on instinct alone. Intuition told her he would feint and charge left, so she rolled to the right gracefully, coming back to her feet in a fluid movement. The movement was also a joy like she had been held back but was now released.

As she turned to face Han, her jaw dropped while his body grew, hands dropping to the floor. She now faced a large, grey wolf. He was raw strength and a force to be reckoned with. But the power she could feel inside herself finally unleashed.

Time slowed. She was consumed by the rage she felt following each nightmare; the power that had been rising within her burst through, and she drew strength from it. In a heartbeat, she leaped at him. She balanced herself carefully as her weight, far heavier than when she left the ground, helped her trajectory perfectly, and she instantly downed the grey wolf. The growl that escaped her was primal, fueled by all the pain and anger she felt.

Aine went for his throat, and Han deftly twisted from under her. When she spun to face him, she realized she was larger than him. Han looked up into her face; she could sense him fighting against her power while she stared him down.

Aine's heartbeat pounded in her ears, slow and steady. She growled again, and put more power behind her stare to force Han to submit. He started to crouch before he exploded towards her once more. Caught off guard, Aine barely moved in time to miss his jaws as they snapped; she heard Han's teeth click as they closed on what would have been her hind leg. He had tried to immobilize her first. Rage powered her further, and she pivoted, surprisingly quicker than his more diminutive form, and heard a snap as her jaw crunched down on his leg. Aine had flawlessly performed the maneuver he had just failed.

Han howled in pain as Aine slowly prowled forward for the kill. Proud and tall, she felt her mind connect to his and sensed the rotten and corrupted cesspool. She sniffed and recoiled as she felt his consciousness, the darkness and filth beneath.

"You are impure and unworthy of your power," Aine thought towards him. Han snarled at her, his energy drained under her scrutiny. His very existence was an offense to her kind. A rabid wolf, unable to submit to a Pack Leader—the very worst of the worst and rarely redeemable. The atrocities they committed broke their ability to recognize a Pack Leader or fit into a pack; Aine was unsure how he could have infiltrated hers. She still couldn't really remember, but she knew what she was. It would be a blessing to the world to be rid of him, and she, as Pack Leader, had the right to carry out judgment. Flashes of what he intended to do to her entered her head and added fuel to her rage.

Aine's full power beat down on him as she met his eye, yet Han still defied her. He was an infection needing to be purged. Aine approached. She didn't want to prolong his pain as the blood leaked from his leg. She pinned his head with one large white paw, and as her jaw encircled his throat, Aine quickly ended his life. She didn't even wince when his neck broke, and he exhaled his last breath.

Aine looked at her pure white legs in front of her and then towards the moon. It was a clean kill; she had no blood on her, and he hadn't suffered. She bowed her head, grateful that of all nights it had been tonight, she went in search of answers. She now knew what she was and that she was a leader—or she had been.

But Aine couldn't remember her pack or who Rolan was. What would Lachlan think? Her horror as she imagined his face when she told him caused her heart to squeeze. She looked at the body of the wolf she had just killed. Would Lachlan understand?

She padded in the direction of his house and lowered herself to the ground once she was a reasonable distance from Han's body, no longer able to smell his offensive odor.

A pain like no other, different from the rage and the betrayal she felt in her nightmares, weighed down on her. It made it hard to breathe as she thought about what would never be.

How could Lachlan understand what she was? He would never accept her. But Aine was no coward, and she would confront him. Then, if she had to, she would leave and find her pack.

Han's words and the mystery still surrounding her rattled around her mind. She had been dumped on the edge of human territory. *Did this mean her pack didn't want her?* She thought. Aine's head lowered to the ground as the rejection by her pack and possibly from Lachlan when he found out what she was, seeped into her.

6

Rolan, acting leader of the Aoibhan pack, faced his people. Old and young gathered to hear his announcement and looked to him for reassurance. Twenty miles from Burntwood Falls, deeper into the woods and in an area difficult to navigate was a shifter settlement called Sumter. Since the disappearance of the Pack Leader, Rolan's mate, the pack had been agitated. Some of the older members displayed their distrust of him openly.

The pack survived over the centuries through anonymity but had to keep up with technology to know what they were up against. Unfortunately, phones didn't work this deep in the woods, but Aine had organized agents who traveled among humans and stayed up-to-date with current events. They chose to stay off the grid for their own protection but often sent wolves out to experience the world as a rite of passage.

The village was made up of tiny wooden houses, sunk into the ground and covered in foliage for disguise. They had managed to incorporate plumbing and some heating via generators. Woodwork was sold to the outside world to fund the settlement, though they traveled far out of the area to avoid drawing attention.

Rolan grimaced. The pack always looked down on him, and yet here he was in front of them as their leader. Now in charge, they had to follow him until Aine was found. Though he wasn't as tall as some of the warrior members of the pack, he was all lean muscle and well-trained, making up for his lack of height with his vicious and precise training style. In addition, he had the benefit of skills from two packs, despite being abandoned by the first.

Rolan ran his hands through his dark hair. Not many remembered his arrival, and most assumed he was born Aoibhan. Aine had helped him initially, she begged her father to let him stay, and Rolan had come to love her for a time. He wasn't sure when it changed, but at some point, he began to resent her leadership and how she used her power. He looked out over the crowd to survey them, the midday sun pouring over the meeting area in the center of the village.

Tensions were high, as always. Rumors of werewolves and shifters circulated for centuries; however, modern beliefs dismissed any truth to such stories due to the vast number of movies and books out there. The underground shifter community encouraged such thoughts and needed them to stay that way. Shifters were scarce, and they had almost been hunted to extinction, thanks to the shifter hunters, famous for their violence and efficiency. But not all shifters believed in secrecy and caution.

Rolan looked out over the small houses. Each had a set of steps down to the house entrance making the homes looked half-buried; the roof on each was covered in foliage and moss.

When the weather got colder, this acted as insulation to keep the houses warmer. The houses surrounded the gathering area located in the village center, with a small school and some communal houses lining the edges. Rolan sneered as he looked over the village. The pack situated here had thrived for generations in modest living. However, they didn't leave and integrate with humans beyond trading—it was forbidden.

Aine's family was powerful and had kept them hidden. Right now, they waited for an update on Aine's disappearance over a week ago. Last night was the full moon, and only those of the Royal bloodline could control their change outside of the full moon. During the pack shift, everyone had sensed a power surge from Aine. The connection with the pack had not been fully broken, as Rolan had thought, and they now knew she was still alive.

Rolan had to hide his rage that she had survived. After Aine had been severed from the pack link, Rolan had no longer felt her power and thought her dead. The pack assumed she had been killed by humans when they ceased to feel her connection; they didn't believe Aine would willingly abandon them. The reconnection with her the night before may have worked in his favor. Rolan growled to silence the pack and waited for their attention.

"As you all know, my mate briefly reconnected with us last night during our full moon shift." Rolan paused to gauge their reactions. "We do not know what this means or where she is; I know as much as you do." The lie came easily.

"Why would she leave in the first place?" one of the younger pack members asked with a shaky voice. Rolan could feel his nervousness and the pack's general unease.

"I don't know, but I promise you, I will find out. No one

misses and wants her back more than I do. Now I, as your Pack Leader—"

"But you are not Pack Leader; that would be Aine. She is pure Aoibhan and royalty. Next in line would be Eloi," the elder Eyolf interrupted. Not many knew that Rolan wasn't Aoibhan, but unfortunately, Eyolf did. He could make Rolan's life very difficult if he opposed his move into the position of Pack Leader.

Other pack members looked at him in confusion. At least they might not listen to the old wolf as he rambled.

"Eloi is too young and is yet to connect to the pack. I will do everything in my power to find Aine and, if possible, return her to her rightful place," Rolan continued, keeping his face blank. "Scouts will be sent to investigate immediately."

"Is that wise? You've been sending wolves out all week. Never have so many been absent from the settlement at one time. This is dangerous; Aine would not have permitted it. Even for herself," Eyolf spoke again, and there were murmurs of agreement from the crowd. Rolan's growl did not have the effect he hoped, and the elder wolf did not back down. Without the pack's acceptance of him as Leader, he would not easily be able to make Eyolf submit.

"The best thing we can do is continue as normal. Complete your duties and keep the settlement running as we always have. Do not be distracted. It is my responsibility as First Warrior to find Aine, and until we do, you will remain vigilant, and I will act as Leader in her place. You are all dismissed." Rolan's harsh command had the desired effect, and the crowd dispersed. He turned to leave as his Second, Mervan, approached, his face grim.

"The scouts found Han in wolf form." Mervan's voice

cracked. "His hind leg had been disabled and his neck broken."

The pack had sharp ears, and this conversation was not one Rolan wanted to be overheard. He gestured for Mervan to follow him as they continued to walk towards the Temple. The Temple was an extensive cave system on the edge of the village; it wasn't used for worship, but the shifters had written their stories onto the walls over the centuries. It was the history of the Aoibhan pack.

Rolan entered the large opening and stared into the darkness. His keen eyes didn't need the light to see, but there were shadow areas into several tunnels that led deeper into the cave. Rolan cocked his head and listened. Once he was sure there was no one there, he continued.

"Have you retrieved his remains?" Rolan wandered deeper into the cave. It wasn't used often, and the smell of rock dust flooded his senses. He found it an ideal area for meetings, ones he held in secret over the last few weeks regarding the pack's future. He smacked the wall and growled deeply once he was out of sight of the main entrance; his body begged to shift as his hands shook. He had to fight to keep his wolf contained.

"No, before they could move him, a family of locals came upon the area, and they had to flee. They thought it best not to be discovered." Mervan carefully kept his face blank, but he looked away. He usually held his composure better, but Mervan was obviously upset, and Rolan could see it in his friend. Han was Mervan's brother, and the fact that they hadn't retrieved the body caused him pain.

"It must have been her—no one else has the power to take down a fully trained warrior. She was supposed to be dead, Mervan. She wasn't breathing when I checked her. Who disposed of the body?"

"Nyko. He's young, but like you said—she wasn't breathing. We all saw that, and even if she had lived, no one survives a Severance with their memory intact." Mervan shifted. He had never doubted Rolan, even when Rolan suggested they sever and kill Aine to take control of the pack's future. Many shifters believed they should be able to live openly. Over the centuries, it had caused wars between shifters, often resulting in more rumors for the humans to spread. The revolution had never gained a foothold to make an impact until now.

"Get Nyko here," Rolan growled and continued to pace. He thought Aine would no longer be a problem. How had the process not worked? The ritual should have left her disconnected from the pack and with no memory. Once she had been severed, the pack should no longer feel her. Rolan would never have been suspected; he had beaten her until she wasn't breathing. How had she survived? All packs were connected via a dream link and could openly share thoughts and memories. It was how they communicated in wolf form and how they passed on knowledge to the next generation. It was impossible to lie during a dream or mind link.

The Severance ritual was only performed as a severe punishment for those banished from the pack. If they found out he had carried it out on their Royal Leader, then Rolan would be eviscerated. It had been a calculated risk to kill her without the pack's knowledge. He had once loved her, but her insistence on hiding the pack made it weak. So Rolan committed the deed for the greater good—it would be better for the pack in the long run. He would lead them into a new age. One where shifters led, able to openly live as what they were meant to be, and humans would cower. That was the rightful place for shifters, the most powerful creatures on Earth. Not hiding in the shadows like beasts. The legend of the hunters had kept shifters down, and now they were dying out.

Rolan snarled and punched the wall. His "mate," the "promised one," had been weak and pathetic. She had adhered to the ancient laws and kept her pack hidden and cowed. Although Aine sent agents out to learn of technological updates and spies to gauge rumors of shifters, she would never take the next step to infiltrate the humans. So when Rolan took control, he did what was best for everyone. They would live how they deserved if only she'd stayed gone.

Nyko bounded into the Temple, breathless and eyes wild. "You wanted me, Master?"

The boy twitched and tremored as he stood before Rolan. Disgusted, Rolan snarled at him, and Nyko dropped his gaze. Nyko folded in on himself, shoulders bent inwards.

Weak. Aine had bred vulnerable people, easy to manipulate and bring to heel. Rolan openly laughed at the pathetic boy before him. Nyko's head snapped up with wide eyes. When Rolan's gaze returned to him, the boy's eyes dropped once more.

"Where did you leave her?" Rolan demanded as he strode up to Nyko and snarled in his face.

"Around the back of a diner about twenty miles away." Nyko trembled, but his gaze remained low.

Rolan growled and stalked away from the boy. "Why did you leave her near humans? They could have helped her!" His patience had ended. The stupidity of one wolf may have cost him everything. Why hadn't the boy dumped her away from civilization and in a ditch to rot?

"I didn't want her to be alone, and you said she was dead," Nyko whined, trembling harder, visibly shaken.

Rolan backhanded him, and there was a loud crunch as Nyko hit the opposite wall. Mervan stepped in front of Rolan before he could approach the boy again, then glanced at Nyko with disgust.

"Get out," Mervan ordered before he faced Rolan. "A missing wolf or death will not go unnoticed," he said in a low voice so only Rolan could hear.

Rolan inhaled and tried to rein in his temper. "This may complicate matters," he breathed. "Will the boy stay quiet?"

"He is not a fool. There may be a way for us to use this. If she has recovered, then we can assume she was helped by humans. There are no other shifters around here. If she is consorting with humans, then she has broken pack law. This may be better than her being a martyr, had the pack assumed the humans had killed her." Mervan put his hands on Rolan's shoulders. "It won't be long until the humans are hunting wolves after finding Han. We can fuel the anger of the pack towards Aine and the humans once they hear of his death and her betrayal."

Mervan's grin was calculated and malicious, unlike his brother, who was half-wild. Han had shown signs of madness, and Rolan was almost relieved that he hadn't been left alive to turn completely rabid. He was lucky to have Mervan as his Second, and despite the pain Han's death caused him, Rolan was lucky Han was no longer a loose cannon. The loss would make Mervan more brutal and calculated.

"Brilliant," Rolan smirked back. "I am so pleased you're not my enemy, Mervan—your plans are diabolical. I will announce her crimes once we've found where she has hidden. If it's with a human, then all the better."

Rolan appreciated how much better this idea was than if they blamed the humans for her death. He would be able to make her suffer by turning the people she loved against her. He could just imagine how good it would feel to see them kill her themselves—the irony of her being accused of consorting with humans when she had tried so hard to stay isolated from them.

Rolan's grin was wicked as he exited the cave, in a much better mood than when he entered.

ELOI'S HEART hammered as she tried to make sense of what she just heard. She looked out from the shadows of a lesser-used exit tunnel. She was small for her age and rarely noticed. As she stood and stretched, Eloi brushed the rock dust off her plain pants and shirt. Her dark hair fell to her shoulders in tangles, fallen out of the messy bun she had put it in earlier. Eloi had always loved to explore the Temple and knew lots of places she could hide there.

She tilted her head and reached out with her power, as her mother had taught her. Her father was mistaken—she could connect with the pack. Eloi felt each shifter in the area to make sure her path was clear, and Rolan was nowhere nearby.

She had developed early and had been shifting with ease for several years now. At thirteen years, nearly fourteen, she was a natural; Aine's daughter, her bloodline strong. Eloi had been suspicious of her father since her mother's disappearance, plagued by nightmares of Rolan hurting her mom and the arguments they had when they thought she couldn't hear. Her heart ached when she thought of her mother, and she had to control herself before she whined in pain.

Eloi and Aine were close. They often slept in the same

bed, and her mom taught her to connect via her dreams. This obviously led to a strong bond, one Eloi hoped to use to find her mom. The moment she had felt the Severance ritual being performed on her mother, Eloi held onto the bond they had with all the love and strength she could muster. Every moment she had, she reached for that connection and sent her strength through the bond. She could still feel her mom and pushed memories toward her every time she felt her sleep. But Eloi couldn't tell if it worked. She had felt nothing in return, and a hollowness filled her.

Eloi crept from the Temple toward the house she had shared with her mother and father. She's lived there for as long as she could remember. But, unlike Aine, Rolan was detached and distant with Eloi, while her mom *always* made time for her. And it just didn't feel like home anymore with her mom missing.

Her parents had argued increasingly over the last year. They were happy once, but Eloi hadn't seen happiness between them in a long time. Her father constantly challenged her mother's decisions regarding what was best for the pack.

Aine had always taken care of the pack needs before hers. She'd become their Pack Leader at sixteen, the youngest Pack Leader the Aoibhans ever had. Eloi couldn't imagine taking on that responsibility in only a couple short years.

Eloi crept, paused, and felt again for any pack members nearby as she passed the other houses. She sighed when she didn't feel her father in their home. She needed her mother to remember who she was and return before her father's plan played out.

Aine would be heartbroken if the pack turned against

her. How could her father do this? He had been vocal about making changes to the pack, and Aine had often heard him out before making decisions. But Rolan pushed more and more of late, he even challenged her in front of pack members. He argued with desperation, often it turned violent forcing Aine to make him submit. Eloi remembered one time that her mom had been so upset when she was forced to make Rolan submit in front of other pack members. Rolan had pushed her into it and left the pack for days in his anger.

Eloi turned the corner and stopped abruptly. Eyolf stood at the entrance to their home and turned to look in her direction. She realized too late that she dropped her mind search after she felt Rolan across the village. She wouldn't avoid Eyolf now but was scared to be seen with him. Rolan was already suspicious of Eyolf after their discussion in the meeting today. She sighed and approached the elder. He seemed relieved to see her and pulled her into a hug when she was near.

"I've been worried about you, little one. With your mother missing, I feared you would disappear after her."

Eloi's mouth turned down. With the way Rolan acted recently, Eloi wouldn't be surprised if she were next. Eyolf's eyes were full of concern as he looked at her face; he appeared to have had the same thought. Eloi felt a surge of gratefulness for his concern.

"I was exploring," she offered weakly and walked through the entrance to her home. The house had an empty feeling; their belongings were sparse, and there were no personal items in view. There was an open kitchen and living area in the main entranceway and two bedrooms separated off each side of the tiny house. It just wasn't the same without her mom.

Eloi and Rolan had avoided each other since Aine's disappearance, which suited her—especially when she had seen what was done to her mother from his dreams. Eloi's connection to the pack was powerful, especially to her mother and, unbeknownst to him, her father, with whom she shared blood. But, unfortunately, she wasn't powerful enough to show the pack Rolan's actions yet.

Eloi stamped her feet and huffed as she crossed to the kitchen. Idly, she played with a cup that had been left on the table.

Rolan didn't realize he had been projecting memories to her in his sleep or that Eloi was sensitive enough to see them. In her desperation, Eloi kept trying to push them to her mother in hopes that if she had lost her memory, it would help her remember. Until now, she thought the Severance ritual was still in effect, blocking her from Aine. But last night, she caught a glimpse of her mom as she carved wood, and her heart soared.

Eyolf cautiously followed her into the tiny house, his eyes darted around to each shadow before he turned to Eloi.

"Have you dreamt of your mother?" he asked. "Like we've been working on? I know your mother wanted you to have a normal childhood, but these aren't normal times."

Only Eyolf and Aine knew how far Eloi had come. Her empathy and connections could make her a target of jealousy, and Aine hadn't wanted her to be treated differently. But, unfortunately, Eloi hadn't managed to catch up with Eyolf to talk alone since Aine's disappearance.

"I wanted to talk to you, but we can't risk Father finding out. I've tried every day, just like we practiced, but something is blocking me. I think whatever Father fed her should have severed her completely, but I kept holding on to that contact, so I think it's still struggling inside her."

Eyolf frowned and waited for Eloi to continue. She hadn't yet had the chance to tell him of the Severance ritual —no wonder he looked puzzled.

"Rolan performed a Severance," Eloi whispered. It felt loud in their quiet surroundings. Eyolf gasped and growled. His face went red, and his eyes changed slightly; this was unheard of in a shifter his age. Eyolf was too old to shift— even that small change was a testament to his rage now.

Eloi growled herself, and her power beat out of her in waves. Her vision sharpened as her eyes shifted in an explicit command to subdue the elder. She had never tried anything like that and nearly sat down in relief when the elder submitted. His face looked just as shocked as she was relieved. If he had lost himself and given himself away to Rolan, they would both have been in danger.

"It is clear, Eloi, that you have a great future." Eyolf took control of himself and looked toward the door. "I cannot believe he would dare such a thing. The elders will hear of this."

"But what if they already know?" Eloi had thought about that already, and it was a well-known fact that some of the elders barely tolerated following one as young as Aine. So even though it was her birthright, and she had been Pack Leader nearly twenty years, it still grated.

"That is something to consider." Eyolf looked at her sadly. "I must go. If your father finds me here, then we both might have a problem. Be safe, youngling."

Eyolf touched his forehead to Eloi's and left swiftly; she was then in a home that no longer felt like home, bereft and empty. She entered her room and secured the door. Weariness weighed on her, and her shoulders sagged. Would her father do the same to her? She feared he would cross any line to become the undisputed Pack Leader.

Eyolf was right; with her mom gone, Eloi was next in line, and Eyolf would make it known Rolan wasn't pure Aoibhan. Rolan knew that; some of the other pack members may push the subject if they doubted him.

Eloi sat on her bed and hugged her knees. She had never felt so alone. Eloi's eyes stung as she stared at the wall in front of her. Polaroid pictures scattered the wall; some of her friends and mom, others of areas around the village she had grown to love. One of her mom's spies had brought a camera back and given it to Eloi as a gift.

The girl braced herself and sighed. She lay on her bed, and stared at the ceiling as she listened to the village around her. All was quiet except the distant river rushing as if nothing had changed. Rolan had yet to return, and she did not want to be awake when he did. What would he do next? Who else could she trust but Eyolf?

She played what she heard at the gathering over in her head, concentrating mainly on what happened in the Temple. She thought of her mother and the bond they shared, imagined her mom in bed next to her like when they practiced connection. Eloi held her mother's face in her mind, her raven hair, and emerald eyes. She reached out as far as her strength would take her mind—perhaps the distance also limited the connection. She pushed as much love and determination as she could into the dream and bond.

"Mom, I hope you hear me." Eloi closed her eyes and pushed her power out once more.

7

Aine woke, less violently than she had in the previous days. She was still in wolf form, surrounded by the comfort of trees; the moon, like a beacon of light, shone high in the sky. A bittersweet feeling squeezed her chest, and a tear formed in her eye. That had been the clearest memory so far, and this was the first time she felt the presence of a child. She recognized the kind old man and hoped he cared for the youngling. But, unfortunately, she only saw them and had not heard any of what they said. Aine growled and huffed as she rose and paced aimlessly through the trees. She still couldn't remember who she was. She only knew she was a Pack Leader and essential.

The only conversation she caught was one in the Temple. Heat flooded her body, and she growled again, so overwhelmed her body shook as she remembered Rolan. Aine now had a name to fit the malicious figure. The one who had forced her to drink the solution she had vomited earlier. Aine tried to cling to the dream, but the harder she tried, the less clear it became. Finally, she stomped her paw and looked down, wondering where her clothes were—she couldn't see them on the ground. They must have shifted with her.

She was a wolf shifter; how could a person forget that? No wonder she was stronger than Caroline or Abbie appeared to be. Aine knew she shouldn't have been able to throw Abbie across the room like she had. She wasn't sure exactly what it would mean for her, but she would have to figure it out sooner rather than later. Her thoughts quickly turned to Lachlan, and her stomach lurched. He would not understand—humans and shifters did not mix. That was ingrained in her; her deepest fear as Pack Leader was that the humans would discover them. That much she remembered. Lachlan would think she was a freak of nature.

Her chest squeezed again, and pure pain ripped through her; she heard herself whine. Aine had been happy the past week with Lachlan and loved the time they spent together. She couldn't remember her past, but she knew she had never felt the way she did with him. He accepted everything about her, even though she didn't even know who she was. But Aine doubted he would accept this.

She looked up to the moon, thoughts of Lachlan reminding her that he would have been home a long time ago and was probably worried. She needed to get back.

It would be faster to run as a wolf, she was still some distance from the diner, and she wasn't sure she could turn back. Aine looked to the moon for strength one last time and bowed her head, thanking it for its light. If it hadn't given her strength, Han would have killed her. She turned to look at the bloody body before she left, astonished that she hadn't got blood on herself. Then she turned from Han, no regret for what she had done, before setting out towards Phil's diner.

LACHLAN WATCHED the sun race towards the horizon, then carefully studied the forest floor, following the signs from the young man they searched for. Craig Jones had left to track the coyotes by himself, and by the time Lachlan arrived, he'd been missing over two hours. Lachlan put together a search party, and what should have been a quick job to make sure the coyotes weren't in the area became a rescue mission. Sweat trickled down Lachlan's back as he concentrated, straining to hear any sound. Each step that took him away from Aine felt wrong but Lachlan continued to examine the path for signs that a human had come through. He had crossed the trail about half a mile ago, the slow pace gnawing at him. Craig's brother, Ricky, shifted next to him as they paused again. Lachlan crouched, closed his eyes, and listened.

"What you—?"

"Shhhhh," Lachlan scolded, ears straining again as a slight moan drifted from a gully ahead of them. He strode forward and looked down to see Craig's pale face. Craig leaned against a small tree, his leg bent at a sickening angle. Lachlan gracefully slid down to the young man, careful not to jostle his leg.

"Craig, can you hear me?" Lachlan watched the boy's face. Craig moaned again, his eyes not quite focused.

"Don't sleep," Lachlan demanded. He looked back up to Ricky and held up a hand as he looked about to slide down with him. Lachlan glanced at the descending sun again and groaned.

"You'll be alright." Lachlan shook Craig as his eyes closed. "Won't be long till we have you back home."

Lachlan kept his eye on Craig as Ricky and two other

men with the search party called for help and put together a makeshift stretcher. They were only a mile from the Jones farm, and it wouldn't take them long to carry the young man back. Lachlan hauled his half the whole way while the others switched out. Over the rough terrain and with the constant switching, it took longer than Lachlan had hoped. He paced outside the Jones' house as he watched Caroline's car pull up; the vehicle seemed to crawl up the long drive.

"Hello, Lachlan," Caroline greeted when she stepped out of the car. "How's the lovely Aine? Good?"

"She's great, and I need to get back to her," Lachlan spoke through gritted teeth and ran his hands through his hair. He had not intended to stay out this long, not with the full moon and Aine at home alone. But, although he couldn't have risked her coming along with darkness falling, he hadn't been able to leave the Jones boy either.

"No sign of coyotes, I hope? Heard Craig took a spill." Caroline tapped her medical bag.

"His leg looks broken. We were careful not to displace it too much as we lifted him onto the stretcher. You'll have to set it. No other signs of injury, but he might have a concussion." The words tumbled out of Lachlan's mouth as he headed toward his truck. A sliver of the sun held on above the horizon.

"Wait! You shouldn't have moved him." Caroline frowned at Lachlan as he tried to leave.

"You wouldn't have got out there, Caroline, and his head injury took priority. You'll mend his leg fine."

Phil noticed Lachlan near the truck and quickly shuffled over, he stammered an excuse to the Jones boys as he ran after Lachlan. Phil barely made it inside before Lachlan drove off without him.

Phil glanced across the cab at him as the truck sped out

of the driveway. "She won't react well if ya turn up all freaked out like this, man, might want to calm down."

"I am calm."

"Could have fooled me." Phil chewed his lip as they ate up the tarmac on their way across town.

The Jones family lived on the opposite side; Lachlan chewed his lip as the town approached. Buildings raced by as he drove faster than the speed limit, his senses on high alert while he watched the road ahead.

"She doesn't know what she is, Phil, and if you changed, not knowing, then how would you react?"

Phil gulped and looked out the window. The full moon was clear in the sky as it rose, mocking the two men in the truck. Lachlan had always loved the moon, but today it was his enemy. Phil fell silent and watched his friend cautiously as they drove on.

"I should never have left her." Lachlan's hands tapped the wheel manically. They finally reached the other side of town; the buildings disappeared quickly, and Phil's diner sat like a beacon in the distance. As they closed in on his house and the diner, Lachlan clenched the wheel harder. The short drive felt like it lasted a lifetime, and he barely skidded to a stop before he abandoned his truck.

The house was dark and felt empty as Lachlan approached and charged through the front door.

"AINE, AINE!" Frantic, Lachlan searched the house, but he knew that she wasn't there the second he walked through the door. No presence came to him, and she hadn't been there for hours, maybe since he left. He grabbed his rifle and gear, his heart squeezing as he felt for the medallion under his shirt. He looked to the moon and prayed he wouldn't have to use it as he turned for the door.

"Where are ya going? Didn't you say they could run for

miles?" Phil followed him towards the diner, then spoke again in a whisper, "If she has shifted, you might be better waiting at home for her. It's all she knows; she might come back."

Lachlan stopped, and a growl escaped his lips. "I know, but I can't just sit here." He pinched the bridge of his nose and closed his eyes. *Where would she go?* Moving out the back door, he headed toward the clearing where Phil found her. His steps were careful in the dark, aware that Phil trailed him.

"I can't leave her out there." His voice was low, and he could hear the emotion, his loss of control. Phil kept his thoughts to himself and followed slowly.

"She was talking about going back to the clearing this afternoon," Lachlan went on. "I'm going to start there. This is where it all started for her; maybe she tried to track back to where she came from. I can't lose her, Phil. I know it's only been a week, and I can't explain it but not knowing where she is...." He trailed off as he ran his hand through his hair and looked around wildly.

Lachlan stopped to inhale deeply; he couldn't plan if he couldn't think. He then moved slower and continued once Phil caught up. Lachlan needed to think like the hunter he was; he took another deep breath.

As they came to the clearing, Lachlan could smell something rotten and putrid, like death. He slowly took out his flashlight to survey the area. The clearing looked menacing in the dark as his flashlight bounced shadows around the trees. It mimicked the look of creatures darted around them. He used a calculated route with the flashlight and searched every inch of the clearing until he came across a thick black liquid on the ground. The flashlight reflected off the surface. That was the source of the smell. Lachlan approached slowly and crouched, nearly gagging, and put his hand to his nose.

"Jesus Christ, that's ripe." Phil coughed as he approached the sludge. "What the hell is that?"

"Don't touch it," Lachlan snapped. He grabbed Phil's wrist as the idiot reached out a hand.

"Seriously, Phil, that reeks; why would you touch it?" Lachlan rolled his eyes, which Phil couldn't see in the dark. He squinted as his eyes watered and looked at the liquid. It had an oily consistency and seemed to glow ominously in the light.

"I don't see her," Phil almost whispered as he looked around the clearing.

"Let's head away from the diner; it makes the most sense. I'll see if I can sense anything." Lachlan gestured with his hand as he straightened up and turned in the direction he had indicated. His whole body tensed as he felt a presence deeper in the woods.

Phil started to speak, and Lachlan held out his hand sharply; he lowered the flashlight and raised his rifle. The full moon was so bright that Lachlan could almost see clearly, as he peered into the darkness once his eyes adjusted.

A small figure stumbled into the clearing, and the faint light illuminated Aine. She was pale and covered in dirt and seemed unsteady on her legs; a twig stuck out of her hair. She held her hands up against the flashlight, and Lachlan's heart stopped. Before he knew what he was doing, he moved to stand before her. He lifted a hand to cup her face and pulled her close.

"Are you okay? You had me worried sick. Don't do that to me, ever again." Lachlan hugged Aine, his heart hammered in his chest, and he noticed she trembled against him, even though her skin felt warm to the touch.

"I need to go home," Aine whispered.

Lachlan's heart swelled when she said the word "home." He held her head on either side to look into her face; Aine's hands were loose around his waist. Lachlan looked up to the full moon and frowned before he blew out a breath. Phil shifted behind him; Lachlan forgot he was there. He held Aine's hand firmly and pulled her towards the diner.

"Come on, Phil, let's get out of here," he said.

Phil still peered at the black sludge on the ground and didn't move. A slight noise came from Aine as they approached it, and she shied away.

"But what is this?" Phil's brow crinkled, and he still stared at the sludge.

Lachlan refused to stop. "Not now, Phil."

Phil took one last look and shuffled after them towards the diner.

"I didn't feel very well earlier," Aine said weakly.

"You threw that up?" Phil's expression changed, eyes wide and mouth open as his gaze flicked towards Aine. She looked sheepish, and her mouth turned down.

"Aine, what happened? Please tell me you're okay." Lachlan pulled her close to his side as they walked. She smiled up at Lachlan as he held her tight and held him back just as tight.

"I'm fine, just tired and want to get warm," Aine timidly replied.

The three of them walked back to his house, and Lachlan sighed with relief when they walked through the door. His arm protectively wrapped around Aine's shoulders; he felt like a weight had been lifted.

The full moon was still out, and she hadn't shifted. But

what did that mean? She showed the skills of a shifter with her strength and sense of smell. That plus the power he first felt coming off her in the diner when they met. His instincts screamed "shifter" at him, and they had never been wrong. But, she was a mystery, and her memory loss would not help him solve it.

AINE SIGHED under the shower as the steaming water hit her skin. She closed her eyes and tilted her head up. She immediately brushed her teeth and could no longer trace any of the disgusting liquid inside her. Instead, her body felt lighter, like the tension she carried for the past week was a weight, and she hadn't realized it. As she washed away the muck from her forest excursion, she wondered what she would say to Lachlan. He hadn't pushed her yet to find out where she went, but she couldn't simply say nothing.

Aine had managed to transform back to human just as she returned to the clearing. She could hear Lachlan shout from a couple of miles away and knew she couldn't appear to him as a wolf. He hunted for the town, and he would probably shoot her on sight if he deemed her a threat to the locals. So how did she tell this beautiful man, who took her in and cared for her, that she was a vicious monster? The warmth from her shower didn't heat up the ice in her chest as she thought of his face changing, with eyes looking at her in disgust.

Procrastination would not help. Aine shut the shower off, the cold absence of the hot water making her shiver. She looked around at the bathroom as she wrapped a towel around herself, hardly able to believe it had been ten days since Lachlan carried her into his house. Her clothes were laid out on top of the toilet lid; she picked them up and sat down heavily, head in her hands as her dark hair dripped water onto the floor.

Despair paralyzed her as she sat. Time passed, and Aine didn't know how long she was there, but the slow drip of water had slowed to a stop. She dressed and left the bathroom; emptiness tightened her chest, making it hard to breathe. She cocked her head and heard Lachlan's heartbeat, slow and steady, and she followed the sound.

Lachlan was on the back porch in his chair, which creaked as he rocked. Aine watched him as he surveyed the yard and the woods. His rifle rested across his lap, and his hands appeared relaxed, but Aine could see the tension in Lachlan's shoulders. She approached slowly, her bare feet made no noise as she halted next to him. Lachlan didn't react; he knew she was there and waited in silence. Aine shifted and let the quiet settle between them, then she swallowed, also looking toward the woods.

She sensed no danger, just the slow sway of the trees as a breeze whispered through the branches. She had begun to trust her intuition and hoped it would save her life as it had earlier. Aine felt no guilt for her kill; the grey wolf wasn't just a danger to her but would have been a danger to the town if she let him live. She started to remember more, but it still wasn't all clear. *Rolan.* Aine tensed, and Lachlan turned his head sharply. The name echoed through her head. Hot rage bubbled up in Aine's chest, and she clenched her fists.

"Why did you go without me? I could have helped." Lachlan's voice was rough and tight. Aine could feel his panic before she came into the clearing. He had been frantic when she heard him shout for her. His worry had slashed through her; she hadn't meant to hurt him.

"I wanted to go alone. I needed to see for myself." Aine shivered, grateful he hadn't been there. She couldn't imagine what would have happened if he had seen her change.

Lachlan turned to face her and took her hands. He put the rifle to the side and pulled her onto his lap. With Lachlan's arms circled around her, Aine relaxed into him. His scent comforted her, musky and of the woods. She breathed him in deeply.

"Please don't do that to me again," he pleaded. "I'd miss you if something happened." A smirk played on his lips when Aine looked up at his face. She smiled at him freely and cupped his jaw with her hand.

"I can't promise I won't try to find out who I am. But I will let you know next time I leave, so you don't worry." Aine would not make promises she couldn't keep, and she would not be trapped by a vow.

Lachlan sighed and looked towards the woods. "I will follow you if you leave without me. We do this together, Aine. Let me help you."

"This might be something I need to do alone. My dreams are getting more violent, and I don't want you to be a part of that. It's not fair for me to burden you with my problems." She pulled away from him, but before she could leave him, he pulled her close once more.

"I'm trying to understand, but I can't do that if you don't let me in." Lachlan held her close and stroked her hair.

Aine looked up into his face and wished with her whole being that they could be a normal couple. But she wasn't normal; she was a creature of nightmares.

She tilted her head and lightly brushed her lips against his. The kiss was sweet, and she held it a moment, the comfort of his heat seeped into her. Her conscience begged her to tell him what happened; if she didn't tell him, it would eat away at her and poison what they had. But she slowly backed away and stood. He would look at her differently if she told him, and she didn't want to lose him.

"I'm going to make some coffee. Would you like some?"

Lachlan's laugh broke the tension. "You're turning into an addict."

Aine smiled at him before she tried to escape into the house, but Lachlan followed.

"Are you trying to stay awake, so you don't dream?" he asked.

"Not really." Aine kept her hands busy setting up the machine. "I find it comforting, like a hug in a mug."

He laughed as she quoted Phil at him. He stood behind her and wrapped his arms around her middle.

"I know you aren't ready to talk to me, and I won't push, but if you need to talk, I want you to know you can trust me." Lachlan kissed Aine on the side of her head, and she felt him breathe in the smell of her hair.

She closed her eyes and melted into him, torn. An image of Lachlan's face, full of hatred and disgust, flashed in her mind. She pulled away and picked up her coffee, then without a word walked down to the basement.

"Mom, can you hear me?" A young girl lay next to Aine with her eyes squeezed shut.

"Yes, little one, you did it." Aine let pride surge down the bond to the little girl next to her; she leaned over to stroke her hair, and the girl jumped as she opened her eyes.

"I did it!" the girl exclaimed, wonder on her face as she grinned up at Aine.

Abruptly the dream ended, and Aine could barely hold on to what had happened. The vision of the girl in her mind caused a severe ache in her chest. The wetness on her cheeks surprised her, and a sob escaped her lips. This dream had been nothing like the others; it was bittersweet.

Who was the girl, a student? Aine laid back in bed again, desperate as she closed her eyes to be back in the dream and that moment. Coldness swept through her as she lay there and stared at the ceiling. Golden sunlight had started to creep into the basement. She thought about what had happened the night before, and determination to find out who she was filled her. But she couldn't talk to Lachlan about it. The thought of him as he looked at her in disgust tore at her.

Aine rose from the bed and dressed for the shed, where she would concentrate on her projects while she thought about her next move. She couldn't hear Lachlan upstairs as she crept out of the house. When she quietly closed the back door, she turned to face the yard and froze.

Lachlan was already up—and shirtless. Her mouth dropped open as she watched him perform a sequence of moves, ones she recognized, that were used to build strength and dexterity. His movements were precise and graceful, a powerful elegance. She watched in silence as his muscles rippled. Mesmerized, she stood completely still, eyes wide as she fought the desire that pulsed through her.

"Enjoying the view?" Lachlan turned to face her as he finished, a cocky grin on his face.

"I...I..." Aine stammered, completely lost for words as Lachlan stalked toward her. His eyes sparkled with his approach.

"Morning, beautiful." He leaned down to kiss her. "Breakfast?"

So much for keeping him at a distance. Aine shook her head and didn't dare to speak; he frowned as she quickly ran to the shed.

She turned for one last look before she shut the door and sighed in relief. The man was so gorgeous, he was going to give her a heart attack. To drive all thoughts of Lachlan from her mind, she picked up the piece of wood she had worked on yesterday morning and got to work.

8

ine had put distance between them since the full moon. It had been four days, and even though he tried to talk to her, she hadn't relaxed into their intimacy as she had before.

Lachlan chuckled, remembering the look on her face when she saw him work out. Since then, Aine spent every day in his shed and carved, often awake before he was, and she stayed out late into the night. He tried to be content with her company and silence, but what was comfortable before now felt heavy and awkward. He couldn't help the tightness he felt in his chest. He knew she hid something from him and tried to wait for her to come to him, but his patience was about to run out. He was drawn to her and needed her closeness; without it, he started to feel empty.

Another day in the shed came, and her silence stretched out before him. She hadn't left yet, but he began to get the feeling she might. Lachlan fought his feelings for her, and now that he'd given in, she pushed him away.

Phil called earlier that day and left a message that

someone at the diner had asked for him by name. He expected it was one of the locals with an order; Phil said the man would be back in the afternoon. It had been a while since he'd been to the shop, and they probably wondered where he was.

As he strode towards Phil's, his mind drifted back to Aine. She had made several children's toys that no one had ordered, and he wondered if the day they gave Cory the chest had made a more significant impact than he realized. Lachlan pushed the diner door open, and his gaze immediately snapped to the familiar redhead near the breakfast bar. The man was tall and lean, with a build similar to his own.

"Girvan?"

"Cousin!" Girvan had been devouring a massive stack of pancakes and dropped the fork he'd been using with a clatter. Lachlan walked forward to embrace his cousin in a hard hug.

"Fifteen years, Lachlan? You don't call, you don't write...." Girvan trailed off but held an enormous grin on his face.

Lachlan felt warm affection spread through his chest; he couldn't believe Girvan was there.

"It's great to see you, cuz, but what are you doing here?" He furrowed his brow and looked around as if the rest of his family might materialize.

"We've been tracking around America; pretty much no more game in Europe. They've all fled to the States. Heard rumors of an uprising around these parts, and since I knew you were here, I thought I'd say hi." Girvan laughed. "Hi!" he added with a goofy wave.

Girvan had always been a bit of a joker; it wound up

Lachlan's father no end. Lachlan was surprised he hadn't grown out of it, but Girvan always said that if he hadn't grown up by the time he reached forty, then he didn't have to. It seemed he held himself to that.

Lachlan sat down in one of the booths, and after he grabbed his pancakes, Girvan joined him.

"Priorities." Girvan indicated his breakfast. "Though I don't get the whole bacon on pancakes thing." He grunted as he sat down.

"How did you find me?" Lachlan hadn't known where he would end up when he left. There was no way they could have guessed where he would settle down. But he already knew the answer.

"Pa kept tabs on me, didn't he?" Lachlan sighed, resigned.

"You think he'd let you run off like that and not keep track of you, huh?" Girvan gave him a sympathetic smile. "You are his heir, after all." Girvan laughed when Lachlan scoffed.

"He has four other sons to step up; he doesn't need me. Finn is the oldest. Hell, he doesn't even like me, not after how I left." Lachlan looked at the table until he heard the kitchen door open. Phil nodded to him as he came through from the kitchen, putting some bacon and eggs in front of him.

"You need it, man." Phil shrugged and disappeared again.

Lachlan looked at the plate and smiled. Phil always looked after him, making sure he ate. He'd probably forget otherwise and ate with relish hoping the food would settle his stomach. The queasy feeling which had started at the sight of his cousin wasn't budging.

"Is he here?" Lachlan glanced up to gauge Girvan's face.

"Not yet."

That was a "yes" then. His father had probably sent Girvan to soften him up before he approached himself. *Shit.* The coincidence did not escape Lachlan's notice. The appearance of Aine with no memory, possibly a shifter, and now his family showing up after fifteen years was definitely suspect. Something must be happening in the shifter community.

"What do you know?" Lachlan's eyes narrowed as he watched Girvan.

"There's a rebellion of sorts among shifters—they usually just stick to themselves unless we hunt them out. There's a new pack, calling themselves the Faction. They believe they should be in charge and that humans should serve them." Girvan slammed his fist on the table.

"This is the whole reason we exist," he went on. "To rid the world of them and stop threats like this before they get started. Don't know what the Americans have been doing over here, but shifters can live in communities." Girvan made as if to spit before he realized he was inside.

"It's not black and white, Girvan, just like not all hunters are good. Not all shifters are bad." Lachlan had this argument with his cousin before. He was the only family member he ever voiced his views to before leaving.

"We need to root out the problem and destroy all the vermin before they rally together and come after us." Girvan's passion had not changed. He spewed the same beliefs his whole family did. Lachlan left because he didn't believe in the whole "it's them or us" mentality.

"That's not my problem, and if you hunt them down, then they will come after you. What would you do if someone tried to kill your entire family?" Lachlan shrugged nonchalantly.

Girvan scowled at him. "Bullshit! It'll be your problem when you're confronted with them. They aren't too far from here."

Lachlan stilled fork halfway to his open mouth. "What do you mean?" He continued to eat but saw his cousin smirk.

"You haven't been paying attention, cuz—there's a settlement in the area. We've seen all the signs, and there are even rumors in local towns about an abandoned village." Girvan looked to his empty plate before he nodded towards Phil. "It's on your doorstep, and *you* haven't been paying attention."

The judgment in Girvan's tone caught Lachlan's attention, and he scowled back at his cousin. "It's not been my fight for fifteen years."

"Make it your fight. Your pa's on his way, and he won't be happy if you don't join us. I know how you left things with him, but you shocked us all that day. He will out you if he must. What's the town going to do when they find out you're a shifter hunter? They won't leave you in peace." Girvan raised an eyebrow in challenge. "Don't tell me you've gone soft and stopped training?"

Lachlan had not. After twenty years of waking up for drills every day to hone his body and mind, it wasn't something he missed often. Annoyed at his cousin's bluntness, he pushed his plate to the side. "No."

"No? You think it will be that easy?" Girvan scoffed. "I came, I warned, and now I'm off. Do the smart thing, Lachlan. Your pa will come one way or another—it's only a matter of time now. You showed just how strong of a warrior you were that day. Even Finn can't take your pa." He lowered his voice, eyes twinkling. "You should have heard everyone after you left; no one has ever taken your pa down so easily."

Girvan continued to eat as Lachlan stared out the window in silence. He hadn't meant to keep his skills to himself; it had become a bit of a game to hide his extra training. He had been young and foolish then. Girvan broke his reverie.

"I know you blame yourself for your mother's death, and running might have been right then, but something is brewing, and we need you now. You were our best fighter before we all realized how good you really were and—" Girvan paused. "—your pa isn't well."

His face scrunched up as if it had caused him physical pain to say the words. He stood, dropped some money on the table, and gave Lachlan a hearty clap on the back before he walked out the door. His cousin was nothing if not dramatic. Phil meandered over to sit opposite Lachlan.

"Your past finally came knocking?" he chuckled. "You're having a hell of a couple of weeks."

"You can say that again," Lachlan sighed.

"Aine still not talking to ya?" Phil looked sympathetic as he picked up the plates.

"She's kept to herself. Something happened on the full moon, Phil, but she didn't shift. I wish she'd talk to me."

"Maybe try and take her to do something else, take her away from the town, and try not to push her. She might need a break." Phil walked back to the kitchen and left Lachlan to mull it over.

AINE HAD BEEN CARVING for days and had built up a collection of children's toys. She knew the obsession with children was important but couldn't remember why. Finally, she threw down her tools and huffed. The workshop was quiet, and the smell of sawdust tickled her nose.

Lachlan had backed off recently, and she wasn't surprised; she had been cold towards him since the day she saw him training. When Aine thought of his body and how it moved, heat infused her, and her stomach fluttered. She shook her head to clear the memory.

She didn't want to push him away but didn't think she could tell him what she was. Sighing, she looked out the open door toward the woods. Since her adventure the night of the full moon, she felt more at peace, despite the awkwardness between her and Lachlan. But she still could not remember who she was or why she had been left by Rolan in the woods.

Lachlan approached; he had come from Phil's diner. Aine caught whiffs of the booth seats and bacon on him from inside the shed; her sense of smell was becoming increasingly potent. As he walked through the door and toward her, she tensed. Then he drew her into his arms and held her tight; she froze, but the closeness melted her, and she inhaled deeply.

"Please don't push me away." Lachlan's voice was soft and cracked.

Aine's heart wrenched as she looked up at his drawn face and frowned. She hadn't realized how much her distancing had affected him. There were dark shadows under his eyes, and he looked pale. Had something happened?

"What's wrong?" she asked softly and reached up to cup his face.

"My family is nearby, and I don't want to see them." His jaw clenched as he spoke, and Aine moved her hands up to run them through his hair. He closed his eyes and moaned in pleasure as she soothed him, his forehead lowering to meet hers.

"Talk to me, Aine. Tell me how I can help you," Lachlan pleaded.

Aine stiffened but didn't back away. He had started several attempts to talk with her, but she wouldn't tell him what had happened. She reached up to kiss him, but he wouldn't be distracted this time.

"I can't because I don't remember," she said finally. "I feel like I've forgotten someone important, and I miss them. It breaks my heart every time I try to think about her." *Her?* The dream of the girl that she had forgotten flashed in her mind. Maybe if she gave in and talked to Lachlan, it would help. She looked up at him and smiled tentatively, causing him to catch his breath.

"Thank you," she whispered, and he grinned.

"I didn't do anything."

"But I just remembered that it's 'her' I'm missing, and I didn't before. So maybe talking would help." Aine smiled as Lachlan laughed.

"That's what I've been trying to tell you!" he said.

Aine felt something shift between them. The distance disappeared, and the tension broke. She finally relaxed against him and allowed herself to absorb his strength and warmth.

"What else do you remember?" Lachlan stroked her hair as he held her.

"A man, I think his name is Rolan. He forced me to drink something, and it made me sick—That is what I threw up in the clearing the other night." Aine's face reddened, and Lachlan looked at her in concern.

"You were forced to drink *that*? No wonder you've been all over the place. Do you know what it was?"

"No, but I think it was supposed to make me forget, which I have but not completely. Bits keep coming back every time I dream." She hummed as his hands continued to stroke her back, and she held him tighter. "I'm scared you will look at me differently if you see the real me," she murmured quietly against his chest, half-hoping he didn't hear.

"I couldn't even if I tried, Aine." Lachlan stared at her intensely, and Aine felt heat creep into her cheeks and neck. They stayed like that for a long time until Aine's stomach grumbled loudly, and Lachlan snickered.

"Let's grab some lunch," he said. "I had a bite at Phil's but can always eat more; want to join me now?" Lachlan took her hand and led her to the house.

AINE WAS SITTING behind the counter in Lachlan's shop as he walked through the door with sandwiches. They had been there all morning, and everyone in town seemed to have come to gawk at her. Gossip had spread like wildfire, especially after some of the boys had seen Cory's chest. They wanted to see the girl who couldn't remember but could carve intricate stories.

Pride swelled in Lachlan when requests came in for Aine to carve the furniture he built. They made a great team, and he was eager to start another project with her. At least it would keep her hands busy.

He thought about everything Aine told him over the last two days. He still felt like she held something back; she hadn't mentioned shifters, but he put enough together to realize she was, in fact, from the shifter village his cousin had mentioned. Maybe she couldn't shift and had been exiled by them. His chest tightened; he needed to tell her about his past, but the time never seemed right.

They spent every waking moment together, and it was more than he had ever hoped for; he wanted to remain in that bubble as long as possible before the real world intruded. He knew he would soon run out of time and that his father would be there. But he savored the precious days he had now before it all came crashing down around them.

"Three more orders, including one from Caroline. She came to check on me, I think." Aine's beautiful smile appeared as he approached her. She seemed more carefree after they'd talked, and there wasn't any more awkwardness between them. He wondered if that would alter when he revealed who he was. He walked behind her and put his arms around her. Before he kissed her neck, he inhaled deeply. She smelled like the strawberry shampoo she had been using.

"We can head home if you want?" Lachlan wanted to get her back so he could have her all to himself.

"No, there's someone not far from here who wants a set of drawers built. They're just trying to decide if they've got time to eat first."

Lachlan frowned at Aine as the doorbell jingled, and Trevor walked through.

"Lachlan, hey, I caught you," he said. "Was just on my lunch break, and Abbie said you were here today. I saw the dresser you did for her brother and want one for my wife. It's our anniversary next month, and I usually forget, so she will be extra surprised." He grinned cheekily and walked up to the counter.

"You must be Aine," he continued. "Abbie said you'd

moved in with Lachlan. Don't move slow, do you, dude? Though I don't blame you." Trevor's gaze swept up and down her, and she stilled; her eyes flashed before she glared at him.

Lachlan could have sworn her eyes changed color, and a low growl sounded. He cleared his throat. "We are just leaving, Trevor, and I think you should, too." He stood to his full height and walked towards the man, who went pale.

"Er, sure, erm—" Trevor's face went blank, and he swallowed hard. "I'll just—"

"I'll call you tomorrow for your order." Lachlan put an arm around Trevor's shoulder and steered him to the door. He wasn't sorry to see him go, and if he lost the business, he didn't really care. He could feel fury building in his chest when he thought about how Trevor looked at Aine. By the way she reacted, she wasn't too happy either; he could feel her crowd his back as he pushed Trevor out the door and locked it behind him. Lachlan turned to face Aine.

"Disgusting man, do you know what he was thinking when he looked at me? How dare he be so disrespectful," Aine snarled.

"No, I don't know, but how do you know?" Lachlan frowned and looked at her eyes. She hadn't shifted on the full moon, and he assumed she just lived with the shifters, but her intuition had started to unnerve him. He looked into her eyes, and despite their anger, they remained green. Lachlan shook his head to clear it.

"I could feel it come off him in waves; it made me feel dirty." Aine rubbed her arms as if she tried to brush away the feeling. Then she smiled. "I like how you made him leave. The fear coming off him when you stood in front of him was funny."

Lachlan laughed with her and put an arm around her

shoulders. "Come on, oracle, let's get home. We can start on some of these projects this afternoon."

Aine giggled, and they walked to his truck. He offered her a hand up into the cab and gave her the sandwiches. As they drove through the town, Lachlan could feel her stare at him.

"What?" he chuckled when she didn't look away. He took her hand and raised it to his mouth for a brief kiss.

"You're really sweet," Aine commented.

"And that's a bad thing?"

"Just how you stood up for me back there."

In truth, Aine had looked like she wanted to rip Trevor to pieces. Lachlan had protected Trevor as much as standing up for her. "I will always protect you if it's within my power. I know we've only known each other a couple of weeks, but I feel like it's been a lifetime," he admitted.

"It's been that hard having me around, huh?" Aine grinned at him, and he watched her from the corner of his eye. Lachlan laughed with her; he couldn't remember a time he laughed this much or felt this open with anyone.

That evening, Aine cooked steak the way Lachlan had shown her a few days before, though she didn't cook hers for as long as his. Lachlan liked his steak rare, but Aine barely touched the meat to the pan before she flipped it and put it straight on her plate. She licked her lips at the bloody juices that now drowned the potatoes already served. Lachlan frowned at her plate but made no comment. They had spent the afternoon in the shed as they prepped their projects, and they'd had a full workload. Hopefully, that would keep them busy over the next few days.

Lachlan put a second chair on the back porch so they could sit together as the sun set. They usually looked out towards the woods in companionable silence, letting the night drift over them. Both had grown used to this peaceful life, and he hadn't heard Aine have any nightmares in a couple of days. Even so, Lachlan still couldn't relax. He felt like they were on the edge of a cliff, with the anticipation felt just before a jump into the abyss.

With Aine's appearance and now his family's, it was the calm before what was sure to be a violent storm.

9

E loi kept her head down since overhearing her father in the Temple. She went to her lessons, did her chores, and kept out of his way. She didn't think Rolan noticed the distance she put between them. She didn't want to remind him of her presence in case he decided to get rid of her as well.

Eloi was exhausted, living in a constant state of fear, and spent her nights frantically trying to push dreams to her mother. It had not been easy living under the same roof as Rolan, after everything she knew. He had stopped being "Father" to her and instead became the man who tried to murder her mother. She knew she had failed the last few days to reach her mom, and her growing fatigue prevented her from pushing out her power very far.

Han's disappearance had not gone unnoticed by the pack, but Eloi had sensed relief, especially from some of the females. Han had been aggressive in some of his pursuits and built a reputation as a bully. She had heard a few women mention he tried to force himself on them. Truthfully, she was surprised the warriors let him get away with it, but with his brother Mervan serving as the Second of the pack warriors, Rolan being First, she shouldn't have been.

Rolan and Mervan had not spoken to the pack about Han's disappearance or her mom yet. Eloi took this as a good sign but worried they were waiting until it would make the most impact. Even without her memory, her mother had outwitted Rolan; he would need to make her look like an enemy to bring the pack on his side.

Eloi started to spend more time with the pack members her age to blend in. There were few teenagers, but she enjoyed it when she helped with the younglings. The group was currently learning about the origin of the Aoibhans and the prophecy that surrounded the Royal bloodline.

She only half-listened; her mother told her the story many times, and she could see the younglings' constant glances in her direction. After all, she was of the Royal bloodline, and expectations of her would be high.

Catori, the Elder in charge of the records and the small library, always dragged out the story in a droning voice. Aine had embellished her storytelling; she had a gift for making you feel like you lived the events themselves. The intricacies and characters she brought to life were a joy to hear. Though this version wasn't as interesting, Eloi did try to listen to Catori in case she heard something important. The students were gathered on the floor of a one-room class-room near the center of the village. It was simple and fit for the purpose, the way the rest of the village was constructed.

The prophecy told that a powerful shifter, half-light, and half-dark, must embrace both sides to bring true unity between humans and shifters. Most of the pack Elders dismissed the tale, as they considered any shifter caught with humans to be a disgrace. The pack law had strictly laid out that they must never show themselves to humans, and the thought of consorting with mankind was vile and disturbing, especially to the older shifters. One of the oldest shifter laws stated that no shifter would mate a human, but the prophecy indicated that someone from her bloodline was destined to meet her True Mate – a human. It went against the nature of shifters, but the younglings always enjoyed the story. Eloi always wondered when the prophecy would come to pass or if it was just another fantasy.

Catori's voice continued to flow amongst the younglings, who all stared up at her in awe. They had all heard this story many times, and even though Catori butchered the tale, they were still mesmerized.

Eloi caught movement as she leaned against the back of the classroom. Outside the window, she watched Rolan and Mervan drawing closer to the meeting area at the village center. A young warrior interrupted Catori at the entrance to the room and demanded they all gather with the others. A sick feeling started in Eloi's stomach; this did not bode well. Slowly, she gathered her strength and pushed off the wall to join the younglings.

As she slowly walked towards the meeting area, Eloi saw Eyolf approach and adjusted her path to walk and stand next to him. His hand brushed hers, and she felt that he was uneasy. Using her power, she drew in the atmosphere around her; tension crackled, and the feel of it was painful. The pack was confused as to why they'd been summoned, and the air felt electric with their uncertainty.

Rolan stood before the pack, and Eloi concentrated harder on her connection to him and his emotions. Triumph and elation flowed between them, and her heart sank. Something had happened with her mom.

Her chest felt tight, like someone's hand squeezed her heart. Fear of what lies Rolan would tell the pack about

Aine seized her. The pack talked amongst themselves, and Eloi could feel their confusion and apprehension coming in waves. She swayed as she tried to make sense of her surroundings. Aine's disappearance had shaken them, and they started to doubt her. Rolan's warriors had been spreading rumors the past few days, which had not helped. Eloi tried to ignore them.

"Pack," Rolan growled and demanded their attention. "I bring news of your leader Aine, and I'm sad to say that it is not good."

Eloi watched his face, which appeared deeply concerned, portraying a betrayed mate. He played his part perfectly. She also noticed his use of the phrase "your leader" and not "our leader." The sick feeling in her stomach worsened, and Eloi swallowed as she reached out her hand to Eyolf and squeezed, the horror she felt in return gripped her chest. Bile rose in her throat.

"Aine has been found, and it is not as we suspected. We thought she had been captured or killed by humans, but it is far, far worse." Rolan looked down with regret in his eyes. He spoke slowly as he continued. "Aine purposefully severed her bond with the pack and has abandoned us. She has forsaken her duties and has taken up with a human in a nearby town. She is living as one of them and no longer embraces her shifter heritage."

The outcry from the pack members hurt Eloi's ears, and she withdrew her power as their cries of rage caused her physical pain. She swayed, and Eyolf held her to keep her from falling.

"Please, please," Rolan begged over the deafening shouts. "There is more." The atmosphere weighed down on Eloi as silence fell for them to hear what else Rolan had to say. The whole crowd waited for the next blow.

"I sent Han, brother to the Second, to talk to her. I had hoped to keep this from you and prevent pain; he tried to reason with my mate to see if she would return and forget the human. I wanted Han to tell her she was needed here, that we needed her. Not to abandon us." Rolan sighed and pinched the bridge of his nose, eyes closed. He seemed reluctant to continue, but Eloi could feel his amusement at his own words.

"I wanted to give her a second chance to take up her responsibility to the pack. But it is with a heavy heart that I tell you...." Rolan paused. "Aine went into a rage and killed our warrior. Brother to the Second."

Gasps of horror surrounded Eloi as the pack cried in outrage, and her eyes stung with tears that threatened to fall. She looked around at the shock and anger consuming the pack. Did none of them think to question Rolan? Her mother wasn't there to defend herself. She had led them for nearly two decades; how could they forsake her so quickly?

Eloi watched Rolan; a dark aura surrounded him, and she paled as she watched faint, dark shadows spreading among the pack. If she hadn't looked for them, she would have missed them entirely.

"I must leave you now to debate with my warriors our next steps. I take full responsibility of the pack in my mate's absence, and I'm proud to step up officially as your leader."

Eloi recognized her mother's dagger as Rolan lifted it high. It had an ornate hilt, carved into the shape of a wolf surrounded by moonlight. The blade was sharp, despite being centuries old. It was a symbol of their pack's leadership and was only to be in possession of the Pack Leader.

"That is not how it works, Rolan." Eyolf's firm tone carried through the crowd. "You are not next in line for leadership, and you are aware of this."

The crowd turned to each other and murmured amongst themselves. Under normal circumstances, the death or desertion of a leader would mean their title fell to their mate if they had one.

"Quiet, old man, and know your place." Rolan jumped down from the stage and stalked towards Eyolf. Eloi shrank into the crowd to ensure she didn't gain any unwanted attention. "I am the rightful leader of this pack, and you will submit or leave."

Eyolf discretely looked to Eloi in the crowd and dropped his eyes to the ground. Rolan's tone implied that leaving would not be an option. Eyolf glanced again at her, and she was certain that if she weren't present, he would have pushed back. Warmth filled her chest; the old shifter refused to abandon her.

"You're all dismissed!" Rolan shouted, his attention back on his warriors. Before any member could object, he turned and walked toward the Temple.

The crowd was stunned by the news, and no one moved. Eyolf tugged gently on Eloi's hand, having reached towards her, and they quickly stalked to the edge of the pack unnoticed. Eyolf no longer had their attention after his submission.

"You need to go and find your mother. This can't be right; she would never abandon the pack. If we can prove she has no memory, then it might save her." Eyolf's voice was quiet and strained as he spoke. "Eloi, I fear Rolan will use this as an excuse to take power permanently and kill your mother for these supposed crimes. I knew he was ambitious, but I thought he would be happy being a mate to the leader. I fear my mistake will cost both you and Aine."

"But she didn't do it!" Eloi squeaked. "Han must have attacked her; that's what Rolan wanted him to do!"

"There's no proof, child, and your mother is severed from the pack. She can't show them what happened. Only you can find her. I know we've not worked on it much, but only you and Aine can shift outside the full moon. Your connection to her is strong, and you can still feel her. Be quick and bring her back to me in secret. We need to find a way to prove that Rolan is setting her up."

"Try Nyko," Eloi suggested. "He seems uneasy with how Rolan is going about things—he's a weak link in his followers. If he left my mother alive and in reach of help near a diner, then there is hope he is not fully converted to Rolan's thinking."

Eyolf nodded and looked at her, pride in his gaze.

"You will be a fine leader one day, Eloi. I'm sorry so much must be put on you so young." Eyolf touched his forehead to hers.

"My mother wasn't much older when she became Pack Leader."

Eyolf chuckled. "True, little one. Now, do not shift until you are past the outskirts; your father may feel it, and you need a big head start. I'll watch and distract the warriors if I can."

Eloi squeezed Eyolf's hand. "I can take care of myself—I don't want to risk you further. You shouldn't have opposed him today. He will be looking for any excuse to get rid of you if he thinks you will cause problems."

Without another glance, Eloi turned and sprinted toward the borders of their village. Fear kept her moving. She hoped her mother would feel her coming and that she could return with her before it was too late. Exhaustion from the past week threatened to overwhelm her, but Eloi pushed deep and kept moving.

"THAT WENT WELL." Rolan grinned as he and Mervan entered the Temple, followed by Mervan's trusted warriors. There were only four for now, but it was enough; they could convert more later. The whole pack would soon turn against Aine with his influence. Once he dragged her back, it was within his power and now his right to execute her. He could then take his rightful place as the Pack Leader and lift the pack to new heights. No more cowering and hiding in the shadows; it was time the shifters came into the light and put humans in their place below those with the most power.

"What's next, Master?" Nyko asked, over-eagerly, his gaze on the ground and his stance tense.

"Spread rumors she's been sneaking out to meet a human lover for months—say you've seen her cross the borders, and she ordered you to remain silent," Rolan smirked as he considered. If the pack thought it had been going on longer, then it would incite them further. It wouldn't be long now until they saw things his way. He had contacts with others, rogues, and outcasts. He could start putting out messages that he looked to expand and offer those with the strength and brutality required, a place with his warriors. The more vicious, the better.

"We should—" Rolan abruptly froze as he felt a shift on the border. His heart stopped.

It was Eloi.

"Rolan?" Mervan glanced towards his leader and frowned.

Rolan growled hard and stormed towards the Temple entrance. "Come, my daughter is trying to run away. She's young—how is she shifting already? Who was watching her?" He snarled his displeasure, and Mervan glanced toward his warriors.

"You wanted us all here. I was watching her, but I've never seen her shift. She must be as powerful as her mother, Rolan." Mervan struggled to keep up, awe in his tone. "Imagine if you could control her! She's young and will be easily influenced."

"We must get her back here!" Rolan's shout was more an animalistic growl as they ran toward the border of the village. His heart soared; with one as powerful as Aine but within his control, he could have anything.

The crowd had finally dispersed, and the remaining members looked toward the group with shock and fear on their faces. The tension rolled off the group as they prepared to hunt.

After the revelation earlier, Rolan imagined everyone was jumpy. The warriors sped up to chase down the rebellious pup, and he could feel their elation at the challenge.

Rolan's grin was wicked; this would be fun. He would keep her close from now on, teach her to respect him, and use his abilities to mold her. After all, she would be the heir of his new pack.

ELOI SHIFTED QUICKLY, driven by her fear and urgency to escape the outskirts. She probably should have waited until she was further from the village, but her emotions put her on the edge of her control. It was a relief to let go and shift into her more powerful form. She usually savored the feeling, a mixture of pain and pleasure, as she became more powerful and agile.

She looked around to get her bearings. She had never

been out of the village and didn't know where to go, but she knew the humans lived to the east. After a short pause to muster her strength, she started in that direction slowly. She then gained speed as the pressure of finding her mother weighed down on her, along with the feeling of being chased. The trees moved quickly on each side of her, and she hoped she would be in time.

As Eloi ran, she could feel the presence of her father bearing down on her. Ice gripped her chest, and she pushed herself harder. He surely wouldn't catch her in his human form, unable to shift until the full moon, but she didn't want to take that chance.

Eloi had never pushed herself so hard and could feel the fatigue of the last week claw at her, slowing her strides. She could hear loud growls and large paws thunder behind her. Shock jolted through her as she felt Rolan's presence in wolf form nearing. *Impossible!* Only the Royal bloodline could shift outside the full moon.

She ran harder as she felt the shock reverberate through her whole body. Rolan had found a way to shift outside of the moon cycle. She had only heard of this through dark, terrible magic, myths that no one believed. She twisted to the right to avoid a tree and whelped as a second wolf snapped at her flank. She turned again to avoid both wolves, quick in her small stature and skidded into a stream. All sense of direction lost, Eloi was filled with the urgency to escape. She galloped along the stream, which was too narrow for both wolves to run together. She panted heavily, unsure she could keep going much longer but willed her limbs to keep going.

Ahead there was a corner, and as she flew up the bank, she gained some ground. Eloi darted through the trees faster than the bulkier wolves, and the sounds of the two adults quieted. She glanced back to see if the pair had lost ground on her, but the distraction cost her. She tripped on some thick roots across her path and tumbled along the hard ground. The air left her lungs as she slammed to a stop.

Before she could recover, her father's large, black wolf form pinned her down and growled wildly. Pain shot through her limbs and a whine escaped her as the giant wolf stomped down harder.

Submit, Eloi.

Rolan's mind connection was stronger than it had ever been, a dark menace bearing down on her. How had he shifted? Eloi whimpered as she looked up and saw Mervan in his wolf form, the rest of the warriors, still in their human forms, sprinted towards them and surrounded her.

Submit.

The command was almost too much to bear and clawed at her mind to force her. But Eloi was Royal, and not many were strong enough to overpower one of Royal blood—even a youngling.

NO!

Eloi screamed in her mind and saw Rolan flinch. She screamed wordlessly in her mind again, and he backed off, shaking his head. Eloi drew more power and stood to face her father.

ENOUGH!

Rolan's command growled in her head, which shot pain through her, and her legs nearly gave out. It took all her strength to stand and face him. He shouldn't have been this strong.

Why do you run, youngling?

Eloi did not answer. Rolan's voice had become soft in her mind like honey, and she didn't want him to realize how much she knew. Rolan snarled at her when she didn't answer and stepped forward menacingly. She could feel Mervan behind her, and the other warriors watched as they prowled and circled the three of them. But she would not cower.

Eloi drew herself tall and regal. A movement behind the warriors caught her attention, and Rolan sniffed loudly.

This is none of your concern, old man.

Eyolf stepped forward into the center of the warriors, and Eloi cringed; he was in human form, too old to shift even if it was a full moon. He was one of the oldest in the pack.

"How are you shifted, Rolan? It is weeks from the next moon." Eyolf drew the attention of the men around him and looked at Mervan.

"Your Second as well, I see. You've not granted the rest of your warriors the privilege, though. I guess you do not trust them with the power you abuse."

Eloi backed up towards the edge of the group, where a gap had formed to take advantage of their distraction. Her heart squeezed as she realized that Eyolf would not make it out of this alive. Rolan had shown what he was capable of, and Eyolf would sacrifice himself to keep her safe. Eloi would not waste it.

I am the leader of this pack, and I have been granted the power to shift outside the cycle. Who are you to question me?

"We both know that's not how it works, Rolan. What have you done?" Horror was evident in Eyolf's voice.

Rolan growled low and prowled towards Eyolf. *Always in everyone's business, Eyolf, you are a meddling fool. What will I do with you?*

Eloi had edged close enough to the gap and had gone unnoticed. That was the advantage of being a pup; everyone underestimated you. Only Eyolf watched her—the other warriors were too concerned with the Elder. He had trained many of them from a young age and had always held their respect. The evident disappointment in Eyolf's eyes had affected the group; all their eyes were on him. Eyolf looked at each of the warriors and held Nyko's gaze the longest.

"It is never too late to do the right thing," Eyolf said quietly. "Come back to the village, all of you. I'm not sure what has been going on, but this is no time to divide."

The warrior shifters looked uncomfortable.

How dare you presume to command us!

Eloi could feel Rolan had lost his temper and used that opportunity to sneak through the gap. But, as soon as she did, Rolan turned and snarled in her direction.

"Run, Eloi!" Eyolf screamed.

Rolan lunged, his jaws open wide, and aimed for her throat.

10

A ine and Lachlan had worked on several projects over the last few days, and Aine accompanied him when he delivered to some incredibly happy customers. She had a way with people, and her kindness showed no bounds. She seemed to instinctively know what they needed, whether it was empathy or a firm word. Lachlan watched as the town appeared to fall in love with her. They complemented each other in their work, and he enjoyed her company.

They had finished Trevor's order, though he had delivered it alone. When he mentioned Trevor to Aine, he could almost feel the rage coming from her. He had refused to let her ride along, worried about Trevor's safety. Fortunately, when Aine carved that order, she said she had thought of the wife and not the man. She had gotten a feel for the woman, who loved her garden and blindly stayed with the man she had married.

Aine told Lachlan that the woman thought she was happy—that she didn't know she could have better and stayed content with what she had. Only Trevor's wife could decide to leave when she was ready, which wasn't now.

Lachlan thought about what she said and wondered how she knew; there were times he thought she must be a mind reader, or at least extremely intuitive. Was that something shifters could do? He didn't know she was a shifter; after all, she hadn't shifted at the full moon. But she wasn't human. If she knew what she was, she hadn't said anything to him, and he hoped that one day she would trust him enough to say something.

It had been three weeks since Aine woke up in that clearing and stumbled into their lives. Phil adored her; the big man constantly looked out for her and let her keep his sweater. Lachlan never felt comfortable with anyone like he did with Aine. He'd never imagined he would share his life in the way he did with her, an equal partnership.

They stayed up talking late into the night, and after the first few nights, Aine had fallen asleep in his bed. Lachlan quietly watched her sleep and fantasized about her staying there with him and waking up to her every day. He must have been a saint to resist taking their relationship further. His need for her grew every day, and he noticed she couldn't help but gravitate towards him.

But Lachlan was distracted by his family; their proximity ate at him, and he knew that if both parts of his life collided, it would not end well. Aine held herself back from him still in some ways, and he knew she remembered more than she told him—he was sure of it. He had given her privacy to let her work it out on her own. But he needed to know if his family would be a danger to her. She had to be supernatural, but he hadn't heard of any creatures other than shifters. He didn't know who he could talk to about it.

Lachlan had mentioned that they should go and check

out the clearing together to try and track where she had come from. He wanted to figure out how she got there and see if this might shed any light on her past. Though they had been there recently, he wanted to go and see if he could find her trail before it had been too long. Aine was reluctant; she shied away from going back, and he suspected something must have happened on the night of the full moon. Maybe she had seen a shifter?

"Morning, beautiful." Lachlan smiled as Aine came down the stairs from his room. She had fallen asleep in his bed again. It had been almost unbearable, the way she looked as she lay next to him. He had to leave and come downstairs before he kissed her awake. Her stunning smile made his grin widen, and he felt his heart swell when she walked up to put her arms around his waist, resting her head on his chest.

"Morning. I can hear your heartbeat." Aine sighed contently, and Lachlan chuckled.

"Let me know if it stops."

She looked up and scowled at him. "It must never stop!" she cried. "Don't say something like that." The horror on her face made his heart leap. She was so expressive and never hid her feelings.

"It was a joke, Aine—as long as I can keep it beating, it will beat."

Aine relaxed and leaned into him. Lachlan lifted his arm and stroked her hair. Catching her scent, he breathed deep and sighed.

"Do you want to go to the clearing today?" he asked. "I think we need to try and see if we can find the trail of you wandering there or the trail of whoever left you." He stared at the wall as Aine stiffened in his arms. It would be the same conversation as last time. She hadn't distanced herself emotionally but still refused to talk about her past.

"No, I don't want to. Not after last time when I was sick."

"What about finding the girl, or woman, that you miss? It's been a couple of weeks since you were sick, and you haven't been ill since."

"I've lost the feeling of her; it's strange. I could feel her so strongly until a few days ago, and now it's like she's gone. I don't know what to make of it."

Lachlan sighed. He didn't want to force her to go. He might have to go and investigate by himself, maybe try, and track the shifter settlement Girvan had talked about. He still held her, and she hadn't backed away when they started on the subject, though, which was progress.

"Do you think she's real or just a figment of my imagination?" Aine looked up into Lachlan's face again, anguish present in her features.

He stroked her arm; at least she was talking about it. "I don't know, Aine, with you not remembering who you are...." His voice trailed off. He wasn't sure what to say to reassure her and decided it was time to take Phil's advice.

"How about we have a day off woodwork today. Go for a walk or into town?" Lachlan looked down into Aine's green eyes, and his face softened. She smiled and glanced towards his lips; he took the hint and leaned his head down to softly kiss her. He had to break the kiss and was slightly breathless when they parted. It felt so intense when they touched.

"Breakfast, and then let's go out," he said. "I'm sure we can think of something to do for fun." He turned to start breakfast. They were eating a lot between the two of them; he was glad Aine had a healthy appetite; it meant she was comfortable. Though she mostly ate meat and eggs, which meant he would need to restock his freezer soon.

"How about we go to the lake?" he suggested as he cooked. "It's great for hiking, and the area is calm. I always relax when I'm there. Not many from town go, especially not during the week."

"The lake? Where's that?" Aine crinkled her brow; he loved it when she did that.

"The other side of town." Lachlan watched as Aine set the table and he dished out the food. He loved the rhythm they had gotten into; they worked as a team with everything and almost instinctively knew what needed to be done without words. He felt like he'd lived with her for years rather than a few weeks.

Aine looked toward him as he watched her; she smiled sweetly and blushed. He laughed and pulled out her chair for her while she gracefully sat down to eat.

"Sounds like a good plan, I like water," Aine giggled, and Lachlan smiled at her again.

AINE WATCHED the town blur past as they drove through. She spent every waking second with Lachlan, and it was so easy. As she gazed out the window, she thought about the last few weeks and how much had happened. When they waited for orders in the shop, she could glean the dynamics of relationships and hadn't felt anything like what she had with Lachlan. There always seemed to be some conflict or agitation in couples—one annoyed at the other for something, most of the time minor. She could always tell Lachlan wanted her to open up about her past and what she remembered, but he was patient and hadn't pushed her.

Lachlan was easy to be around, and she wished she could stay with him forever, but she could feel her past approaching. She hadn't had the dreams over the past few days, and she felt disconnected from what she had seen. The dreams were so hazy and hard to remember. However, she could feel a dark presence coming. Aine wondered if it was the man who poisoned her—if he knew she was alive. The thought made her shiver, and she rubbed her arms.

"Cold?" Lachlan asked. Aine shook her head.

Would he believe her if she told him she thought the dreams were real, more real than being with him? Aine had touched on the subject a few times, and Lachlan appeared to believe her, but the more she thought about it, the more it all sounded crazy. She'd watched other people in town and figured that none had her ability to sense the way she did. If they did, they certainly wouldn't argue as much.

Aine watched as the scenery changed; the comfortable town buildings slowly transformed into open countryside, then trees and mountains. The drive was much longer than any they had ever taken before, and Aine felt lighter as they drove away. The mountains were huge; it made her feel small in comparison. She glanced over at Lachlan and watched his hair moving in the breeze from the open window. He was such a kind man, in total opposition to what she expected when they first met.

When they arrived at the lake, the air was cooler and felt fresh compared to in the town. Aine drew in a deep breath and reveled in the scents around her. There was a mixture of various floral essences, and she could smell the clean water in the lake. She still felt warm in the shorts and t-shirt she wore. Lachlan was right—it was peaceful here. She could sense smaller wildlife but no other humans in the area.

"I can see why you like it here." Aine watched Lachlan as he got out of the truck. She wondered how he had found this place. She had realized she didn't know much about his past or him; they had only met three weeks ago, but she knew *him*. His presence in the house had been pure, and she could feel his character when she drew on that strange feeling within herself, as she had in the house.

She couldn't explain how she knew, but there was a darkness to him. Aine felt it was in his past and involved his family, but he hadn't pushed her for information, so she wouldn't push him.

Lachlan turned to smile at her as he closed the truck door and put his arms around her. He looked deep into her eyes, and Aine felt a jolt of heat rush through her. She felt like her heart had stopped and started again. She had to stifle a giggle and felt her face heat.

"Shall we go for a walk?" Lachlan chuckled as he ran a thumb over her cheek.

He snorted when Aine kicked off her shoes. She found them so constrictive and wanted to feel the ground beneath her; it felt more natural to her as she walked. The shore of the lake beckoned, and she strolled over to look out over the calm, crystal-clear water. She stepped forward and closed her eyes as the coolness on her feet soothed her.

She could feel all the menace and agitation she had felt when exploring her past melt away. Her eyes drifted shut, and she lifted her face to the sun as she drank in her surroundings. Aine instinctively knew she had never been to an area that radiated so much peace. She couldn't feel another human for miles, just nature, and silence.

Lachlan followed her to the shore and stopped short of the water; he held out his hand toward her, and she quickly stepped towards him. He tilted his head to the mountains and gently pulled her with him.

≈

AINE AND LACHLAN spent the day together, not thinking about work or her lack of memory. Instead, they enjoyed each other's company and explored the surrounding area. Instinctively, Lachlan kept to the shore and avoided entering the woods. However, Aine often came back to dip her feet in the lake's water as they traversed the shore. Happiness radiated from her, and Lachlan couldn't help but smile and laugh.

During the afternoon, when the sun was high and the air had warmed, he laid out a blanket on a patch of soft grass, and they ate sandwiches while watching the birds curiously approach. His heart warmed as he caught her relaxing in the afternoon sun.

"I like it here," Aine sighed, a small smile on her face.

"We will have to come back." Lachlan gazed at her.

"Maybe…" Aine's voice trailed off as she looked out over the water and frowned slightly.

Lachlan could feel her conflict like he felt his own. He wondered if she kept a secret like his, one which she thought would hurt him. He took a deep breath.

"Aine, I need to tell you something."

She turned to look at him. "Not now, Lachlan; this day is perfect as it is." Her eyes had a mischievous glint as she quickly got up and ran towards the water.

"Aine," Lachlan warned halfheartedly. He laughed when he heard a loud splash, and Aine's head appeared above the water.

Pulling off his boots and socks, he made a show of tugging off his jeans when he felt Aine's eyes on him. Then, slowly, he pulled his shirt over his head before he ran after her. His muscles bulged as he threw his clothes onto the blanket and approached the lake.

Lachlan's eyes took in Aine as her clothes clung to her

body, every curve accented by the wet garments. His mouth went dry, and heat shot to his groin; he felt relief when he hit the cold water in the lake. Aine gasped as he dove into the lake next to her with a big splash.

LACHLAN'S BODY caused water to cover Aine, and she laughed. When he surfaced, it streamed down his naked chest and his body glistened in the sun. She felt her eyes widen and struggled to close her mouth as she watched his muscles ripple.

He swam towards her and pulled her down into the water with him. Aine's breath caught as Lachlan gripped her hips and pulled her close. They floated and stared at one another, and the world seemed to disappear around them. She felt her stomach flutter; Lachlan slowly leaned forward and kissed her, and she tasted the freshness of the lake water on their lips. Her movements turned desperate as Lachlan deepened the kiss. His tongue thrust into her mouth with urgency, and she pulled him towards her hard. His body didn't give against her; his smooth, muscular back felt incredible beneath her hands as she stroked him.

Rough stones caught Aine's bare legs as they drifted towards the shore. In one movement, Lachlan lifted her from the water without breaking the kiss. Aine gasped against his mouth when he carried her over to their blanket. His face parted from hers as he gently lay Aine down, positioning himself over her and cupping her face. Aine shivered as water dripped from his hair onto her chest.

"Aine, I can't put into words how important you are to me. I need you."

Lachlan smiled as Aine grabbed the back of his head

and pulled him down to her. Her core throbbed with need, and she could barely contain herself. He shifted so his weight didn't hurt her, and she could feel a hard bulge against her thigh.

When she looked up into his face, his eyes were devouring her body. The top she wore had gone see-through in the water and her nipples were hard. Lachlan growled as he kissed her again possessively. His hand slid up her thigh and caressed her skin; he explored her body as he lifted the wet top over her head.

Lachlan moved off Aine to take off his boxers, and she quickly undid her shorts, tugging them off. She drank in his naked form and swallowed as he moved to kiss her again. Her hands slid up his incredible chest, and her whole body flushed with heat. She wasn't disappointed as she explored and kissed him. The noises that came from him encouraged her further, doing strange things to her body.

"Tell me you want this," Lachlan breathed in her ear.

"Tell me you don't," Aine laughed.

In answer, Lachlan pulled her sports bra over her head and threw it away. Aine cried in protest until he took her nipple into his mouth. Everything tingled and tightened at her core as she ached for him. She leaned back against the blanket and tried to concentrate as she reached down to take him into her hands. He hissed at the first touch and moaned loudly as her hands caressed him.

"You'll be the death of me," Lachlan breathed, gently kissing down her body as he explored every inch of her. Aine pulled back and gasped as Lachlan kissed her hip just below her belly. The feeling was intense. He gently stroked her core with his finger, feeling her wetness, and used his thumb to stimulate her clit.

She leaned back and cried out as pleasure washed over

her. She was completely open to him, her hips bucking against his hand as he reached an exquisite rhythm.

Lachlan smiled when he felt how ready she was for him. He positioned himself above her. As he slowly pushed himself into her, Lachlan kissed her to catch her scream. Aine felt overwhelmed with every touch as she stretched around his length.

She started to move with Lachlan as he rocked into her, deeper with each thrust. Her nipples rubbed against his muscular chest and intensified the pressure in her core. Aine felt like she was on a cliff edge and would tip over any second. When he reached down to touch her, her whole body shook with the force of her orgasm.

Lachlan cried out as she tightened around him and released himself into her. He shook slightly and breathed hard as he gently lowered his weight onto her, careful not to crush her. Aine's chest heaved with exertion, and she looked up into his dazed face.

"That was unreal." Lachlan shook his head to clear it but failed. His eyes were sex-glazed, and he smiled at her lazily. "I'm not sure I can move."

Aine's laugh was breathy and sultry when she lifted her hand to caress his jaw. "I don't think I can either."

With an effort, Lachlan gently pulled out of her and reached for the bag he'd brought with them. Another blanket appeared, and he covered them both. He pulled Aine into his arms, and they laid in the afternoon sun, their skin glowed in the light. Content, Aine closed her eyes to savor the moment.

She knew the time would come when she would have to leave. She needed to find her pack; even if they didn't want her, she knew that the man in her dreams would ruin them. She had a sense of foreboding that refused to leave her, and she cared about Lachlan too much to endanger him. She would give herself this last day, then leave.

Aine lay her head on Lachlan's shoulder; he immediately reached up and started to stroke her hair. She moaned, then sighed; it felt incredible. The slightest touch from him sent shivers through her and made her heart flutter.

She knew her feelings for him were dangerous for them both, but she couldn't help it nor explain why to herself. The attraction between them was so strong, it was impossible to ignore. It would only make it that much harder to leave.

She tried not to think about that as she felt Lachlan's warm skin against hers. The comfort and heat from the sun, combined with Lachlan held against her, soothed Aine as she drifted to sleep.

11

Aine saw a pale young wolf run through the trees; she panted heavily, and Aine could see her struggle to move forwards. The exhaustion radiated from the youngling in ripples. Dark shadows from the trees surrounded her. The desperation of the wolf came off her in waves as she slowed. The shadows moved quickly around her, and Aine's chest tightened as they began to close in. It didn't take long until the young one fell, unable to continue, at the mercy of the group.

Aine could see two giant wolves, one grey and the other black as night; four human warriors caught up and positioned themselves to encircle the little one. Aine screamed out for the pale wolf to run; her mouth moved, but no sound came out. In her desperation, Aine tried to will herself to move forward but couldn't shorten the distance between them. Her mind screamed wildly, blind panic overwhelming her, while she could do nothing to help the youngling.

Another came forward from the darkness, an older man Aine recognized. Her heart swelled, and she felt a fondness toward him. The old man appeared to plead with the group, his arms moved quickly, though he never gestured toward the young wolf.

She could see the younger wolf use the distraction to move towards the edge of the group. The old man held the group's attention as he drew them away from the pup. Aine watched as the pale little wolf tried to slip away. When almost out of the larger group, the black wolf, his fur the color of midnight, turned to suddenly lunge for the smaller, pale youngling as she tried to sprint out of the circle of warriors.

Aine felt the ground drop out from beneath her and tried to put herself between them, but her body was still held fast, and she could not move. A scream tore from her throat, the sound finally breaking through, and the need to protect the youngling over-whelmed her. Aine's heart wrenched as the jaws of the black wolf bore down towards the neck of Eloi.

"ELOI!" Aine screamed as she jerked awake. She pushed hard against Lachlan, who held her in place.

When she had started to twitch, then flail in her sleep, he'd tried to wake her. Blood smeared his chest from where she had scratched him. Fear had gripped Lachlan when she wouldn't wake, and he tried to make her comfortable, but after a while, she had started to claw and scream. He hadn't known how to help her other than to hold her down to prevent her from harm.

"Calm down." Lachlan tried to soothe her, but his voice was laced with panic and sounded loud in his ears. Aine paid no attention to him and continued to struggle; he held her with one hand and blindly reached where he had dropped his shirt earlier.

"Eloi!" Aine screamed again, the sound animalistic, not one any human was capable of. She pulled hard against his grip, stronger than was possible as Lachlan tried again to calm her.

"Please, Aine," he begged, "you know me!"

As he held her back with both hands again, her bones began to bend and twist within his grasp; Lachlan could hear them grind and shift. Claws grew from her hands, and Aine's beautiful face lengthened. Pure white hairs sprouted over her body, and her eyes glowed a dark amber.

"Aine?" Lachlan's horror was evident in his voice as fear seized him. She hadn't shifted on the full moon—how could she be a wolf? He could feel her strength and wasn't sure he could take her if he let her shift entirely. Most shifters he could, but he struggled with her now, and she wasn't even half-shifted.

He desperately reached for his shirt again, but Aine pulled against him. Her control was incredible; she had been strong for a human, and he should have realized that. Now he knew she was a shifter, and she must be an extremely powerful one. Lachlan needed Aine to recognize him; otherwise, she would kill him. What had caused her panic? She had been crying out in her sleep, but what had changed?

Lachlan's heart hurt as he realized the choice he faced. His chest was tight as he reached again and finally grabbed onto the medallion he had dropped with his shirt. The metal felt warm from the sun, and Lachlan gripped it hard in his hand, trying to hold Aine with the other.

"Don't make me use this, Aine!" He called her name again and hoped that it would get through to her. Her eyes were wild as she fought him—she was more wolf than human now, and if he didn't act soon, he would lose his grip on her. Lachlan's heart broke.

"Forgive me."

He held the medallion to Aine's forehead while he gripped her with his other hand and watched as she fell limp under him. A bright flash of light hurt his eyes, and he had to blink to clear his vision. His beautiful Aine was human again, calmly laid out as she had been before as if nothing had changed. Lachlan screamed in frustration as he let her go. He felt his muscles slowly relax from the strength he'd had to use to keep her contained.

A growl of frustration escaped him as he stood and gazed down at his Aine. Had she known what she was and kept it from him? Who was Eloi? Had she faked the memory loss? He quickly picked up his jeans and shirt and dressed.

Lachlan wiped his hands on his pants and paced the shore of the lake, the haven now tainted. He thought shifters had no control without the full moon and that they couldn't shift any other time. Had his family gotten it wrong for centuries? Lachlan turned to the woman that had become his everything; he would wait for her to wake and get some answers. But he couldn't believe she had purposefully deceived him. *Had she lured him in to trick him?* It would break his heart if she had. He slowly returned to where she rested.

Lachlan gently lifted Aine off the ground, wrapped her in the blanket, and carried her to his truck. He would need to get her to safety; with his family in the area, she would be in more danger. He belted her into the passenger seat and picked up their belongings.

His family would kill her without a second thought; he would not see her dead, even if she had betrayed him. He would have to figure it out once he got her home, think of a place they would never think to find her.

Their return journey was painful in contrast to their peaceful drive out that morning. The road appeared to continue forever as he slowly drove to his house. Once Lachlan had Aine back in the home, he carried her down to the basement and laid her gently on the bed. Her face was relaxed in sleep and showed no signs of the events of the afternoon.

When he first met her, his instincts had been right; he was a fool to convince himself otherwise. Lachlan ran his hands through his dark hair and heard Phil enter his house upstairs. His friend made his way down, and his face paled when he saw Lachlan. Lachlan had called him from the lake to tell him what had happened.

"Not like you to be this out of sorts." Phil's voice was filled with concern.

Lachlan pulled to blanket across Aine to make sure she was covered.

"Do you want me to call Caroline?"

"No, this isn't a natural sleep and in all honesty, I don't know when she will wake up." Lachlan ran his hand through his hair again in frustration. "The medallion has only ever been used to incapacitate before elimination of a shifter. We've never let one wake before. I'm not even sure she will awake but I had no choice." He stalked up and down the basement, nervous energy coursed through him.

"You only ever killed them." The horror in Phil's tone shook Lachlan, and he stopped. Shame filled him as he looked at his best friend.

"It's why I left, Phil. I hated the life I was born into. It was unnecessarily cruel. I argued with my father about terminating them all—that there must be some good. It's why I had to leave; I disagreed with killing them because of what they were. I should have known I would never escape." Lachlan paused. Phil knew rough details about Lachlan's past, but he had never told him specifics. Phil was too kind to hear about the innocents his family had slaughtered.

"My father is here, Phil, and I don't think he will let me leave this time. The family has been hunting down a pack called the Faction. I have heard of them before—they are supposed to want all humans enslaved and for shifters to rule the world. Then, it all sounded too farfetched, but now I'm not so sure. If that's why my father came for me, it must be real."

Phil's face paled; from what Lachlan had told him, he wasn't surprised the big man was spooked.

"Is that why your cousin is back at the diner?" Phil whispered as if Girvan might hear him.

"He's there now?" Lachlan turned quickly to face Phil, who nodded weakly and shrugged. Lachlan ran his hand through his hair and growled in frustration. He sighed and ran up the stairs to get changed. Dirt and silt crusted his clothes from their afternoon at the lake; the perfect day felt like a dream now.

As Lachlan reluctantly strode towards Phil's diner, he took in a deep breath of the evening air to steady himself. His face blank, he pushed the door open, the room was empty, but for his cousin sitting in the booth, they had spoken in a few days ago.

Despite the food being shoveled into his mouth, Girvan showed no emotion as Lachlan slowly walked towards him and sat down opposite.

"More pancakes?"

"What can I say? They're good, and I need the fuel." Girvan shrugged.

Lachlan stared at him; the silence made most uncomfortable, but he used it as a tool.

Girvan sighed and placed his knife and fork neatly in

front of him. "Your pa needs an answer. He's discovered pockets of a rebellion in cave systems through America. He's sending out units of hunters to investigate, but there aren't enough of us."

"I can't." Lachlan kept his voice level and face blank. Girvan's mouth drew down, resignation clear. The food left on his plate, his cousin rose.

"I knew that would be your answer, but I'd hoped not. Finn is more than your pa can handle. I think your pa can see that feeding him power over the years was a mistake. He picks fights with other hunters and is unnecessarily cruel to any of those under him. Please reconsider." Girvan's eyes showed strain as he almost begged the last part. Lachlan felt a headache start behind his eyes; he closed them and breathed deep.

"I'm dealing with something here, and it's just as important. Give me a week to think about it." Maybe he could leave Aine with Phil, get them both to safety. If the hunters' attention was on him, they would never know about Aine.

Girvan grimaced.

"It's the best I can do." Lachlan moved toward his cousin and embraced him. The smell of leather under the shirt Girvan wore was familiar, and Lachlan wasn't surprised at the weapons he could feel his cousin carried.

"Stay safe," Lachlan muttered. His steps felt weary when he returned to his house. Torn, he stared into the darkness, stars winking down over him while he considered his next move.

Guilt ate at him as he remembered why he'd left.

12

***

Fifteen years earlier...

Lachlan drove his old truck towards the farmhouse; a meeting had been called by his father, Liam. Liam was the head of his family of hunters. The O'Reilly family didn't hunt normal animals—they hunted and exterminated shifters. Lachlan swore as the farmhouse came into view. It was a pain in the ass to get to, and he hated these meetings. Nothing was ever resolved, and the family usually went around in circles, fueled by hate.

Quickly Lachlan parked and got out of the truck; he stared up at the evening sun and prayed this wouldn't take long. The white house before him looked calm in contrast to the arguments that normally raged inside. The house was encircled by a large wood and open fields beyond that. Entirely isolated, it was the perfect location for the hunters to meet.

Lachlan opened the door and strode down the hallway. He nodded at the warriors who let him through, all part of his father's group. His father stood at the head of the meeting table in what once was a dining room. There were blank spaces on the faded wallpaper where pictures had once hung.

"The time to act is now! The vermin are nearly exterminated in this area!" Liam repeatedly banged his fist on the table.

"You say that every year, when will it actually be true?" Liam's brother Garry challenged.

Lachlan looked at his uncle. The two had been in a power struggle since they were teens and rarely agreed. If one said white was white, the other would argue it was black until they both resorted to violence to make their point. Lachlan took his place behind his father and next to his brother Cillian to lean against the wall. Lachlan was older by two years, and Cillian was the only brother he felt was reasonable. His cousin Girvan stood next to Garry, amusement on his face as he watched the two men argue.

"We could use the artifacts," Liam countered. "If we have them, other hunters must have them too. If we pooled our resources, we could be more efficient in our extermination. We can use them to identify shifters living among humans. One touch incapacitates them."

Artifacts had been passed down in Lachlan's family, the medallion he wore around his neck being one of several. The history of the artifacts had been lost, but they had been used to take down wolves.

"How long have they been at this? And where is Finn? Shouldn't he be here?" Lachlan hissed as he looked at Cillian, whose rapt attention was on the meeting. Lachlan had to elbow him and repeat the question. Cillian shrugged and turned his head back to their father.

Lachlan frowned. It wasn't like Finn to miss a meeting and throw his weight around. Finn had become more dramatic over the last year.

"He's probably torturing the trainees again or with the captive." Cillian shrugged.

Lachlan shifted; suddenly, he knew precisely where Finn would be. Finn was the eldest of the five brothers and expected to take his father's role as head of the family when the time came. Finn was more brutal and vicious than any of the other warriors. He enjoyed anything that caused captives pain before they were executed.

Lachlan looked out the window towards the outhouses. A teen shifter had been caught the day before; they only kept her alive so that they could find the rest of her pack. Lachlan felt bile in his throat as he thought of his brother's methods for finding the location.

Steps slow and silent so as not to draw attention to himself, he crept out the side door. Once outside, he approached the outhouses and looked to the sky. The sun was slowly reaching towards the horizon, and it was a full moon tonight. If the rest of her pack were going to rescue her or attack the hunters, it would be tonight. There would be a well-laid-out trap in case that happened. Lachlan came to a halt and felt dizzy; a weariness washed over him.

"Are you okay?" Lachlan's mother was at his side moments after he stopped.

"I'm fine, Mother, just lightheaded."

"When did you last eat?" Briana frowned at her son. It didn't matter how old he got; his mother would always try to look after him.

"About an hour ago. Have you seen Finn? Is he with the girl?" Lachlan turned to look down at his mother. She glanced towards the outhouses.

"Don't go there, Lachlan. You know what he's like, and I can see what it does to you. Finn enjoys making you squirm. It'll be worse for the girl if you're there." She bit her lip. "You need to speak to your father. The last of the hunters are here, and I think he wants to head to the pack's location tonight."

"Is he crazy? It's a full moon." Lachlan's whole body tensed; he could feel the adrenaline course through him. "They will be at their strongest."

"He thinks they won't expect it and that they will go after the shifter here. Leaving the weak behind. He..." Briana paused. "He plans to take the young and old, force a surrender from the whole pack. You know he won't let them live; he will execute them all."

Lachlan felt his stomach drop. If a shifter got out of hand and killed a human, then fair enough, but killing for the sake of killing was wrong. No matter the species. If the pack hadn't harmed humans, then the hunters had no right to exterminate them.

"It's time to choose a side, Lachlan," his mother whispered softly. She put a hand on his back. "I know you hate this life, but if you are going to act, the time is now."

Lachlan's mind went numb; he rarely expressed his opinion. Was his own mother encouraging him to act out against his father?

"I..." Lachlan didn't get to finish. His mother had turned towards the house as if she hadn't even spoken. She had never been soft or shown weakness, but Lachlan could see now that she wasn't comfortable with this life. It was in her eyes as they almost pleaded with him to stop it all. It was probably where he got his doubt from.

He turned to look to the outhouses. This had to stop. His mother had warned him not to go in there, but if he was going to help the shifters, he would need an ally.

Lachlan checked his weapons. As a show of strength, his father demanded they were all armed to the teeth, even when at these meetings. Always prepared, they could not allow the showing of any weakness at any time. So Lachlan strode with purpose and flinched when he heard the screams ahead of him.

As he entered the area where he knew the girl was being held, he had to hold his breath against the smell of blood and vomit. The girl was chained to a chair in the corner, her clothes filthy and her arms covered in blood. Her once-blonde hair hung in dirty rat tails to hide her face as her head hung.

Finn stood twirling a dagger between his fingers, silver-plated for the sole purpose of causing more pain.

"Ah, Lachlan, here to join in?" His brother lifted an eyebrow in challenge.

"Father wants you at the meeting," Lachlan informed the youth, who had looked back toward the girl. The look on Finn's face caused Lachlan to clench his fists. His eyes were sharp with cruelty, and his mouth grinned as he went for another slice along the girl's arms.

The girl looked up at Lachlan as he spoke. Her eyes shone and silently pleaded with him to help her. Tear streaks ran through the dirt on her face; she cried out, her face contorted, as the dagger sliced down her arm. Lachlan turned to see Finn watch him. His face sneered as he twirled the blade again and strode over.

"Pathetic." Finn spat and shoved Lachlan as he passed by.

Lachlan reacted without thinking—one fluid movement and his brother was in a headlock. Finn didn't know what hit him. The two had always fought, and their hand-to-hand sparring was a spectacle to behold. Lachlan had held back for years; he had known that he would need to surprise his brother one day. He shifted to a sleeper hold, and when

Finn was unconscious, he lowered him to the ground. The young girl stared at him, eyes wide.

"We do not have long." Lachlan approached the girl, but she cringed away. "If you want out, you have to trust me and do as I say, quickly."

Lachlan knew he could take the girl by force, but they didn't have time. She looked up at him, and in one moment, her eyes changed from fear to awe. She smiled and instantly looked younger. Lachlan barely contained his anger at his family and their brutality. Efficiently, he unchained the girl and lifted her out of the chair, putting her on her feet.

"I never believed you existed," the girl whispered quietly. "The kind warrior."

"I don't know what you're talking about, and we don't have time." Lachlan gently pulled her arm for her to follow him and exited the building out of the side door they rarely used.

He headed for the woods nearest the ocean. The warriors wouldn't be guarding the woods there, and he could sneak around to the cove. He'd seen the weakness in their defense when they put it together and kept quiet. It was at that moment Lachlan realized he had planned this from the start. He was confident he could sneak around the warriors in that area, especially if they took to the trees in spots where the patrol was light.

Lachlan turned back as the girl stumbled; her bare feet had faltered. She was tired and looked beaten in body, but her eyes were keen and seemed to radiate an unexplained joy. He lifted her and carried her until they reached a point where a patrol would pass in a couple of minutes. He had memorized the routes, as he usually did for each meeting. Now he could use the patrol plans to help the girl escape.

Lachlan looked at his watch. "In a minute, a warrior will

pass by here—we need to climb the tree and wait for him to pass. Once he does, we won't have long to slip through the gap in the patrols. Do you think you can move quickly?"

He looked down at the girl. She was so small, and he began to doubt she would make it. But he couldn't regret his choice; if the pack had no reason to come for the girl, then their home wouldn't be left unguarded. She needed to get back to them quickly and warn them.

He looked to the horizon as the sun crawled closer, then back at the girl. Her face was determined, and she nodded.

Lachlan jumped and reached up to a thick branch, his body strong; he pulled himself up easily. Once he was settled on it and certain it would hold his weight, he reached down for the girl. She felt like she weighed nothing as he pulled her up. She scrambled onto the branch next to him and laid out, as he was, to spread their weight. Lachlan held his breath, hearing soft footsteps approach, and the girl cocked her head.

A dark-haired warrior from his uncle's clan passed by nearly five feet from their tree. Lachlan almost breathed a sigh of relief; his uncle's clan tended to be careless and didn't take patrol seriously. After the warrior had passed, Lachlan counted to thirty in his head before he gracefully dropped to the ground. He reached up for the girl, but she jumped down beside him with a grace that shocked him.

"As the full moon draws near, my strength returns," she said.

"You can shift so young?" His voice low, Lachlan pulled her along quickly; they did not have long.

"Yes, though I'm an exception. At fifteen, I'm the youngest able to shift."

"You don't look fifteen," Lachlan teased. Hopefully, the girl would be less scared of him if he joked, though she hadn't shown any signs of fear since they'd left his brother. The girl pressed her lips together, brow crinkled. Amusement shone on her face as she tried not to laugh.

Together they silently ghosted through the woods. After an hour, Lachlan stopped; they'd gone about five miles, which was a miracle considering the girl's state. He could feel a presence ahead and stepped in front of the girl, his hand out to hold her back.

"Wait." The command in Lachlan's voice made it rough, and the girl stiffened. He listened and held himself ready.

A shadow flew from his right with an animalistic cry, and Lachlan swiftly stepped to the side, putting himself between the girl and the threat. A boy landed face first in the dirt, and instinct gripped Lachlan in the presence of another shifter. In his whole life, when he'd been threatened by a shifter, his entire body filled with adrenaline and instinct tried to take over.

His father had taught him that his family had been hunters so long, the survival instinct was ingrained within the bloodline. Without pause, Lachlan subdued the boy and held him down, mainly to keep him quiet.

"Stop!" The girl sprang from behind Lachlan and crouched beside the boy. Lachlan immediately released him and stepped back.

"Stay down; he's the warrior the elders talked about. The one that will save us." She put her hand on the boy's back and applied pressure. "This is my brother." Fondness crept into her tone. When she looked up at Lachlan, he had taken another step back to give them space.

"Do you know your way from here?" Lachlan asked. He needed to get back and face his family. Finn would no doubt embellish Lachlan's actions, and he needed to prepare himself.

"Yes, we can make it back, but...you can't go back there. The other one will tell them what you did." The girl looked up at him, eyes wide.

"I must face them; I can't just leave." Pain lanced through Lachlan. "My mother is back there. Get to your pack, my family knows they will attack tonight, and they plan to take your settlement while the warriors are here." He shrugged and smiled at the girl. At least these two would be safe.

"If you ever need anything, approach the pack and ask for Ciara." As the girl spoke, her eyes glowed amber. The small boy looked between them both, confusion on his face.

"Let's go." Ciara turned to the boy to help him up. "We need to stop the pack attacking."

"It's too late."

The horror in the boy's voice hit Lachlan hard in the gut. He turned to look up at the full moon in the sky; and when he turned back, he faced two brown wolves. They were young, but the boy must have been older than Lachlan first thought. He had to be in his late teens, judging by the fact he could shift.

"Go!" Lachlan shouted as he took off towards the farm. A loud howl and the sounds of rifles came from that direction.

Lachlan breathed hard as he reached the perimeter around the farmhouse. Ice gripped his heart as he looked at the chaos across the grounds. The wolves must attacked as humans before the full moon, counting on the shift to turn the battle in their favor. It was clever and had meant the hunters hadn't had a chance to attack their homestead, and the hunters had not been prepared.

The farmhouse was on fire, and Lachlan needed to find

his mother. Women were considered equals and hunters to be used in the fight; she wasn't defenseless, but Lachlan worried. As he ran towards that area, another howl called out over the skirmish. Every wolf nearby turned and ran.

Relief flooded Lachlan; the retreat had been called. Ciara and the boy must have made it to the pack and let them know. He ran to the nearest group of warriors.

"Are there wounded? Are they safe?" he called to them.

"Dunno, everything broke out so quickly. Got them on the run, though," the brown-haired warrior grinned.

Lachlan turned away before he could grimace; he was the only one who knew the real reason behind the retreat. He strode towards his father as he saw him push through a crowd near the fields. As he approached, Lachlan could see the medics running towards the injured in that area. His stride faltered when he realized that some of the trainees were among the wounded, then saw his father crouched beside a figure on the ground and froze in horror.

Lachlan's mother lay on the ground, covered in blood that still gushed from her neck, the contrast stark against her white shirt. Lachlan didn't remember moving, but he was beside his mother in a heartbeat.

"Mother." His voice was tight, and he held his hands against her wound.

His father stood, rage seeping off him, and he growled as he strode away. Lachlan held his mother's hand to his chest, and his eyes stung. His mother struggled to speak, but only a loud gulp sounded as she lifted her other arm. Briana's eyes softened; her hand stroked his face, then fell to the ground. The light left her eyes, and the movement of her chest stopped. Glassy eyes stared at Lachlan, and his world fell apart.

Lachlan didn't make a sound, and he couldn't hear

anything around him. He held his mother's hand, and silent tears slid down his face.

"Where were you?!" Liam screamed when he stopped inches from Lachlan's face.

Lachlan's vision went black for a moment as his father backhanded him across the room. He could see double, and everything blurred as he hit the floor. He felt weary and did not have the strength to stand. He shook his head as he tried to focus on the laminate.

He'd stayed beside his mother until they had started to move the injured. She was the only casualty of the night, and Lachlan felt responsible. Not for his actions—he did not regret getting the girl to safety—but he should have been there to protect her.

Liam breathed hard as he raised his hand again; Cillian grabbed him to pull him back. Lachlan had never seen his father lose his temper. It was a sign of weakness to lose control. Lachlan tried to gather himself and spat the blood he could taste out on the floor.

"You should have been with her. What is the use of a warrior son if he can't protect his own mother?"

Lachlan stared up at his father. Liam's eyes were murderous, and his face red with fury. Finn chose that moment to walk through the door.

"Well, he was letting the shifter go, of course, betraying his people in more than one way," Finn smirked at Lachlan as he walked to stand behind his father. "I told you he was weak."

Lachlan's father froze, as did Cillian. Both looked like they'd been struck. Weariness forgotten, Lachlan was quickly on his feet, his whole body tensed and ready to fight. He watched as his father's face turned an even darker red, and he roared. Lachlan could see the glee in Finn's face as his father took a step forward.

The old man froze when he noticed Lachlan's stance, then he pointed at his son. "You are a disgrace! You should have been here to protect your mother, not consorting to get her killed!" His voice boomed with every word, and Lachlan felt each one hit him hard. His father was right. He should have protected his mother.

"Your hatred of the shifters drove them to attack us. The rabid need to be put down, but the rest could have been left in peace. They had not harmed anyone until you drove them to it!" Lachlan held his voice firm as he spoke the words.

"No harm? They killed your mother!"

"They wouldn't have been here if Finn weren't torturing the girl. For God's sake, she was fifteen. He is out of control; she should never have been taken!"

"You are out of control, Lachlan—you took me out to free her!" Finn joined Lachlan's father and crossed his arms, then spoke quietly. "I should kill you for it."

"I'd like to see you try!" Lachlan's words were fierce; he could feel the anger burn in him. Cillian looked between the three of them, conflicted. "Cillian, this hasn't got anything to do with you. You should go."

Lachlan watched the concern on his younger brother's face. There was little chance Lachlan would leave this room alive against Finn and his father, but he didn't want to put Cillian in a position where he would have to choose or must fight him. Cillian nodded once before leaving through the door behind him; Finn and Liam were between Lachlan and the door. Finn turned to watch their father, still the lapdog who needed instruction.

Liam launched towards Lachlan, a move motivated by anger and grief. Lachlan read it easily and countered. He shoved his father towards the wall as Finn followed up on the attack. Unfortunately for him, he hadn't learned from earlier and still underestimated Lachlan. In two moves, Finn was unconscious on the floor for the second time that night, and Lachlan turned to engage his father.

"Lachlan, you've been holding back." Liam's anger abated slightly at the surprise.

The two men circled each other. Without Finn to distract him, Lachlan knew he could beat Liam. He drew himself to his full height and reveled in the strength as he felt it course through him. Lachlan didn't want to harm anyone in his family, but he would survive this. He would find Ciara's pack and learn more about shifters, try to understand them, and make the decision for himself as to whether they were the threat his father believed they were.

Lachlan watched, and time seemed to slow as his father attacked. It was almost too easy. Lachlan had trained by himself and never shown anyone his full potential. Instead, he had sought trainers from other clans and didn't reveal his identity if he could help it. The fight was quick, and both moved with grace and power. If the circumstances had been different, Lachlan would have appreciated the beauty of their strikes and counters, but he could see his father grow more and more frustrated. Eventually, Liam pulled a dagger, fueled by his anger, and Lachlan was forced to disarm and subdue him. As he held his father's arm in a hold which had him kneeling on the floor and unable to move, Lachlan spoke.

"I am leaving."

He pushed his father down and took a step towards the door. Finn was still unconscious, and their father was sprawled next to him. Lachlan showed no fear as he turned his back on them and walked out into the night. He knew he never wanted to return.

13

resent Day

Eloi curled up tighter in her ball; she remained in wolf form, hidden in the hollow of a tree. She had just slipped by Rolan and his warriors. When Eloi had glanced back, she had seen Eyolf held them off and kept them distracted. The human warriors had not known what to do. She saw them torn—obey their old teacher or obey their new Pack Leader. Rolan had taken the dagger held by the Pack Leader, and for the moment, it seemed no one would dispute his claim.

Eloi had to find her mother. She had fled as far as she could, but when she looked around, she didn't know where she was. As night fell, she had hidden in the hollow and shivered until she eventually slept a little.

As the sun rose, Eloi's stomach gnawed at her insides. She hadn't been able to eat much over the last few days, too troubled by the events at home. She took comfort in the fact that her fear had caused a burst of her power to thrust out towards her mother, and she swore she could feel Aine as it did. Aine had screamed her name; she was sure of it. Her mother was still alive, and now Eloi must find her. Fresh determination filled the pup.

A natural pool of water had formed just outside of the hollow, the damp wood tickling Eloi's nostrils as she strained to rise. Aches and pain in her muscles she had never felt before almost stopped her forward motion, but she had work to do. She paused to take a drink from the pool before she looked to the sky. East, she must continue east.

Once she had figured out which direction that was, she trotted slowly at first and hoped that she would be able to pick up her mother's trail. Her stiff limbs started to ease as she kept going, one step at a time. Her mother had always said, *"When things are hard, Eloi, and getting through them seems impossible, break it up into little bits and take one step at a time."*

Eloi smiled inwardly at her mother's saying; here she was, a small wolf who traveled through a strange forest, doing exactly as her mother said. She took one step at a time. The sounds of the animals around drifted into her consciousness, and she was soothed by the calmness around her. If her father and his warriors had managed to follow, then her surroundings would be too quiet.

EYOLF TRIED NOT to move his head. Every time he did, he felt nausea rise and dizziness overtake him. He needed to keep a clear head. He knew he was being held near the meeting area. They rarely needed isolation areas or prison cages in Sumter, but he wasn't surprised that Rolan had locked him up.

He had seen Rolan's ambition when he was younger but

never thought he would try to seize leadership. He had genuinely seemed to care for Aine, and she had always kept control of his viciousness. Eyolf had tried to counsel Aine against mating with Rolan, but the two were in love. Other than them being young, which wasn't uncommon in their pack, he couldn't think of a reason for them not to mate. His instincts pushed him to oppose the union, but his instincts weren't strong enough for him to act. Eyolf regretted his decision now.

Leaning against the wooden bars of the cage he was in, Eyolf closed his eyes. He kept his breath shallow as another wave of nausea hit him. The warriors had seized Eyolf after he helped Eloi escape, then beaten him to the point that he thought he would be killed. The fact that he was alive was no comfort, not after what he'd seen from Rolan and his men.

He thought about Aine and hoped that Eloi could find her. Rolan must have planned for a while to perform the Severance ritual on Aine to be able to gather everything he needed. While the Royal bloodlines had used it on outcasts so they could no longer connect to the pack through mind links or dreams, no one had ever tried to sever one of Royal blood.

Eloi had reached her mother's dreams, which alone showed how powerful the young wolf and Aine were. Unfortunately for Rolan, he underestimated them—the two of them would be a formidable pair, and Aine had kept Eloi's abilities hidden. Eyolf now wondered if Aine had already been suspicious of Rolan.

Sharp pain behind Eyolf's eyes made him groan, and he rolled his head as he tried to distract himself. He could hear the rest of the pack gathered in the meeting area. The pack murmured as Rolan, and his group of warriors approached the front; there had never been so many meetings in such a short time.

"Pack, I have called you here to update you on Aine. Unfortunately, I again only have bad news." Rolan's voice was strong and level. The pack appeared mesmerized by his words. "Aine has taken Eloi, your future Pack Leader, with the help of one of our own. We have yet another traitor." Rolan dropped his head to look over at Eyolf held in the cage.

"One of your elders has conspired with Aine to help her escape and live a human life. They have now taken Eloi against her will." Rolan's voice wavered, and the crowd gasped. Horror reverberated through the village.

"I must go now to work with the warriors to return her safely. Eloi is my heart and my only child. If any harm comes to her...." Rolan trailed off and paused. "I beg you, if any of you have any information on her kidnapping, please come forward. For now, we need to leave the traitor alone. He is dangerous and will kill any of you if he has the chance."

Rolan quickly turned and left the stage. After yet another announcement that left the pack shaken, they stood stunned, almost unable to will their own limbs to move. No one approached the cage that held Eyolf, and for that, he was grateful. He would need the time to recover. He couldn't understand why they believed Rolan. But with Aine missing and now Eloi's disappearance, Rolan could use the upheaval to his advantage.

Eyolf sighed as he rested his head against the wooden bars again. He would heal faster than a human, but it would take longer than a wolf in its prime. Old age was such a hindrance. Since he hadn't received any food yet, or eaten in a while, the situation was dire. He closed his eyes and tried to reach out to Eloi, but his head felt heavy, and the pain behind his eyes intensified before he succumbed to blackness.

ROLAN COULDN'T BELIEVE his luck; his plan had come together so well. Out of habit, he strolled toward the Temple and now looked at the walls that displayed his pack's history.

Rolan caressed the leadership dagger. With Aine gone and now blamed for Eloi's disappearance, the pack would have no choice but to follow him. He just needed to make sure Aine was dead and bring Eloi under his control. Eyolf was a fool, and if no one spoke to him, the others would never know what Rolan had done to earn his rightful place as their leader. He could imagine the changes he would make—they would bring themselves out of hiding and take their proper place as rulers of the humans. Humans were weak, and they didn't deserve the illusion of power they believed they had. Rolan grinned at the thought.

If Eloi was as powerful as he suspected and he could control her, then she could influence not just his pack but others as well. Aine and Eloi's bloodline was legendary, and it was rumored that they could exert influence in their dreams. Rolan's chest swelled with pride as he realized what he was about to achieve. He had wanted to be Pack Leader since he knew he had secured Aine's affections. He did love her or thought he did at one point. However, since Eloi was born, he realized it was Aine's power he had loved, and that was no longer enough. If only he had been able to take it from her.

The female should not be the leader—the title should

have fallen to him once they mated. Rolan should have been in charge. It was his right as the male of the house.

Mervan entered the Temple and nodded when he saw the look on Rolan's face.

"Everything is working out well; now we just need to find Aine." Mervan approached and smiled. It was the first smile Rolan had seen since Han's death. Hopefully, when they were established, with Aine truly gone and his brother avenged, Mervan would return to his old self.

"True, at least the pack won't question us killing her now. They will think she deserves it." Rolan grinned. He had used dark magic to try and influence them and hadn't believed it would work completely, but it had helped.

Mervan nodded again and looked to the Temple entrance as the other four warriors entered. After they had subdued Eyolf, he could see that some of them were uneasy. Especially Nyko—Rolan had seen the doubt in his eyes, and the young pup had left Aine alive.

"Second thoughts?" He questioned the four but stared at Nyko. The boy immediately looked to the ground and mumbled his agreement. Two of the others grinned at the outcome of the day, and the third held his face blank. James never gave much away, but Mervan had assured Rolan he would follow.

"You four were the first to see the weakness in our pack and align with its true leader. For this, you will be rewarded and hold positions of honor by my side." Rolan glanced towards Nyko again. The boy still looked down and defeated. Rolan probed with his mind and could feel Nyko's doubt. However, his actions meant that he would have to stay loyal to Rolan now, and Rolan could easily control him. The leader shrugged and returned his attention to the others; if Nyko stepped out of line, it would be easier to dispose of him now that the pack trusted him to lead them.

"Now, it's time you learned to shift outside the full moon. I kept it from you until I was certain you could be trusted, but we will need to be at full strength with Aine alive. She is powerful, and we won't be able to take her unless we are all her equal. Then we must bring her back here and make an example out of her." Rolan's eyes gleamed. "Are you ready to begin?"

"Eyolf said it was dark magic, and it was forbidden," Nyko said quietly.

"If it is forbidden, then how come Aine's family line can shift when they want? Don't we all deserve the same?"

Strong agreement came from the warriors, and Nyko dropped his gaze again.

"It's time for you to become what you were meant to be, and once we are all strong, we can take the nearest human town as our own and show them who should really be in charge."

Rolan's men cheered, and he held his head high, as the leader of a powerful pack should.

ELOI HAD NEVER FELT SO tired and hungry in her life; her feet had started to drag, and she ambled forward. One step at a time. She found a log to crawl inside and slept there last night. She hadn't eaten in two days, and as she walked, she could feel her energy drain away. She tried to hunt a rabbit, but after years of others hunting for her, she had failed miserably. Her failure to find Aine and her hunger had not helped her melancholy. As her second day dragged on, Eloi's vision started to blur, and she drank again from another puddle. At least she could keep hydrated, despite the sour taste of the water.

Eloi finally entered a clearing and froze when she smelled blood. However, it wasn't the blood that gave her pause—it was her mother's scent. Joy warred with fear as she took in the scene. There was no body, but a lot of blood was spread across the area. She swallowed hard before she sniffed again; her mother had been there, but it wasn't her blood.

She sighed in relief and sniffed the ground nearby. By the smell of it, this was where Han had been killed. It looked like Rolan was right, and her mother had killed him, but there must have been a reason. Rolan had tried to kill her mother, so it made sense that he sent Han to try and finish the job. Her mother had probably defended herself.

Eloi studied the scene as Eyolf had taught her, and from what she could tell, Han had maneuvered to higher ground and pounced towards Aine. That was an aggressive move, but it made sense that he struck first. She continued to smell the area and found the spot where her mother had entered the clearing. At least now she had a direction to follow.

Her heart swelled with hope, and she padded in that direction. She had only gone a few steps when she heard a voice, and three men approached. Eloi quickly darted towards a thicket and ran for cover. She crouched in the spot and held her breath as the group of men approached. Squeezing her eyes closed, she prayed they wouldn't see her.

"This is it, Phil; this is where we found it last week. It had been here a couple of days, but it was a full-grown wolf; its neck was broken. What could even do that?" The man's voice got louder and shriller as he spoke. The men studied the area, and the evidence of blood still soaked into the soil.

Eloi could feel it fill her nose as the scent drifted towards her.

"I've seen the body. I know it was full-grown." A large man crouched towards the ground then looked up to the edge of the clearing, where Eloi knew her mother had come from. His brow crinkled, and he looked back at the ground and he swore under his breath. Eloi didn't think the other two men would hear, but she could. Her ears pricked forwards to see if she could catch more from him.

"Maybe it was killed by another wolf, and they were just passing through the area?" Phil's voice was low and uninterested. He looked in the opposite direction, toward where Eloi had entered the space. She wondered what he was thinking.

"There's been rumors of wolves and large dogs round here for generations but never this close to the town. There is a straight line to your diner, Phil; it's only a few miles from here. We need to act now before someone gets killed. Aren't you worried?"

"That's a bit extreme. No one has seen a live wolf in the area."

"What about Lachlan? He's the hunter! He can help us track them...right?"

Eloi felt a shudder of fear tremble through her when she heard the mention of a hunter.

"I'll talk to him, but he's been a bit busy since Aine arrived." Phil shrugged, but Eloi could see and almost feel the tension in his shoulders.

She had to stop herself as she nearly yelped at the sound of her mother's name. This man knew her mother; fear gripped her. Aine was with the one they had called a hunter! Her head drooped when she realized Rolan was right; her mom was with the humans.

Eloi looked up towards the large man in front of her and gathered herself. His gaze had turned back to where Aine had stood, and he rubbed his chin with his hand, turning to face the two men.

"I heard she stumbled into your diner." The man who hadn't spoken yet grinned at Phil. There was a hint of amusement in his voice.

"Aye, she had no memory either. Something bad happened to that girl. I don't think she wants to remember." The large man scratched his chin and looked back to the way they had come. Eloi's heart stopped. The thought of her mother not remembering her made her legs wobble, causing her to nearly collapse. What if she had come here for nothing?

"Let's get back," Phil said. "I know you've called a meeting, and you'll want to be on time. I'll go and get Lachlan. You're right; he needs to be there."

Eloi looked after the large man as he left the clearing. If she followed him, then he would lead her to Aine. She was so close, and she would make her mother remember. She couldn't have forgotten everything, or Eloi wouldn't have been able to feel her.

One step at a time.

"LACHLAN!"

Phil's voice echoed in the basement, jerking Lachlan awake. His neck protested when he stretched it out; his head had rolled back as he slept. The chair had not been a good choice to rest.

His eyes flew to Aine in the bed, whose face was still relaxed in sleep. She was unbelievably beautiful. For two nights, he'd watched over her, and she was yet to wake. He wished she had trusted him enough to tell him. Lachlan sighed and stood; Phil watched him.

"Ya okay?"

"Yeah, just tired and worried." Lachlan stretched out his back and walked over to Aine. As he looked down on her sleeping, he brushed her hair from her face and felt her forehead.

"The fever has broken," he said with relief and relaxed for the first time in two days. "It won't be long until she wakes."

"Dude, I know this is going to be bad timing, but you need to get to this meeting. You're expected, and the town is going crazy. It won't be long before they take matters into their own hands."

"I can't leave her." Lachlan brushed his hands through his hair. He couldn't remember when he last showered, but his hair felt awful, so it must have been a while.

"I know, I'll stay, but you need to defuse this. If there really are shifters out there, they will get themselves killed."

Phil had him there. Lachlan had gone to look at the body they'd found, and it was too large for a regular wolf. His heart sank at the sight of it. Another shifter had killed it; he was sure of that.

He looked towards Aine. Was it her? Lachlan swallowed hard and turned to Phil. The night of the full moon, she had been shaken and filthy. He hadn't seen any blood on her, but the killing blow had been a broken neck.

"I'll go, but you need to watch her. If she wakes, you call me immediately."

Phil nodded solemnly as Lachlan walked up the stairs. Shower first, then he would go and stop the town from getting itself killed.

14

Aine felt like she had been plunged into water and drowned; darkness surrounded her, and she desperately tried to crawl upwards in the hope of light. She knew she was asleep—the scene from the forest with the youngling played in her head again and again. She needed to help Eloi, her daughter. How could she forget her daughter? No matter how hard she tried, she could not wake up. She was in a prison in her own mind and being tortured by the image of Rolan's lunge. Rolan, the man from her other dreams, the one who had poisoned her. She remembered him now. Her mate, *her husband*, she thought with disdain.

They had met the day Rolan arrived in their village, a runt who took up more resources than he was worth, according to him. He had been abandoned by his pack. Aine had seen the sad eyes on the small boy and begged her parents, the Pack Leaders, to help him. No one deserved to be abandoned by their family.

"Papa, he's so young. You can't just leave him by

himself," she begged in their small home. Her parents didn't believe they should live any different from the rest of the pack because they were in charge. It was more her mother's influence than her father's, but Aine loved their tiny home. She was proud of her family line; her grandfather had stepped down as Pack Leader to Aine's mother, Arwen, his only child. Arwen shared the leadership with Solus, Aine's father. Aine would be next to lead.

"Young one, we don't know his pack. The boy won't tell us where he came from, and until he does, we don't know why he's here. It may be that he's telling the truth, but this pack hasn't survived this long, hidden from the hunters, by being reckless." Solus ruffled her hair and smiled at her before he approached his mate. The look on Arwen's face was beautiful. Aine had always hoped she would find a love like theirs.

"He could stay for a trial?" Aine tried. "Wait until he proves himself honest?" Her eyes dropped to the floor when her father turned around to look at her.

Solus smiled at his daughter and lifted her chin. "Don't look down, child; you need to be confident in your suggestions. There is no such thing as a stupid idea. I will talk with the boy and get a feel for him. Your mother may be able to mind-read him and see what his upbringing has been like. He is young, so we may be able to teach him our ways."

Aine remembered her father's smile. He was strong and encouraged strength in her. Aine's mother was so gentle with her, but in public, she had to take on the face of a leader.

Arwen had been a good leader, and Aine could feel the loss of her strength and presence as much as she did the day her parent had died. Arwen had died in childbirth; her son was stillborn, and it had broken Solus. The Royal bloodline was incredibly powerful but had issues with fertility for generations. Only one child ever survived, and the attempt at a second often killed the mother. Arwen had been stubborn and determined to overcome the odds when she fell pregnant. She couldn't bring herself to abort her unborn child.

Later that day, Solus and Aine's grandfather had been out with the warriors on a hunting trip. Their grief drove them to shift and try to distract themselves; it was a full moon, and they needed to take advantage to replenish the pack's supplies. They sometimes traveled further to ensure the ecosystem around them would continue to thrive. If they constantly hunted locally, the animals would learn not to come to the area, which would advertise the pack's location to anyone who knew how to look for the signs.

Aine's father and grandfather had not returned, both shot by a human who didn't know any better and had been out hunting regular wolves. Rolan had been with the warriors that day and returned to give Aine the news.

She was left alone at the age of sixteen. The leadership role had been thrust upon her, and she had worried the pack would not follow a teenage girl. But her parents had trained her well. She was a strong leader for the pack, especially with Rolan as her Second. They had been inseparable since the Pack Leaders had given him permission to stay. Aine had trained with the warriors most of her life, encouraged by Solus, and invited Rolan to train with her. She had earned her place as the First after she worked her way up the ranks. She had been the youngest to hold the title, though not for long. None of the warriors doubted her or

Rolan when he ascended to Second; he earned his place along with her. It had been Aine's proudest day when her father promoted them both.

She couldn't remember when her feelings for Rolan had changed from friendship to love, but she realized one day that she couldn't fight them any longer. Rolan had always found an excuse to touch her and had supported her fiercely when she became Pack Leader. He became the only person she could rely on; all her friends treated her differently once she took on her responsibilities, and she had felt very isolated.

Aine compared how she felt for Rolan with the feelings she had for Lachlan and realized she hadn't known what love really was. In her desperation to find what her parents had, she had mistaken Rolan's love for her power and forced the relationship with Rolan to be something it wasn't. No wonder they had grown to resent each other.

But that was no excuse for what Rolan had done to her. How had she been so blind to his ambition? He had only ever been attracted to her power, and when that wasn't enough anymore, he had taken what was hers. She needed to get it back.

But not before she found Eloi. She had a sick feeling in her stomach. The guilt ate at her as she remembered her forgotten daughter. Even in sleep, Aine could feel a tear roll down her cheek. She needed to wake. She could feel her body, but something kept her eyes firmly closed. She silently screamed in her head; as the frustration built, Aine reached out with her mind and searched that way for her daughter. The last image she had of Rolan lunging played in her head again. The scene made her heart hurt.

Images of Eloi, still as a wolf, formed in her mind. Aine

could feel the hunger and tiredness in the youngling, and her heart squeezed. Her daughter tripped and staggered but kept going. *Eloi, I will find you, I promise. One step at a time.*

Aine's energy wavered, and she slipped into unconsciousness. Her last thought was that next time, she would wake fully and go to find her daughter.

AINE GASPED as she finally emerged into the real world. Pain lanced through her head as she sat up with a jolt; she felt like she had fought for days inside her own mind. She could almost cry at the relief as it washed over her, but the urgency to move gripped her. She flung the blanket off the bed and quickly stood; she stumbled and held out a hand to grab the chair next to the bed to right herself.

There was no one in the room, and she couldn't feel Lachlan in the house. Aine looked out the window and saw that night had fallen. At least now that she remembered, she could use her power and awareness to defend herself.

She felt a tug toward the woods and quietly crept up the stairs. She still couldn't feel Lachlan, but Phil was outside on the porch. As she reached the top of the stairs, she prowled to the backdoor. She smelled tobacco as it drifted in the air and realized why Phil must have stepped out and left her. It had been luck that Aine woke when she did. Aine took a gulp of fresh air as she left by the back door and sprinted toward the woods.

A surge of power and joy raced through Aine as she shifted easily; she relished the power and energy. She had missed this without knowing she had missed it. She reached out with her mind for Eloi, her head throbbed as she strained in every direction. She hadn't used her powers to their full potential in over three weeks, and her stamina had reduced.

Aine trotted in the direction of the diner, the clearing she had been found in. Eloi was close, but her presence was weak. Aine's chest felt tight as she moved in the direction she could feel her daughter. She sniffed the air and could smell her baby in the area. Aine slowed and searched, her eyes locking on a small, ghostly shape that limped toward her.

Aine ran as fast as she could, her heart leaping with joy as she saw her daughter. Eloi's head rose at the noise of Aine's paws as they pounded on the ground. The fear in her eyes was instantly replaced with elation as she looked up at her mother. Both shifted simultaneously and grabbed each other in human form. They held on tight, and Aine sobbed as she clutched her daughter in her arms.

"Eloi!" Aine cried as she held her little girl.

"You know who I am." Eloi's tear-streaked face looked up at Aine.

"Of course I do, I've been dreaming about you for weeks."

Eloi shook as she held on to her mother. "Rolan made you forget, and I was scared you wouldn't know me."

"We are together now, it will be okay." Aine stroked the girl's hair as they sat on the ground and rocked.

"I did what you said, Mom—one step at a time." Eloi smiled through her tears, and Aine grinned back.

"I am so proud of you, baby. I thought Rolan had you, and here you are. Let's get you safe and fed."

Eloi tensed and shrank back as Aine spoke. "But you're living with humans! Why, Mom? You always said we needed to stay away from them."

"I know, it's complicated." Aine sighed. What would Lachlan think? She had been unconscious since she shifted in front of him, but he had stayed nearby. Would he still feel the same about her? She stood and helped Eloi to her feet.

"It's not far from here." Aine took the girl's hand, and they slowly walked back toward Lachlan's house. She hoped they would be safe there; she owed Lachlan an explanation. If he turned her away, she would find somewhere to go. At least Eloi would be able to tell her what the mind of the pack was.

Aine felt a gaping hole in her center where the presence of her pack would typically provide comfort. The loss weighed on her, and she would have to find a way to reconnect with her pack. She felt the pressure of her responsibilities settle on her shoulders. The last few weeks had been incredible, but now she remembered who she was, and the reality of what she needed to do almost overwhelmed her.

She would not let Rolan win.

LACHLAN FIDGETED as he sat at the front of the hall; nearly everyone from the town was crammed in, and there were a lot of people and noises. He was uncomfortable with such large crowds, which was why he lived out near Phil. It had suited him—he hated when he was called into these meetings. As Lachlan looked around, he could feel the tension; there had been animal attacks in the past but nothing as serious as a wolf. The usual coyotes looked harmless compared to wolves.

The crowd quieted as the librarian of the town, Toby, took to the stage. "As we all know, the body of a large wolf was discovered in the area about a week ago."

The room erupted as everyone started talking at once. Lachlan sighed; it was going to be a long night. He closed his eyes and let the turmoil drift around him. He needed to get back to Aine. Her temperature had dropped, so it wouldn't be long until she woke. He hoped he was back in time.

"Settle down, settle down." Unfortunately, Toby failed to subdue the crowded meeting from the front of the hall. Initially, they ignored him but eventually, the conversations died down, and the room was quiet again.

"Lachlan, do you have any suggestions?" Toby's voice was unsure as he looked toward Lachlan, sitting near the front.

He still had his eyes closed, and his head leaned back. He was tired and still worried about Aine. Finally, Lachlan opened his eyes and looked around the room, his eyes taking a moment to focus. Everyone stared at him, some with suspicion and some with hope. He was still the outsider of this town, particularly in times of strain. They didn't care if he knew they thought that.

Lachlan stood and walked towards Toby, his body heavy with exhaustion; the last thing he wanted was to have to talk the town out of doing something stupid. He waited until everyone was quiet.

"The last thing you want is to risk your lives chasing wolves that might not be out there," he said. "Has anyone seen a live wolf? There is just the body you found and no evidence that a pack lives nearby."

"There have always been rumors!" Trevor shouted from the back of the hall. "For generations, we've heard of the wolves living west of here. I've even heard humans live with them." He nodded and looked around to see what reaction his statement would get.

"My grandpa used to say the humans were the wolves. Like werewolves," Sandy Trumane, one of the teachers at the high school, added.

Lachlan was stunned. He hadn't heard any of these rumors. If he had, he would've realized a long time ago that there were shifters nearby. He would have to talk to Phil; he wondered why the big guy hadn't told him. Especially since he knew Lachlan's past and what his family did.

"Really?" Lachlan had to look dubious and tried for nonchalant. "Werewolves?" he chuckled. The town was safer not knowing what could go bump in the night.

"If it makes you feel better, I will try and track the dead wolf's movements and see if I can find evidence of a pack. I'll need a few days, and if I do find any evidence, I'll call another meeting, but the last thing you want to do is antagonize a whole pack of wolves if there is one. Or stumble around the woods getting lost. The likelihood is they will just move on if they are passing through unless you provoke them." Lachlan's face was blank as he looked out at the town's population. He prayed they listened to him.

The hall broke out into arguments; from what he could tell, many of the men talked about putting together a hunting party. None of them were hunters. A few had firearms they liked to take out into the woods and shoot, but Lachlan knew they only went for the use of the guns rather than to hunt animals. If they approached a pack of shifters armed, they would all be killed. Lachlan was concerned that the pack would then be slaughtered with his father not far from the town. He couldn't decide if that was a bad thing—he considered how they must have treated Aine. He thought back to the state she'd been in with faded bruises when Phil had found her. Did a pack that treated its females like that deserve to live?

"Let me take a look around first, it'll save you wasting your time getting lost at least." Lachlan knew the draw of the hunt, a change in this sleepy town, would appeal to a lot of the younger men. And he wasn't sure if he could diffuse the situation. The town seemed too riled up.

"Take a group Lachlan; what if something happened to you out there?" Toby's words were quiet next to him and couldn't be heard by anyone else over the rumble of voices in the hall as the town spoke amongst themselves. Toby was a sensible man, and Lachlan knew the town would defer to him if Lachlan could make him believe there was no threat.

"I'll be fine. But, Toby, if the younger men go out there and there is a pack, they will all be killed. Wolves can be vicious, and they will tear them apart, even if they do carry guns. So you need to downplay this."

Toby nodded as he heard the worry in Lachlan's voice. "I'll give you a couple of days and call another meeting. In the meantime, I'll try and talk to some of the more boisterous. See if I can get them to leave it for now; half of them are lazy anyway. They probably won't be bothered if the appeal of seeing a real wolf isn't guaranteed."

Lachlan breathed. "Thanks, Toby."

"How's Aine? Paige said you two looked...cozy." Toby winked at him.

"She's not been well, actually, and I could do with getting back to her. Are you done with me?" As Lachlan spoke, the massive doors at the back of the hall banged loudly, and a large, dark-haired man made his presence known. Lachlan stiffened and felt adrenaline pump into his body. It had been fifteen years since he'd seen his father.

"Seems to me you have a bit of a wolf problem." Liam's voice carried loudly, echoing across the room. The whole hall went quiet, and Lachlan swore under his breath. Toby glanced towards him nervously.

"Lachlan, my boy, good to see you. What? Not even a 'hello' for your old man?" Liam grinned at Lachlan. Girvan followed Liam through the door with Cillian, and Lachlan was relieved to see that Finn wasn't with them.

"It's been a while," Lachlan replied, he walked towards the two men. His body was tensed and ready in case his father started something. As he drew closer, he saw the gleam of amusement in his cousin's face. Cillian's face remained impassive Lachlan was pleased to see his little brother.

"I need you, son. You can try and downplay this, but you know what it really is."

The whole town's attention seared into Lachlan; every eye was on the three men in the middle of the room.

"Don't do this," Lachlan said quietly and drew himself up to his full height. No longer a cowed boy, he looked into his father's eyes. "Leave the town out of it, and I'll come with you, help with this one pack." He spoke under his breath and saw the triumph flash in his father's eyes.

"Girvan, stay with him," Liam ordered. "I'll call you when you're needed."

Lachlan's heart sank as Liam turned towards the door. He couldn't bring Girvan home with Aine in the basement. Cillian didn't say a word as he followed their father.

"Just tell me where to be, and I'll be there!" Lachlan shouted after him. He needed to set the boundaries now that his father knew what he was capable of. He wouldn't be used in his father's schemes.

"You will do as you're told!" Liam turned back and glared at his son. "It's time you took your place. You will be my Second from now on; had I known what you were capable of, I wouldn't have wasted my time on Finn. It's time you lived up to your responsibilities."

Lachlan could feel the gaze of every person in the room fall on him. The tension in the air could have been cut with a knife while every person held their breath and watched Lachlan stare down his father.

15

L achlan gritted his teeth as he walked through the front door of his house. It had taken some time, but he had persuaded his father that he did not need a babysitter. The front door closed with a click, and he leaned his head against it with a soft thud, taking a deep breath. He had never managed to stand up to his father as he did today, but when he had left to live away from the family, it had made him feel like he needed to be his own man.

"Phil?" Lachlan called his friend's name, puzzled when he got no answer. He repeated the call; Phil had said he would stay with Aine until he got back. He rushed down the stairs of the basement, and panic gripped him; he froze at the sight of the empty bed.

Aine was already awake. Guilt held him in place. He should have stayed after the fever broke. Lachlan looked around wildly and expected her to be somewhere else in the room, but it was resoundingly empty. He heard the back door slam hard, followed by loud footsteps. Phil was back. He sprinted up the stairs and saw Phil, looking frazzled.

"I'm sorry, I only went out for a smoke, and I didn't hear her leave."

Lachlan felt his face heat with anger and his muscles tense. He was already on edge after the confrontation with his father. "Go home, Phil. You can't help now."

Phil's face fell, and he shuffled towards the door; he looked like a kicked puppy. Lachlan turned to his friend and put a hand on his shoulder.

"It's not your fault," he said, softening his tone. "If she wanted to leave, you wouldn't have been able to stop her, even if you could have heard her. I shouldn't have left knowing she would wake soon."

"I'm sorry, dude, I thought ya needed to be there."

"I did, more than you could have known." Lachlan paused to look at his only friend. "My father was there, and I don't think I'll be able to stay here much longer."

Phil put his hand out and gripped Lachlan's shoulder. "There will always be a place for ya here. I know some of the town folk are a bit funny about outsiders, but you're one of us, and they won't forget what you've done for them over the years."

Lachlan grimaced. Phil gave them too much credit. While Phil returned to the diner in case she showed up there, he hurried to his room to change his clothes and get into some better boots. If Aine had taken off into the woods again, he would need to be quick.

The back door opened again tentatively, and Lachlan stopped.

"Lachlan?" Aine's voice called softly from downstairs, and Lachlan felt the tension melt from him, breathing a sigh of relief as he turned. He ran his hand through his hair and quickly descended the stairs.

Aine stood near the back door and clutched a young girl

to her side, her hands shook slightly as she held the girl with an iron grip. The girl couldn't have been older than fifteen and was filthy; she looked like she was about to collapse, and the simple shorts and t-shirt barely covered her.

"Are you okay?" Lachlan said roughly, his throat tight. He left the distance between them, so she wasn't spooked.

"I'm fine, but Eloi here needs food and rest. Is that…" Aine swallowed. "Is that alright?"

She looked directly at him and didn't drop her gaze; her bearing showed confidence and determination. Something was different, but he would have to wait to find out what. Aine's worry for the young girl was evident in her face, and he could almost feel a bond between the two.

"Of course." Lachlan crouched so he was level with Eloi. As he looked in the girl's eyes, he contained the reaction his body instinctively felt in the presence of a shifter. Even a young one. "My name is Lachlan, this is my home, and you are safe here."

The girl's eyes glowed amber as he spoke to her, which didn't surprise him as he remembered Aine's shift near the lake. That she could shift so young was a surprise. Aine must have quite a story to tell.

"Lachlan." Aine paused and took a breath. "This is my daughter, Eloi."

AINE WATCHED Lachlan's face carefully after her declaration. He had kept it blank once he saw her standing with Eloi at the back door. She saw a brief flash of shock in his eyes, but he continued to look at Eloi as he spoke gently to her.

"Hello, Eloi. Would you like a burger? I can ask my

friend Phil to bring some over, he was worried when Aine left and is probably stress cooking. In the meantime, why don't you ask your mum to get you cleaned up, and then you can get some rest."

Lachlan's voice was careful when he talked to her daughter, as an equal but softly so as not to scare her. Aine could have cried; she felt the sting of tears in her eyes. Instead, she stroked Eloi's hair and kissed the top of her head. Even though it had only been a few weeks, her daughter had grown.

Aine took the girl's hand and pulled her upstairs. Eloi's eyes were wide, and Aine could see the glow in them as they skittered around the house and tried to take everything in. The poor child barely held on to her control, but she managed to somehow. Aine couldn't be prouder of her baby girl.

Once Aine had cleaned up Eloi, who was fascinated by the shower and hot water, she dressed her in some pajamas Madison had given her in the shop. The pair then went to meet Lachlan in the kitchen.

Phil hadn't stayed, probably warned by Lachlan to give them space, but had dropped off enough food to feed more than the three of them. Aine took a burger from Lachlan, unwrapped it, and handed it to Eloi, who sniffed it hungrily. Aine thought about how simply her pack lived; she would change that. Over the years, she sent agents out in the world to keep up with news around them and some of the technology, but they lived too far off the grid. Now she knew that she could be around humans; they needed to modernize what they had.

Eloi ate quickly and moaned continuously through her meal as she sat at Lachlan's kitchen table. Aine thought back to the first time she'd eaten a burger with Lachlan and smiled. She could feel him watch her; he showed no emotion, and she could sense the tension between them. She wanted to make sure Eloi was cared for first and had somewhere she could rest before Lachlan confronted her. The awkwardness she felt between them made her ache and hurt her heart. Things had been so easy before the afternoon at the lake.

"How are you feeling?" Aine stroked Eloi's hair again and crouched next to her chair, grateful that she was safe and Rolan hadn't harmed her baby.

"Good, this is incredible. Can I have some more?"

Aine chuckled and reached out for another burger. Phil had brought enough to feed an army; Aine wouldn't be surprised if Eloi ate the lot herself.

"Can I have some more, *please*?" Aine said automatically and rolled her eyes as she handed Eloi the burger. "Eat slowly, or you'll choke."

She caressed the girl's cheek; she couldn't keep her hands to herself. Then she looked towards Lachlan again. He didn't look angry as he watched them both, but he wouldn't look her in the face. Aine sighed and turned her attention back to Eloi.

Once Eloi had eaten her fill, and the little wolf's eyes started to droop, Aine helped her stand and guided her down to the basement. It would remind her of home, as it had Aine when she first arrived. Their houses weren't exactly underground but camouflaged so heavily they almost felt like they were. Eloi snuggled close to Aine as she held her and sighed.

"I'm so happy I found you, Mom. Eyolf will be happy you're okay."

Aine's heart clenched at the thought of her old mentor. She wondered what Rolan had done with him after Eloi escaped; surely she would have felt it if Rolan had killed him.

It didn't take long until Eloi gave in to exhaustion, her breath steady as she slept soundly. Aine stayed a few minutes and stroked Eloi's forehead. She was exhausted and would probably sleep until morning. Aine knew she was putting off going to see Lachlan, but she had missed her little girl; she felt a warmth in her chest staring at her beautiful daughter.

Eloi had her father's hair and eyes, but the rest was Aine. The girl stirred but didn't wake as Aine kissed her forehead and brushed the hair off her face. Then, she braced herself and slowly made her way upstairs.

She paused on the bottom step and closed her eyes; she was sure Lachlan would let them stay the night, but if he asked them to leave, Aine would understand. She took a deep breath before she continued up the steps and entered the kitchen. Lachlan didn't turn to look at her.

"Hi," Aine said as she leaned against the basement door. It closed behind her with a soft click.

Lachlan cleared the table and put the rest of the food in the fridge. Aine wasn't hungry, her stomach was in knots, but she didn't look down and didn't fidget. It was going to break her heart to leave him. Lachlan ran his hand through his hair in agitation before he turned to face her; it looked like he'd done that a lot today. She'd noticed he did it when he was frustrated.

"Hi," he spoke quietly as he finally looked at her and then at the floor.

Aine pushed back the hurt when he still couldn't look at her, but was surprised when he continued speaking.

"I'm so sorry I hurt you. I just knew that if you fully shifted, you might hurt someone. You seemed crazed, and I didn't know what to do...." His voice faltered.

"You knew?" Aine's voice was loud, pain lancing through her as it dawned on her. Lachlan had taken everything in his stride when she did weird things. It made sense now she thought about it. Her heart skipped as she realized he accepted her for a shifter, even before she knew she was one.

"No, not for certain. I felt it when you first arrived—do you remember how I reacted? It was instinct."

Aine nodded slowly, not understanding how he could have known.

Lachlan looked at her helplessly. "But when you didn't shift on the full moon, I thought I was wrong. I didn't know how you'd take it, with you having no memory and not knowing what you were. I should have warned you, but I got called away. By the time we got back, you were gone."

He took a step toward her but stopped when Aine stiffened against the door.

"I thought I was going crazy," she whispered, remembering Eloi asleep downstairs. Aine gestured to the back door and welcomed the cool air as it drifted over her heated skin. She continued to walk to the back of the yard and opened the shed door. Lachlan entered without a word. Aine gathered her thoughts before she spoke again.

"I did shift on the full moon," she said, "but I changed back before I saw you. I didn't know how to tell you."

Lachlan dragged his hands down his face. He looked defeated, then surprised when he registered her words, that she had shifted back. "Shifted back? I've only ever seen shifters turn on a full moon. I didn't even know it was possible."

"I think the full moon triggered my shift for the first time since I woke up behind the diner." Aine leaned against the workbench. Lachlan still stood near the door but showed no signs that he would leave. "It is when we are strongest."

"Do you...do you remember everything now?" Lachlan asked cautiously.

"Yes, while I was unconscious, it all came back. I was poisoned by my husband."

"Husband?!"

Lachlan's shock reverberated through Aine, and she flinched; now that she remembered her power, she was more sensitive to others' feelings, though she had never felt the emotions of humans before. She thought back to how she had been able to read everyone in the town.

"I'm sorry, I didn't know I was married." Aine took a step forwards as if to comfort Lachlan but stopped herself. Even if she weren't married, a human and shifter could never be mates. It was forbidden.

She realized they had both obviously hidden essential details from each other. She had never told Lachlan about when she shifted on the night of the full moon. Was what they felt for each other even real if she hadn't truly known him, and she hadn't remembered who she was?

Aine sat down hard on the stool she usually worked at and picked up a piece of wood to run her hands over it. Lachlan sat across from her; he looked off to the side, still stunned. The silence between them stretched, and Aine's heart hurt. She sighed.

"I don't know where to start," Lachlan said.

Aine looked up into his face. It was closed off, and he

stared out the window. "How do you know about shifters?" she asked.

"I've studied shifters for many years," he answered vaguely; he still stared off, now at the tools on his wall.

"And you knew what I was?"

"I suspected at first—well, Phil did, which is why he called me. I've been raised to hate shifters, but I don't believe shifters are bad. You *were* aggressive when we first met." Lachlan's laugh was cold. "I didn't want to risk anyone in the town. I've seen the results of a crazed or angry shifter firsthand."

Lachlan shifted on his stool, his mouth turned down, and he looked everywhere but at Aine. "How can you shift and then shift back during a full moon?" he asked. "It was my understanding that the moon controlled the shift." He finally glanced towards her.

"It does for most shifters." Aine scrunched her brow and leaned back on her stool, which creaked. "But I'm different, I'm from a Royal bloodline. My ancestors were born to be Pack Leaders and able to shift at will. We don't broadcast it, as other packs have forced our females into breeding with them in the past. My ancestors put a stop to that, but it nearly caused a war."

Lachlan looked away again, his jaw tight. "They took females and forced them? I remember the history of the great shifter wars but didn't know what started it. There were many casualties." His voice was stern as he spoke through gritted teeth, and she saw his fists clench.

"It was a long time ago, my grandfather's grandfather's generation....I think." Aine could see Lachlan relax before he tensed again, and his head snapped to look at her.

"Pack Leader." Surprise edged Lachlan's tone, and his eyes were wide.

"Yes." Aine looked him in the eye and held her head high. He smiled at her, and she felt the tension leave her body as he chuckled.

"I've been living with a Queen." Lachlan's voice held amusement, and Aine laughed too; she felt some of the distance between them lessen and the tension disappear. But sorrow permeated through her. She knew that she couldn't allow the relationship to continue. What she had with Lachlan over the last few weeks was precious but should never have happened.

"If I had remembered who I was then, I wouldn't have allowed us to get so...." Aine paused and looked down. "Intimate."

Aine looked back at him across the workbench. She had wanted what her parents had and thought she found it once with Rolan. How wrong had she been? Being with Lachlan had shown her that she could live with humans and that two people in a relationship could be equals, not having to force each other to submit. But her laws did not allow it.

With Rolan, she constantly had to remind him she was Pack Leader. He had supported and encouraged her in the early years but then tried to manipulate her, especially in the last few years. Aine hadn't liked that he wanted to lead the pack, and he challenged her to make dangerous changes. How could two people be partners when constantly fighting each other for dominance? It made each person miserable or resentful. Lachlan hadn't been honest with her, but she hadn't told him either when she shifted. Or what she was going through. They both thought they were doing the right thing to protect each other.

"What a pair we make, both scared to let each other know what we knew." Aine laughed and looked at Lachlan, who shrugged and let out a breath.

"I know, I just didn't want to burden you with something that might not be true, with everything that you were going through. I'm sorry you didn't trust me enough to tell me about your shift."

"I was worried it would change how you felt about me." Aine held her breath but didn't turn away. Instead, she waited for his reaction; she needed to know, even if they couldn't be together.

Lachlan took a deep breath before he spoke. "No, Aine, nothing could change that. I love you, and I want to help. But I know how shifters feel about human relationships."

Aine's heart stopped and swelled; her chest felt tight, and she couldn't swallow. "I...I love you too, Lachlan. I didn't know what love was before. I thought I did, but I was so wrong, and it has cost me everything. We can't be together." Her eyes stung, and a tear rolled down her cheek.

Lachlan quickly stood and was immediately by her side. He wrapped his arms around her to hold her as she cried and kissed her head. Aine had never been able to show weakness to anyone, and the fact that she could be comforted by this man made the moment much sweeter. She didn't feel weak as she let her frustration and anger at Rolan's actions flow out of her. Instead, she breathed in Lachlan's scent and took the strength he offered.

"I don't understand why not," he said. "We both feel it. The very first moment I saw you, I felt like I knew you. Even if it was impossible."

"Like a mate bond." Aine shook her head. "I felt it too, but a shifter can't be mated to a human."

Lachlan stroked her hair and soothed her. Aine looked up at his face, and he smiled at her, love shining in his eyes. Then, gently, he leaned down to kiss her forehead again. They stayed like that for a while in comfortable silence. Her heart ached as she felt her tears dry and the sting in her eyes lessen.

She looked up into Lachlan's face, reaching up to stroke his jaw. Aine felt a jolt through her when he smiled. He lifted his hand to cup her face and tilt it towards him. The kiss was sweet at first, but as she pressed her lips back on his, she deepened it. She knew she should leave before anything further happened between them, but she couldn't stop.

Lachlan moaned as she opened her mouth to him, and his tongue caressed hers. Then, without breaking the kiss, he lifted her up onto the workbench and pressed himself against her; Aine's legs opened to him. How could something so wrong feel so right?

Lachlan reached up to the back of her neck and kissed her passionately again. Aine felt her stomach flutter and her core tighten against him as he pinned her against the bench. When he broke the kiss and looked at her, Aine felt overwhelmed with the love and wonder in his eyes. She should push him away but couldn't bring herself to. Her skin tingled as they had kissed. She reached down and tugged his shirt up, feeling hard muscle as she pulled it over his head and running her hands down his chest. Lachlan shivered and moaned as her hands stroked further and further down. She could see the evidence of his need by the bulge of his jeans against her crotch.

Aine ran her fingers along the seam on the top of his jeans; her knuckles grazed over his hip bone. Lachlan watched as she let her hands wander up his sides, along his chest and shoulders, before cupping his face. He leaned down to meet her lips when she pulled him in closer for another kiss. Aine pressed her thighs tightly at his sides, desperate for some friction when he pressed against her.

Lachlan placed his hands on either side of her on the bench, caging her in. Their breath came fast and mingled as they kissed. Aine ached with each touch and could feel her nipples harden against his naked chest.

Lachlan reached down to pull at the thin tank top she wore; he pushed the material up to bare her midriff, his thumbs caressing her bare skin. She gasped as he leaned down and kissed her hip, just above where her shorts began, while he deftly undid the button and zipper.

Aine felt pleasure rush through her and moaned at the feeling; her entire body felt like it was on fire. She pushed herself against him, satisfied to feel friction in her most sensitive area. Lachlan's moan took her pleasure higher. She could feel him smile against the skin on her bare shoulder as he reached up to cup her breast. At some point, her sports bra had disappeared. His thumbs brushed against her ribs and grazed just under her nipple. It pulsed, desperate for his touch. Aine's chest heaved as another of Lachlan's kisses took her breath away.

"You are so beautiful, Aine." Lachlan stared down at her, and she reached up to brush his hair across his forehead.

"You are too, Lachlan. I've never felt this way before." Aine smiled at Lachlan's self-conscious laugh. "I don't know how we will make this work. We shouldn't be doing this."

She grinned up at him and lifted her hips to brush against his groin. Lachlan moaned when she reached out to undo his jeans and cup him with one hand while pushing his pants down with her legs.

"I don't care, Aine, don't stop," Lachlan growled as he nearly lost control.

He lifted Aine off the table to help her out of her shorts and cupped her ass before setting her on the bench again, completely naked. The smell of sawdust and the feel of the bench on her bare skin comforted her. Lachlan quickly backed up to pull his jeans and boxers off. Aine licked her lips and leaned back on her arms as she saw him standing before her.

He was incredibly toned and muscular, solid, and toned in all the right places. Lachlan stalked towards her, the heat in his eyes taking her breath away. He pushed her legs open to settle her thighs on his hips, her weight still on her arms, and leaned back as she opened for him. Lachlan then stared intently into Aine's eyes and pushed his tip against her.

She felt more turned on as she looked at him, gasping as he waited for her to stretch around his length. She tilted her head back as his full length pushed deeper; she had been ready for him, but the surge of pleasure as he pressed into her still shook her. Lachlan's hands ran up her sides, one hand teasing her nipples when he bent down to kiss her. Aine reveled in the feeling of him inside, an ache for movement overwhelming her.

"Please, Lachlan." She begged him to move, pushing her hips up for some friction.

Aine leaned back on her elbows and closed her eyes, relishing the feeling of his hands as they moved up her skin. As Lachlan started to move, pleasure pulsed through her, and her body began to shake. He stopped and grinned when she scowled at him.

Lachlan brushed his thumb over each taut nipple, the other hand massaging her clit when he started to move again. Aine's whole body felt wound up, heat coursing through her. She closed her eyes to concentrate on each touch and caress. Her body hummed with pleasure as Lachlan's powerful rhythm pushed her close to the edge. The taste of their mixed scents in the air was heady and made her feel powerful.

Aine pulled her knees up, her legs stroking Lachlan's sides as she opened further to him and felt him deeper inside her. He groaned, chest slick with sweat, and pushed deeper inside her. Each powerful stroke took them both higher.

Aine's body pulsed when they moved together, skin on skin. Just when she thought she couldn't take it anymore, Lachlan drew himself out and slowed the movement, taking her pleasure to a new level. Then his speed increased without warning, and the pressure on her clit intensified.

Aine fell over the edge, shaking and crying out when she felt Lachlan stiffen and groan. She tightened and pulsed around his length as they came together. Aine's arms shook as she tried to hold her weight.

AINE SLEPT naked beside Lachlan in his bed as he looked down at her. They hadn't bothered with clothes when they returned to the house. He had taken her again in his bed last night before they eventually fell asleep. Now he was on his side, resting his head on his elbow. His mind raced with everything she had told him.

Aine was a shifter, Pack Leader, and Royalty. Lachlan could barely believe what she told him. After he left his family in Ireland, he had found Ciara and spent time with her brother and their pack. He didn't blame them for his mother's death, not entirely; they were desperate, and his father had pushed them to the attack. Instead, he blamed himself for not being there to protect her.

But he had never felt entirely comfortable with them and spent time with other packs through Europe, then America. Most had been wary of Lachlan, but he had carried a letter from Ciara's Pack Leader, which had eased their suspicion. He had finally settled where he thought there were no packs and no hunters, a fresh start away from his violent upbringing.

Aine and Lachlan had talked through the night. He spoke of his travels between packs and all he had learned from them. But he didn't tell her he was a hunter. He was deeply ashamed of his past with his family, and he didn't want her to hate him for the shifters he'd killed. Some were dangerous, and it needed to be done, but he knew many had been innocent. Especially now that he knew she felt the same as he did, he didn't want to risk the look of horror on her face when she realized what a monster he had been, just like his father.

Lachlan had never known it was possible to shift outside of the moon cycle; no wonder her bloodline had been sought out by others. One could breed an entire pack who could shift at will. Aine had told him about her mother, how their bloodline struggled, and usually only had one child. It seemed her ancestors had fought the abductions, but many females had been lost. In the end, the Pack Leader at the time had limited the knowledge, made others believe the ability had died out to keep them safe, and Lachlan didn't blame them.

He would do everything in his power to protect her and Eloi. A surge of possessiveness towards them both made him more determined. Things had just gotten a lot more complicated with his father in town, but he would keep them safe.

16

Rolan roared with fury as he woke. He hadn't sought to connect with Aine since he had severed her from the pack. He didn't think it would be possible, but she was so powerful, she must have overcome the ritual somehow. The images of her with a disgusting human replayed in his head, and he punched his fist through his bedroom wall. At least now the pack would side with him; he would bring the human and Aine back here to be executed. He couldn't allow her to speak, and he must be quick—if she reestablished her link with the pack, then his plan would fail. It was impossible to lie during dream shares, so they would know she told the truth.

Rolan dressed quickly, venting his frustration by throwing a chair across his bedroom—the bedroom he had shared with Aine. Rolan shuddered with disgust. It grated on him that their home wasn't grander. As Pack Leader, Aine should have claimed the best accommodation and taken what was rightfully hers. Instead, she had been content with their tiny home, raised their daughter with the same values. That would change when he got hold of Eloi.

He would mold her into a stronger wolf and heir. She would take what she deserved.

Rolan closed his eyes and called on his trusted warriors to meet him in the Temple. The more he used the dark magic, the easier it had been; he could now connect and shift more easily. As Rolan walked through Sumter, he tried to feel the mood of the rest of the pack. He was irritated he didn't have the power Aine had. He tried to figure out a way to take her power before he severed her from the pack, but there was nothing on how to drain another in everything Rolan had learned about the dark power. *Pity.*

The feelings he could gather from around him gave him a sense of unease and doubt. Rolan could sense from the few close to him that they still didn't accept him as their leader, but fear would keep them in place for now. Once Aine and her lover were executed before them, they would follow him. He grinned, imagining the outrage as they realized their leader had abandoned them and fallen in love with a human. It was the most sacred of their laws, and Aine had broken it.

One of the younglings walked on the path in front of Rolan and immediately dropped his gaze, crouching low. The bitter taste of his fear saturated Rolan and he grinned at the reaction, passing the boy without a word. He could at least control them by fear if needed. As he entered the Temple, the damp smell of the cave tickled his nose. He approached his warriors.

"She is sexually active with the human," Rolan spat out, not surprised to see the disgust on his warriors' faces. Mervan spat on the ground. Nyko's face paled and looked sick, the horror plain on his face.

"The pack will not argue when I kill her now." Rolan felt his rage rise inside him as he thought of her naked with the human. He felt sick to know he had touched her and that she now lay with another.

"I know where she is now as well," he continued. "There is a diner on the outskirts of the town. I believe where you dumped her, Nyko. The human lives in a house not far from there. Better yet, Eloi is with her. We can take them both, and I'll bring Eloi back here. If I can influence her and she speaks out against her mother, then the pack will follow me. I will be their rightful leader."

The warriors bowed their heads in agreement. Nyko still looked green.

"We will take them tonight. Have you all managed to shift outside of the moon cycle?"

All the warriors nodded, except for Nyko, who looked sheepish. Rolan growled at the young warrior.

"It didn't feel right, I couldn't make it work." Nyko's voice was weak and his eyes downcast.

"No matter, someone will have to remain human to restrain them. We will attack tonight and bring them back here." Rolan went to the back of the cave and drew out the restraints he had stored there. He felt elation at the thought that by tomorrow, this could all be over. He handed the restraints to Nyko, who shied away from the oily colored metal; they were designed to restrain even the most powerful shifters.

"Nyko, in human form, and the rest of us will shift." He smirked at his men before he dismissed them and turned to leave himself. First, he needed to talk to Eyolf and persuade him to be reasonable. He'd managed to keep the others from him, but if he could convince the old man to say that Aine had taken Eloi, then it was another nail in Aine's coffin. Though staying with a human and forsaking her pack was damning enough, it would help his case as he took over.

The old wolf looked forlorn in the corner of his cage. Rolan had constructed one next to him to hold Aine when they eventually returned with her; he would not fail.

"Well, well, old man. Have you had time to think about what I told you? You must see how what we are working towards is for the good of all shifters."

"I won't lie for you, Rolan—you do not deserve what you have taken. What you want to do is madness and will be our doom. You know there are still hunters out there."

Rolan scoffed at the man's dramatics. "Even for Eloi?"

Eyolf looked up at Rolan, the color drained from his face.

Rolan snickered. "I knew she was a weakness for you. If you tell the pack my version of events, then I will not harm her, and you can still work with her. *Once* she's under my control."

Eyolf swallowed hard. "You can't just take the leadership and rule in fear. The pack will rise up against you. Aine and her family have led through kindness and empathy. You will breed weakness into the pack. Fear is not strength."

"I don't think so." Rolan frowned, and his face heated. "When I show them how they've been limited for generations, how they will be able to shift at will, everything will change. Once they trust me and take me as their rightful leader, I will lead them into a new age. One where we rule the humans and put them in their rightful place."

"You can't ignore the hunters! I know there are still many who hunt shifters. They won't let you terrorize and enslave the humans."

Rolan scoffed, and Eyolf fell silent. "The Hunters are weak. The Americans haven't had any that are really active for generations." His grin was feral. "They won't know what hit them."

"You're naïve to think that you will succeed. The European hunters are vicious—they've driven shifters to America or slaughtered them. You don't think they will come here?"

"I'm not alone, old man, others are gathering. You think I infiltrated this pack by accident? I was sent here. The more followers the Faction have on board, the more likely we are to succeed. This has been years in the making." Rolan watched horror envelope Eyolf at the mention of the Faction; he felt it as it swept through Eyolf and came off in waves. The old wolf didn't show it outwardly, but Rolan could sense his terror and fed on it like a drug.

EYOLF WATCHED, frozen in shock, as Rolan walked away. He had heard rumors of the Faction; they had been a small group that believed shifters should be in charge. Around for centuries, they had never been taken seriously, but their methods were gruesome. Humans outnumbered shifters and had better technology. If shifters went up against the humans, they would be annihilated. Hunters still came after shifters, especially in Europe. Though America had been safer, Eyolf wondered if the Faction recruited refugees from other countries to bulk their numbers and gain traction with their idea of revolution.

Eyolf had been silent while Rolan's warriors constructed the cage meant for Aine next to him. He'd waited and bided his time, until one of the warriors had dropped a tool near his cell the day before. He'd quickly slipped his hand through a gap in the wooden structure and snatched it. It was used in wood carving and would suit his purposes. Now that Rolan was gone, Eyolf could get back to work.

He'd found a weakness in part of his cage, and with time and patience, he would be able to deconstruct that area and escape. With time, anything could be broken. Eyolf looked around, and when he was sure there was no one in the area, he returned to working on the weak corner. He quietly hacked at the location and pulled away sections of wood as they came loose.

He had no doubt that Rolan would bring Aine back; she was only one person, and he had his warriors. But, when Aine was back, Eyolf needed to make sure he was prepared to help her and Eloi in any way he could.

AINE WOKE to the feel of sunlight on her face and a soft caress on her cheek. As she stirred, she felt Lachlan kiss her forehead. She smiled, her eyes still closed, and sighed with pleasure. She snuggled closer to Lachlan's warm chest. His arms circled her and held her gently.

"Morning, beautiful," Lachlan whispered in her ear, kissing her softly on the side of her head. Aine opened her eyes and turned to look into his arctic blue ones. He smiled back at her and reached his hand to stroke her face again.

"Sorry I woke you," he said gently. "I think your daughter may be up. I can hear movement downstairs."

Aine cocked her head and heard the fridge door open. She sighed and pushed back the comforter. "If you can hear that from up here, you have great hearing. If I didn't know any better, I'd think you were a wolf." She chuckled as she dressed in jeans and a soft blue shirt.

"I want to get to know her." Lachlan hadn't moved from

the bed. Aine pulled her hair out from under the shirt and turned to face the gorgeous, naked man sprawled before her. Her body tightened as she thought about the night before.

"I'm glad," she said. "I was so worried it would be a problem for you."

"Why would you having a daughter be a problem? She's an extension of you, so I'm sure I will love her." Lachlan grinned, and his eyes sparkled with amusement. "Let's hope she doesn't give me as many headaches as her mother."

"Ha, she is my daughter, after all." Aine beamed at him before she turned to the door. Reluctantly, she went downstairs, wishing she could have stayed and maybe participated in more of what they'd done last night. But her daughter came first, as she should.

Eloi was on tiptoe, head in the fridge as she sniffed around loudly. Aine figured she must have smelled the food in there and gone to investigate. She smiled as she approached her daughter and felt a thrill as she hugged her from behind. Even though Aine hadn't remembered her until Lachlan had knocked her out, she felt a large void in herself. She had missed Eloi without even realizing it. Her mind drifted to the young wolf carving and all the children's toys she'd made.

"Sit down, little one; I'll get that for you."

Eloi turned and grinned at her mother. "I was hungry and didn't know where you'd gone." She hugged Aine and sniffed loudly, then crinkled her nose. "You smell like the human." She looked at her mother, uncertainty in her eyes.

Aine led Eloi to the table, her gut clenching as she realized what she needed to tell the girl.

"Eloi, I need you to know something." Aine sat next to her at the table. "What did you think of Lachlan?"

"He's kind for a human, he's not scared of us. I didn't feel any fear, but...." Eloi looked up at her. "I could feel his love for you. And....you love him, too."

Aine nodded and prayed her Eloi would understand. "When I was found," she began, "I couldn't remember who or what I was. Lachlan, well, he told me last night that he knows of our kind, and he knew what I was when he saw me. He helped me to keep the town safe, and I think he did it to protect me, too. You're right; I do love him." She held her breath.

"Then I like him. I know it's not going to be easy, but he makes you happy. I've never seen you happy with Rolan."

"I don't think it will be easy either, Eloi. I will have to leave him. Humans and shifters can't be together, and the pack will never accept him." Aine's brow crinkled, and she looked over at her daughter. "When did you stop calling him father?"

"When I saw what he did to you in his dreams. He doesn't know I saw him, but he's evil, Mom. I spied on him in the Temple and heard his plans. He's going to try and challenge the humans."

"Eloi, how did you manage that?" Aine's heart stopped in her chest at the thought of what Rolan would have done if he caught her.

"I'm small, so he never saw me when I listened in on his meetings," Eloi told her mother. Then she explained what she'd overheard and shrank from the horror she could feel coming from Aine.

Aine held her tightly. "He could have seen you! Why would you take the risk after knowing what he did to me?"

"Because we needed to know, and I needed to find you." Eloi's control fled, and she burst into tears. "I missed you so much, Mom." The two clung to each other. "What are we going to do?"

Aine could feel her daughter's despair and didn't have any answers. Then, finally, Eloi explained the rest that happened after Aine had disappeared—how Rolan had told the pack about Lachlan and that she had severed herself.

"I need to reconnect with the pack, and I'll need your help, Eloi." Aine's mother had taught her how to bring a wolf from outside the pack into it, like when Rolan became one of them. It had to be one of the Royal lines who connected them, which meant Eloi was the only one who could help her.

"You've been so very, very brave, and I'm so proud of you, baby," she said. "I just need you to help me one more time." Aine smiled at her daughter.

"What can I do?" Aine looked at the eagerness on Eloi's face. She was so strong for one so young.

"Normally, we'd need a full moon, which isn't for another two weeks. But I think that we are both strong enough to try now. If it doesn't work, then we will have to wait for the full moon. Do you think you could try for me?"

"Of course, Mom, we can do anything together." The faith in Eloi's mind made Aine's eyes sting, and she hugged her daughter again.

"Let's get you some breakfast." Aine grinned. "Wait until you try bacon."

Lachlan, Aine, and Eloi spent the day together, some time in his shed and in the afternoon Phil came over from the diner to meet Eloi. She recognized Phil as the man she followed from the woods, the one who led her to Aine. Phil laughed when Eloi said she followed him back; Aine put her arm around her daughter as she told the story. Later, after Phil had left, they returned to Lachlan's kitchen, and Aine had Eloi sit down at the table.

"I'm going to teach you something my mother taught me when I was about your age," Aine explained. "Our bloodline is incredibly special. There are not many packs that can connect their minds and dream share as we do or who can shift outside of the moon. My grandfather believed that we are descendants of the original shifters and that these shifters learned to create other shifters using dark magic. The dark magic was linked to the moon, which is why shifters can only shift around the full moon." Aine paused and looked up at Lachlan, who listened intently.

"I didn't know any of this—what I've learned of packs is from the Europeans. Mainly around Ireland and then France. They can't—dream share, did you call it?—or shift outside of a full moon," he said.

Aine frowned, then continued. "I'm not sure why but our ancestors have always had this ability. I told you about the war which started and why it's important to keep it a secret. I worry that Rolan has told others outside the pack and that we may be in danger."

"Are there any others in the pack who may have the ability?" Lachlan crossed his arms and leaned against the wall of the house.

"No, our bloodline has always struggled to have more than one child. I believe it's nature's way of balancing our abilities. I don't think I ever told Rolan that." Aine looked worried as she glanced back at her daughter. "My mother told me how our ancestors connected to others to form packs as a way of protecting themselves. We've also always felt the need to be in a community and live amongst others of our kind. Only those of our bloodline can connect those outside the pack. Eloi, I will show you how, but you need to connect with me and then with the pack. That should link us all together again."

"What if I can't? What if I'm not strong enough?" Eloi fiddled with her hands in her lap and looked down.

"Baby girl, your connection to me is so strong. I think that's what stopped me from forgetting you completely. The other part is our bloodline—no one has ever tried to sever a Royal before." Aine smiled and stroked her daughter's face, then lifted her chin. "If you can't now, we will wait for the full moon and try then. There's no problem with that at all; it just means Lachlan will be stuck with us longer."

Lachlan snorted. "Fine by me." He smiled at them, then walked over to ruffle Eloi's hair. "I don't doubt you, kid. After what you told us about your escape and the information you gave us about Rolan, you'll help your mum one way or another."

Eloi beamed at him. The three went out to the yard to make their first attempt at the reconnection. Lachlan watched as Aine and her daughter sat cross-legged in his backyard. Aine had explained how being out in the open air would strengthen the connection.

"Ready?" Aine asked gently, across from Eloi.

"Yeah." Eloi smiled and put out her hands. Mother and daughter held hands and closed their eyes.

"I need you to concentrate on our connection. You've been doing it naturally most of your life, so that shouldn't be a problem." Lachlan watched as Aine's mouth twitched into a smile, and Eloi frowned in concentration.

"I feel you, Mom."

Aine smiled, and Lachlan could see the joy on her face. "I feel you too, baby; now reach out to the pack. I know it'll be hard because they're so far away. But you've been working closely with Eyolf. If you connect to him, you should feel the rest of them."

Eloi's frown deepened, and sweat started to form on her forehead. Aine's smile relaxed into a frown; Eloi gasped but didn't open her eyes.

"Eyolf is cold and hungry. They have him caged—I was worried they'd kill him, but they kept him locked up."

Lachlan watched Eloi's hands tremble in Aine's.

"I can feel it too," Aine said. "You're doing so well. Now reach for the rest of the pack and keep breathing. Once you can feel them all, I will be connected."

Lachlan held his breath as he watched the determination on the young girl's face.

"Almost there, Mom." Eloi scrunched her face up in concentration, and both their chests heaved. Lachlan watched in awe; he realized he was probably the first human to ever witness something like this. His body tensed, and the girls held their breath. He counted in his head to distract himself, feeling the tension in the air.

Suddenly a loud crash sounded across the yard as a giant wolf, black as midnight, raced towards them.

17

Lachlan's instincts and muscle memory kicked in as he prepared himself to fight; he looked around the yard at the scattered tools and wood. He could feel the skin-warmed metal of the medallion against his chest. He was glad he put it on while dressing, even though he would never use it again on Aine and never on Eloi. He'd wanted to be prepared. He worried about Rolan since Aine told him about the betrayal by her mate.

The black wolf before him crouched and growled as it turned to face him. The wolf's mouth curled into a cruel snarl as a smaller wolf leaped into the area to support him. Lachlan's muscles tensed as he looked at their odds. Two shifted wolves against him; odds were not in his favor. Or at least not if he were alone. He looked across at Aine and Eloi, who still appeared to be in a trance. Fortunately, the two wolves were fixated on Lachlan—he wouldn't be able to count on the girls for help yet.

There was a gleam of anger in the black wolf's eyes as he stepped forward and bore down on him, hackles raised. Lachlan took a step back toward the side of the yard, away from where the girls were. There were weapons stored around the house and grounds; old habits die hard. The movement caused the wolves in front of him to growl and tense. Then, in a graceful move and speed not possible for most humans, Lachlan darted across to the back porch and had a hunting knife in his hand before the two wolves could react. Their angry snarls made him grin. He crouched into a fighting stance; it had been too long since he'd had a good fight.

The smaller of the two wolves started to flank him, brown fur bristled as he approached. The black wolf used the distraction to charge, but Lachlan was prepared for the move. His family had trained him to fight shifters in their stronger wolf form, as well as their human form. Lachlan blocked the large shifter with a move that used the wolf's momentum to throw it into a wall and fluidly turned in time to use the same move on the smaller wolf. The smaller of the two landed dazed, but the large black one recovered quickly.

"Rolan, I presume?" Lachlan smoothly moved to put himself between Rolan and his girls. The thought jolted him but felt right. They were his girls now, and he needed to protect them.

Rolan's response was an angry snarl with a flying leap. Lachlan easily blocked Rolan again and ran his knife along a muscular black shoulder. The wolf released a sharp whine but knocked him to the ground with his next lunge. It took most of Lachlan's strength to hold back Rolan's wolf form, which snapped at his throat. He needed to get off the ground; it was the most challenging position to fight a wolf.

Suddenly the weight which held Lachlan down disappeared as a small, pale wolf form catapulted in from his right to knock the large wolf aside. Lachlan marveled at the bravery of Eloi, who shook herself as she got to her feet, slightly dazed. He looked towards Aine, who still sat with her eyes closed, then to the smaller brown wolf who appeared unconscious in the corner. He flipped the knife between his hands in an attempt to distract Rolan.

"Behind me, Eloi," Lachlan said.

The young wolf stepped back but came to his side and growled at her father. Her side moved quickly as she breathed heavily and brushed against his thigh. Lachlan didn't dare look away from the wolf that snarled before him but was in awe of Aine's daughter. He was proud to fight beside her to protect the woman he loved.

When Rolan charged at them both, Lachlan could almost feel Eloi's intentions and adjusted his movements around her. As Rolan fought them, Eloi and Lachlan were in a graceful dance and appeared to get the best of him when a swift kick from Lachlan's boot threw the black wolf against the porch.

Rolan managed to gain his footing with a wolfish grin, large jaws opened, and his head tilted back. An ear-splitting howl echoed around the yard, which caused Eloi to whimper and Lachlan's ears to hurt. In mere moments, three more wolves surrounded them, snarling and growling. Lachlan wished for the first time in years that his family was here to back him up.

A cry from Aine behind Lachlan made his stomach lurch, and he turned without a thought. A young boy, only a little older than Eloi, held a knife to her throat, and her hands were bound by large, black cuffs with a thick chain between them. The surface looked odd and shiny, like oil and water combined into a congealed sludge.

Lachlan looked at Aine and expected her wolf form to erupt. But when nothing happened, he realized something was very wrong. He adjusted his position so he could see all the enemies in the area, which was difficult. Eloi whimpered next to him but held her ground.

"Surrender now, or I have been commanded to slit her throat," the boy said.

Lachlan looked at the boy; his young voice shook, and eyes pleaded for him to obey.

"The cuffs prevent shifting," the youth went on, "taking any strength the shifter has and using it to cause pain if they resist. With Aine's strength, the pain will be intense."

Lachlan could see sweat pour down Aine's face and neck. By the looks of it, she already fought the cuffs. Lachlan wondered why the boy helped by telling him what was going on but still held the knife against her neck. He could almost feel the fury coming off Aine in waves; he had never seen her so angry.

Eloi whimpered again when Rolan growled and snapped at her. She trembled as the gaze of the black wolf bore down into her. Lachlan dropped the knife and put his hands on the young wolf's back.

"Stand down, for now, there's nothing we can do outnumbered," he whispered softly, but with the wolves so close, he had no doubt they all heard him.

Eloi tensed under his hand and growled again, the vibration rumbled through Lachlan's hand. He dropped to his knees and put his hands behind his head, hoping Eloi would follow his lead. It grated on him to be so submissive, but Lachlan had more chances of helping his girls if they took him alive with them. Plus, he still had his medallion to use as a last resort.

Rolan shifted to human as he approached Lachlan. He wasn't a bulky man, dressed in simple shirts and pants with an ornate dagger at his waist, but he was muscular. His dark eyes bore into Lachlan with a feverish fury. His eyes and hair matched Eloi's.

"And here stands the man who stole my mate." The hatred in his voice was almost toxic.

"I heard you betrayed her and tried to kill her." Lachlan didn't try to hide his disdain.

"Disgusting, I can smell her on you."

Lachlan tensed as Rolan neared him; he felt exposed, having never been so vulnerable. "I will have to take you as evidence to show the truth of her crimes to the pack. You have both made it extremely easy, but I can't have you fight back. You're too good of a fighter."

A sharp pain erupted in the back of Lachlan's head, and darkness spread through his vision. He tried to fight it but slowly gave in to oblivion.

AINE'S HEART hurt as she watched Lachlan crumple before her. She was in awe of him as he held his own against the shifted wolves beside Eloi. He looked lethal and powerful; she had never seen anything like it. By the time she had come out of the trance enough to help, she felt Nyko clasp the cuffs around her hands. She wasn't sure if the reconnection had worked, the cuffs would block her connection if it was there. But when she tried to connect to the pack with Eloi, power had rushed out of her. She hadn't recovered fast enough and had failed Lachlan and Eloi.

The cold steel of the knife at her throat bit into her skin as she turned her head to look at the man she had once called mate.

Aine could feel darkness surround Rolan; he had a faint aura. The fact that he had shifted and obviously taught his warriors to shift meant he had used forbidden magic. She swallowed as Rolan approached but refused to drop her gaze. Even cuffed, she wouldn't be forced to submit.

"Hello, wife," Rolan drawled and lifted his hand to her face. Aine reacted without thinking and tasted blood as she bit into his hand. The blood tasted tainted and bitter—she had been right. Rolan had called on the dark, forbidden magic.

Aine shuddered as she considered the consequences of his actions, and Rolan growled, yanking his hand back. Aine's head snapped to the left as he backhanded her. She laughed as blood dribbled down her chin, then she turned to sneer back at him.

"You can't control me, Rolan, you should know that by now." Aine spat at him and smirked as the bloody glob hit him in the face. "So desperate for a power you could never earn or control."

"Take her and her disgusting human. Search the house and see if there is anything we can take, and then we need to get back to the village. The sooner they are sentenced to death, the better." Rolan turned back to Aine. "And then, *wife,* you will see what my true power really is. Your pack is ready to destroy you. I don't know how your memory returned, but you won't have it for much longer."

Aine's stomach clenched as Nyko lifted her from the ground. Rolan couldn't possibly have turned the pack against her in a month. Some of her power must have returned as she could feel the misery in the boy, but also the fear of what would happen if he didn't follow orders. She almost felt sorry for him, but when she looked back to see what would happen with Eloi and Lachlan, her sympathy fled.

Eloi had laid down protectively by Lachlan and growled

as Mervan and the warriors approached to pick him up. The girl remained in wolf form; her poor daughter probably didn't have the control to shift back right then. Aine couldn't blame her. Their situation was not good. Mervan kicked Eloi aside and heaved the heavy man onto his shoulder.

Mervan followed Nyko and Aine out to the back of the yard before he dropped Lachlan on the ground. Aine looked at Rolan's Second and realized there was no hope of help from him. Mervan turned and grabbed her by the throat; she didn't struggle as his gaze burned into her.

"What? No 'Why are you doing this?'" Mervan mocked as he gripped her harder and pushed her to her knees. "Not so high and mighty now, you stupid bitch. You'll pay for what you did."

Mervan's eyes glowed orange as he glared at her and squeezed. Aine felt dizzy as he threatened to cut off her air.

"I've seen him deteriorate recently. He was rabid, Mervan; why weren't you looking after your brother? Han attacked me! What was I supposed to do? Stand there and die?" Aine struggled through clenched teeth.

"Yes, you don't deserve to live." Mervan reluctantly threw her to the ground and stormed off toward the house when he heard Rolan bark his name. His eyes flared darker, and his hands shook as he struggled with his control just before he turned from Aine.

Nyko sighed as Mervan stalked away. The proximity of the Second warrior made the young man nervous.

Eloi quietly slunk toward where Lachlan lay. Unable to help, she laid back down with him after he was unceremoniously dropped on the ground. The gesture made Aine's heart squeeze; it was apparent her daughter had fallen as hard for her gorgeous man as she had. If the girl had feared or not liked him, Aine would have left him. It would have hurt like hell, especially because Lachlan would have understood that Eloi was her priority, but she would have done it.

"I don't need to ask why they are doing this, but why are *you* doing this, Nyko?" Aine tried to look at him, but the boy kept her head facing the house. Eloi let out a small cry next to Lachlan and nuzzled his arm.

"We deserve better," Nyko spoke quietly but sounded sad. "This was the only way; you left Rolan no choice."

"Sure, killing me and manipulating my pack was the only option. But, did you ever think that I have my reasons for keeping the pack isolated and safe? You don't think we've tried to integrate in the past and had to learn from our mistakes? My own father and grandfather were killed by humans."

Nyko stayed silent.

"Rolan, you may want to take a look at this." James, one of Rolan's four warriors, appeared in the back doorway of the house.

Rolan had stared out at the woods at the end of the yard; he could see why the human lived here. He scowled as he looked at Aine and the unconscious human, watched over by Mervan and Nyko. Maybe he would claim the house as his own when they eventually took over the town.

He turned to look at James. In his thirties, James was one of the strongest warriors in the pack, and Rolan was lucky that Mervan had managed to groom him. He followed James into the home.

"We found it in the shed," James said in the kitchen, gesturing to the table.

Rolan looked at the large chest and the weapons within. "He's a hunter," he hissed.

Of all the humans to find Aine when Nyko had left her, this wasn't a coincidence. *Why is he here? Are they looking for Sumter? Do they know what we are planning? Are there more?* Rolan's thoughts churned quickly; he would have to inform the others. The hunter had fought ferociously. Without the support from the other wolves, Rolan would have struggled. He took a deep breath and tried to calm his mind. His hands reached for a set of solid chains on one side of the chest; careful to not come into contact with any of the other weapons, Rolan pulled them out.

"Restrain him. I will have to interrogate him when we get back to Sumter. At the very least, we need to know if there are more."

James nodded and took the chains outside to the back-yard. Rolan ran a hand through his hair and sighed. Hope-fully, this was nearly over—he could kill Aine and finally be the undisputed pack leader. He couldn't wait to come back to this town and take over these pitiful humans. Once they were enslaved, Rolan could start to live the life he deserved.

Rolan walked back outside. Eloi had still not shifted back; it was not uncommon for young shifters to get stuck if they were in distress. Rolan wasn't surprised at her form; he was surprised, however, that Eloi had fought with the human. He thought back to the fight and was pleased with how strong and brave his daughter had become. Once he could control her, she would be a valuable asset.

"What were you planning to do with the hunter, Aine?" he asked. "Take the pack back?"

"Hunter??"

Rolan watched as Aine paled, then he started to laugh hard.

"You didn't know? Seriously? You've lived with him for a month and didn't know he was a hunter?" Rolan chuckled harder at Aine's puzzled look at Lachlan. Nyko looked horrified and backed away from the hunter, dragging Aine back with him.

"The fact he's a hunter is another nail in the coffin. I won't even have to persuade the pack, they will want to kill you themselves for selling us out."

Eloi lifted her head from Lachlan but didn't move. Rolan's humor soured. The girl couldn't have been with the hunter for more than a day, and she was attached to a man that would rather destroy them.

"Eloi, the hunter was probably using you and your stupid mother to find our pack and destroy it. You both could have caused a terrible massacre if I hadn't arrived," he said.

Eloi huffed and put her head back on the human's arm. The girl was as stupid as her mother. That would make her easier to control.

Rolan turned to see his warriors exiting the house, Mervan still fuming as he watched over Aine. Rolan should have expected him to be furious when he confronted his brother's killer. He put a calming hand on Mervan's shoulder. "Are you okay? Keep it together a little longer, and you can be the one to end her." He watched Mervan's face; the man was in control.

"Let's get this over with." Mervan strode past Aine and led the way into the woods. James lifted Lachlan from the ground and ignored Eloi when she growled at him. With her mother bound and the hunter unconscious and chained, the girl would have no choice but to follow them back to the village.

PHIL SHOOK hard as he watched the group leave the yard. Lachlan hadn't moved, and the small wolf looked forlorn as she and Aine were marched into the woods. He needed to help, but what could he do? If Lachlan couldn't fight them, then Phil had no chance.

He clutched his phone in his hand as it trembled. He had come around to sit with Lachlan and the girls; they had all seemed happy when they were at the diner earlier, and he wanted to join them. It was nice to see Lachlan smiling for a change.

When the wolves had attacked, Phil hadn't made it to the house yet. So when he arrived, he hid in the hedge around the side and watched as his friend and poor little Eloi had surrendered. Phil had pulled out the crumpled card Lachlan's cousin Girvan had given him when he stopped by the diner after the town meeting. Then he took a deep breath as his hands still shook and slowly dialed. Girvan had said that if Lachlan was ever in trouble, he should call.

"Well, that doesn't look good."

Phil dropped his phone as Lachlan's cousin appeared next to him; he hadn't heard the man approach. "Nice to know you would have actually called me," Girvan said.

"Indeed," a deep Irish voice said behind Phil, who spun and held his hand to his chest, his heartbeat thudding loudly in his ears. The hulk of a man, who claimed to be Lachlan's father, stood in the drive. "At least one of you has some sense. How long has my son been living with a wolf?"

"Nearly a month," Phil stuttered. "She's not dangerous, she's kind even. You should see her with the kids in town."

"Sure," Liam said dismissively and glanced up at Girvan. The man didn't appear to have heard Phil.

"Follow them and stay in touch," he ordered. "This is the break we needed; now we will know where they've been hiding and can wipe them out. Once you know their location, call it in. I'll get Finn and Cillian."

Phil looked at the older man and immediately regretted the decision to call them for help. Liam's eyes glinted with bloodlust and the thrill of the hunt. The older man didn't seem interested in saving his son.

He gulped and looked at Girvan and could see the concern on Lachlan's cousin's face. But he left to follow the wolves without a word. When Phil turned back to Liam, he had vanished.

18

Any hope Aine had left died as she felt the horror and anger coming from what had been her pack. As they entered Sumter, there was a large crowd gathered. Rolan smiled and reassured some of the pack members as he passed. She was disgusted at their lack of loyalty; it had taken Rolan only a few weeks and several lies to turn them against her.

The warriors were gathered in the meeting area, where cages had been constructed, and a large pit was dug out. They had never needed more than one cage, and that had been rarely used. To Aine's horror, Mervan dropped Lachlan into the pit; there was a loud thud as he hit the bottom. She was yanked back by Nyko as she lurched forwards.

"Don't." Nyko's objection was quiet and more of a plea than a command.

Aine looked around for any ally but only saw stern faces in the crowd. Nyko led her to the cages and gently pushed her into the one on the left. Rolan still worked the crowd, he smiled and moved among them. Appalled, Aine looked at her new accommodation and was shocked to see Eyolf leaned against her bars to her right. She ran forwards to crouch beside him, her hands clinging to the rough wood that separated them.

"Eyolf, I wasn't sure you were alive after Eloi escaped!"

"Oh, good, you remember, I was worried for a while there. Have you managed to reconnect to the pack? Your mother said only another of your bloodline could reconnect the pack; I tried to send Eloi to you." The older wolf looked tired as he spoke.

Aine cupped his cheek through the bars. "Eloi found me. Fortunately, I'd gotten my memory back by then. We tried to reconnect, but I'm not sure it worked. We were interrupted. I can feel the Pack's emotions, though—and I've been feeling the emotions of the humans in town since I woke up a few weeks ago." Aine sighed and spoke desperately. "Why have they turned against me so easily?"

"Rolan used their fears against them. I think he uses dark, forbidden magic to influence them. You're so strong and have done so much for them. A lesser person would have broken under the responsibility by now. Things have not been easy since your grandfather died." Eyolf shifted and laid his head against the bars. "You took everything on so young, and with your power, you haven't had a moment's peace."

Aine leaned against the bars next to him. "What has happened since Eloi escaped?"

"Rolan told them that you left to live with a human and then kidnapped Eloi." Eyolf coughed, and Aine groaned.

"I guess I can see how they believed that since I did live with a human before I knew what I was. And Eloi did end up with me." Aine's chest tightened as she thought about Lachlan. She couldn't believe he was a hunter. Why hadn't he told her? The betrayal stung after they had spent the night talking. Even after she had told him everything, he still didn't trust her. The thought hurt, and she closed her eyes.

Eloi had been taken by Rolan; she had managed to shift back as they neared Sumter but hadn't said a word as her father took her away. Aine worried that Rolan knew how powerful their daughter had become and would use her against them. A tear tickled her cheek as it fell down her face before Aine remembered how Eloi had protected Lachlan, even after Rolan announced he was a hunter.

"How long has Rolan been using the dark magic?" Aine suddenly remembered that Rolan and all his warriors had control over their shift.

"I don't know. I only discovered it when Eloi escaped. I could see the madness in him, though, when he questioned me." Eyolf paused to cough again. "I wouldn't be surprised if it's been years."

The thought sobered Aine. Eloi was strong, but she was young. Aine didn't know if she would be able to withstand Rolan should he use dark magic to influence her. Aine didn't know much about it, but her mother had warned her that it could cause good people to turn evil. She wondered if that was what had happened to Rolan. When they first fell in love, he was sweet and always put her first. How could a person change so much?

A noise disturbed Aine's train of thought as Nyko skirted round the back of the cages. He moved silently, checking every direction carefully before he approached where Eyolf was slumped near the back of his cage. He handed the old man some food through the bars before moving across to Aine and did the same. The chains and cuffs clinked as Aine took the food. She could smell the barely-cooked deer when he first arrived and was grateful for something to settle the sick feeling in her stomach.

"Have you thought about what I said, Nyko?"

Aine paused when Eyolf spoke. The old wolf hadn't touched his food and stared intently at the younger boy. Nyko bowed his head and mumbled something; Eyolf chuckled. "Not so hard to figure out, was it?"

"Figure what out?" Aine quickly forgot about her food and unsettled stomach. Nyko looked up at her, eyes shining with unshed tears.

"I'm sorry, Pack Leader. Rolan was wrong to do what he did. We... well, I... thought that we deserved better, to be free. But we should have tried to talk to you...." Nyko trailed off and looked around quickly before his gaze fell to the floor.

"You didn't kill me, though, did you, Nyko? You left me somewhere for someone to find and help me. Rolan can be persuasive it seems; he has the whole pack fooled right now." Aine reached for the boy, the touch meant to soothe, and when it worked, her hope sparked again. If she could do that, maybe she could connect to the pack—perhaps the reconnection had worked.

"Be ready." She looked Nyko in the eyes as she lifted his chin. "We aren't done yet."

ELOI CROUCHED IN HER ROOM; it had been her place of peace once, where she came to relax and be alone. Now it was a prison. Rolan had left her in there before gleefully going to calm the pack down, and when she checked the corner she could usually squeeze through to get out of the back of their home, it was sealed shut.

The girl sat on her bed in despair, her knees drawn to her chest and her chin rested on them. She had gone to save her mother, and she felt like she had led her father straight to them. Eloi shifted to her side and let the tears fall, exhaustion swept through her, and slowly she drifted to sleep.

Eloi wasn't sure how long Rolan had been gone, but she jumped awake when the door opened. He finally entered her room. It was still light outside but seemed to be later in the day. Rolan came to sit on the end of her bed. His approach was careful, like that of someone trying to coax an animal.

"Why did you run away, Eloi?" Rolan sighed, almost defeated. Eloi knew too much to believe it to be real.

"I know what you did to Mom. I saw you in the Temple with the warriors. And you projected in your dreams." Eloi snapped her mouth shut; she didn't know why she had said that, but she couldn't stop herself. Aine had told her to hide her abilities from Rolan. She fought to stay quiet in case she said anything else.

"Ah, that's a problem." Rolan's brow creased in contemplation. "You are my daughter and my heir. I need you to trust me when I say what I did was for the best of the pack. We need to elevate ourselves. We are worth more than living in the back end of nowhere and scrambling to survive."

Eloi didn't trust herself to speak, so she stayed silent. Rolan rose and held out his hand.

"I need your help. Don't worry; you don't have to say anything, but the pack needs to know that Aine has been consorting with a hunter. She put them in a lot of danger, and we need to make them aware of that. There could be others out there."

Eloi tried to stay on her bed, but an odd sensation ran

through her; she watched her hand reach out to take his. Hate bubbled inside her as she rose from the bed and followed her father.

Rolan led her to the Temple, where the pack had gathered to wait for them. Eloi watched the crowd as they approached and noticed their rapt attention. No one spoke as Rolan stood before them.

"Pack, we have rescued my daughter and now hold her captors as prisoners. My warriors discovered a plan for hunters to massacre us all. We have stopped it for now."

Gasps ran through the crowd, and everyone started talking at once. Rolan put up his hand and the pack silenced.

"The human Aine was...with...." Rolan paused and swallowed hard, the disgust evident on his face. "...is a hunter. Aine and the hunter planned to return to Sumter and kill us all."

Eloi snapped her head to her father and paled. She tried to speak, but her mouth wouldn't open. She couldn't make a sound. She could only watch in horror as her father continued.

"The fate of Aine and her lover," Rolan's voice became twisted, "is in your hands. She is already severed from the pack. We can either exile her or execute her. The choice is yours."

Eloi could feel anger and horror simmer through the crowd as Rolan spoke. Her stomach dropped out as the pack started to shout.

"Execute!"

"They must die!"

"Kill them before they kill us!"

The girl's gaze swept the crowd as she looked for any that would object.

"As you wish." Rolan bowed his head, his hand never left Eloi's as he turned and tugged her gently with him. "See, my daughter. Their fate is decided, and you acted beautifully; there is hope for you yet."

Eloi's eyes stung as tears threatened to spill. The strange sensation overwhelmed her again.

"Yes, Father."

AINE SAT in the center of the cage, hands cuffed in her lap, and studied the chains around her. After Nyko left, she realized that she shouldn't have been able to use any power with the cuffs, but even now, she could feel it leaking from her. The cuffs had stopped her control of it but hadn't stopped the power completely. When she tried at Lachlan's house, the intense pain that overtook her had nearly caused her to blackout.

She hadn't cried out or shown any sign of the pain; her father had taught her that when she was a child. Aine was unique—she could put the pain in a compartment of her mind so she wouldn't feel it. Her father had never caused her more pain than a pinprick on her finger; her mother had never let him try anything further. But it had been enough to teach her the concept.

Now, as she watched the surface of the cuffs shine in the drops of evening sunlight leaking through the ceiling of her cage, she contemplated how she could use her power despite them. Aine closed her eyes and reached inside herself; in some ways, her ability had embarrassed her, so she didn't use it much. Besides feeling those around her, she never tried to influence her pack or reach further than their village. But since Lachlan had touched her with the medallion, she could feel it simmering under the surface, ready to explode outwards.

Aine reached within herself to draw everything she had into her control. It felt slippery with the cuffs on. But once she started, she couldn't stop. Her skin tingled, and her fingers twitched the longer she held it. She concentrated on the cuffs and imagined them shattered; all it took was a thought. Power rushed through her and disappeared; the weight of the cuffs fell from her wrists, and they hit the ground. Aine opened her eyes with a grin at Eyolf, but her face fell when she saw his shocked expression.

"Your skin was crawling with darkness, like smoke. Aine, you haven't been using the darkness, have you?" Eyolf's voice hissed; his face was pale. He held a carving tool and looked to have made a hole in the corner of his cage.

"What? No!" Aine felt horror shoot through her with a jolt. "Never, I just concentrated on trying to use my power to get the cuffs off. I was trying to trick them into thinking I wasn't a wolf. They react to what we are." She had been shocked to see the cuffs when Nyko put them on her. They had been with the pack since before anyone could remember and were only used when they severed someone from it.

"I can't...I can't think about this now. I need to try and connect to the pack. They know that you can't lie through dreams. If I show them what Rolan has done, then no one will trust him." Determination filled her as she thought about her pack, then she felt sadness when she thought of Lachlan. Aine couldn't understand why he had hidden that he was a hunter. She felt so stupid, why would someone who studied shifters have a medallion that incapacitated them? She should have suspected something, but had been blinded by her feelings for him.

Once again, she sat in the center of the cage, eyes closed, looking inside herself. Without the cuffs, her power was more accessible. As she reached for it, a white flash in her mind shocked her, and she put her hands over her eyes. When she opened them, she was surrounded by white, and her mother stood before her.

"Mom?" Aine cried and threw herself into her mother's arms as she smiled. They squeezed each other hard. "How are you here, Mom?"

"I'm not really here, darling, but I know you need help. I need to be quick. Our bloodline is special, Aine, and you need to use it now. What Rolan has done is unforgivable, and you must stop him. Unfortunately, there is more at risk than you know. You have the power to gift our pack the ability to shift, but only those loyal to you and the strongest in the pack."

"But that's the dark magic—Rolan is using it now. And the pack hates me! Rolan has turned them against me."

"This is different; what Rolan is using isn't natural. You were born with this magic, Aine. All our ancestors were capable of using it, but only you are strong enough to keep it under control. And maybe Eloi if you train her well." Aine looked at her mother's beautiful face as it shone with pride.

"You have grown into a magnificent woman, my child," she continued. "I am proud to be your mother. I'm sorry I did not live long enough to see you grow."

With those words, Arwen faded, and Aine hugged herself, tears spilling over as her eyes closed.

When Aine opened her eyes again, she was sitting in the cage and hadn't moved. Tears still streamed down her face, but at least she knew what she had to do. Or at least try to do. She just hoped that when Eloi had tried to reconnect her to the pack, it had worked.

She closed her eyes a final time, leveling her breath, and dug deeper for her power than she ever had before. As she pushed it out from her body, the feel of it changed. It no longer was a fight to push it out as it had been; the power almost felt like it wanted to spread out from her.

First, Aine sought Eloi and could feel a dark parasite in her mind. It felt repulsive and had an essence of Rolan. Anger pulsed through her, which fed the power as it spread from her to Eloi, obliterating the darkness that controlled her mind.

Mom!

Eloi!

Thank you. I couldn't help. I couldn't speak when I wanted to, and then when I could, I said things I didn't want to.

The relief which came from Eloi was a balm to Aine's worry.

I need to win our pack back over. Can you get away from Rolan? Trick him if you must. He will still think he controls you.

Anything for you, Mom. Now get our pack back before they do something we will make them regret.

Aine mentally chuckled at the vehemence in her daughter's mental tone. She gathered her power for the most significant push she had ever attempted. As the power stretched to each pack member, Aine could feel the same dark parasites infecting them. She felt the power in herself build, fighting her restraint. It wanted to destroy Rolan's influence. As each pack member felt her reach them, they froze and stopped what they were doing.

Aine showed the pack what Rolan had done to her. She fed them her pain from the betrayal, the confusion when she woke with no memory, and the love she felt for Lachlan when he and Phil had shown her kindness. She showed the pack how they helped her, even when they suspected what she was. The power pulsed through her to every member in her pack and dissolved the influence Rolan had over them.

Aine could feel the darkness rooted deep in Rolan, Mervan, and the three warriors they had taught how to shift, but she didn't think she could remove it. They were lost to her.

The emotions scattered in her mind as the pack absorbed Rolan's betrayal and manipulation. She held those feelings with her power within them. As the pack's loyalty shifted back to her, she could feel those who were remorseful and those who were still uncertain. The longer she held the power, the more she had to fight it for control. It had started to feel slippery in her grasp; sweat beaded on her forehead and ran down her back. It wanted to grant everyone the power of her bloodline, but she had to be careful who she chose.

Brow furrowed in concentration, Aine examined every pack member. She chose warriors who had served under her grandfather, also those with the greatest potential from the younger warriors. Eyolf shuddered next to her as he felt the power skim across him before it settled in his core. Aine pushed the power into those she could trust and granted them the ability to change at will. The power still tried to escape as she pulled the majority of it back within herself. She sagged as she forced it down and felt it fade away.

With that complete, Aine had one more thing she needed to do.

Her anger swelled as she thought of Lachlan. He was a hunter and had betrayed her. Was she a fool to believe he really loved her? As she thought about him, she started to feel his presence in the pit. She frowned; Lachlan was human. It shouldn't have been possible for her to feel and connect with him like the rest of her pack. But, using a small amount of power, she thought about Lachlan and her connection to him. Even if he had betrayed her, she might be able to use him to escape.

Lachlan?

Aine? Lachlan's mental voice sounded muffled and groggy. He must not have been conscious long.

You're a hunter. Aine felt her disappointment throb through their link; he recoiled in shock as he made sense of her words. She felt his shame and grief as he relived his last memory of his mother. Her mouth dropped open when she relived the night he had helped the young wolf-girl escape. Through her shock, she nearly let the connection drop.

Lachlan, I'm so sorry about your mother. I don't know what to say.

You saw that? Lachlan's confusion felt almost as bad as his realization that the memory had been shared. Aine sensed his vulnerability and was ashamed of her violation. She shook her head.

I'm not used to linking with humans, and you fed me the memory. I should have warned you that could happen. I'm glad I know, though—you have no reason to be ashamed.

We have a lot to talk about when we get out of here. Where is here?

We are in Sumter. Rolan took us back to the pack, but he is about to get more than he bargained for. I just showed them his betrayal.

Aine felt Lachlan's grin.

Come and get me then.

On my way, handsome.

Aine opened her eyes and looked at Eyolt. A dark grey wolf stared at her through the bars and grinned as much as a wolf could grin, making Aine laugh.

"You're welcome, old friend." Aine chuckled again when

Eyolf barked at her; she could feel his joy. Older shifters lost the ability to shift as they aged, and it had been a few years since Eyolf had been able to enjoy his wolf form.

Aine turned to her cage door and pushed with all her strength, putting a small amount of her power behind it. She felt satisfaction when the cage door burst off its hinges as the sun set and night fell.

19

As Aine walked out of her prison, she saw the darkness surround her on the edge of her vision. She embraced it, fueled by her anger. Nyko approached and dropped to his knees. The young wolf felt defeated, and guilt spread off him in waves.

"Forgive me; I can't believe I was so wrong." His eyes were downcast, and Aine could sense his remorse and sorrow at his actions. They crept through the young shifter like ice spread over a lake.

She placed a hand on his shoulder. The darkness and shadow that had surrounded her drew back inside. It took a great effort to keep them there. "Come along, there's work to be done." Her voice sounded deeper as she spoke, and she saw the surprise in his face when Nyko rose. Aine pushed the power through her hand into the young man, and he shuddered. His features contorted and strained as he shifted into a small dark brown wolf. She laughed as he shook himself out, and she sensed his surprise and joy.

"You are obviously loyal to me, Nyko. If you are, the ability to shift as you wish will remain with you. This is different from what Rolan tried to give you. Once you begin to doubt or fall back toward Rolan's way of thinking, you will lose the ability."

Nyko nodded, his tongue lolling out the side of his mouth. He playfully bounded toward the edge of what was the pack meeting area.

Aine looked at the large pit in the center; Eyolf had slipped through the hole he made and stood beside her. She clenched her fists as she stalked toward it. The last time she had seen Lachlan, he had been thrown down unconscious. Aine wondered why he hadn't attempted to climb out.

As she looked down, she realized the pit they had dug was deep enough that if three men stood on each other's shoulders, they still wouldn't reach the edge. There were no marks on the smooth sides, though Lachlan had started to dig handholds into it. Aine smiled down at him and chuckled.

"How are you doing down there? Is it my turn to save you?"

"Haha, very funny, you going to let me up?" Lachlan crossed his arms and scowled at her. Aine was pleased that the events of the day hadn't dimmed their connection. It was forbidden for her to mate with a human, but as Pack Leader, she could change that. Aine could see a lot of change in the pack's future.

Nyko shifted back to his human form and ran over to the pit's edge, pushing a heap of rope on the ground and over the side. Aine watched the rope ladder unroll down into the hole.

"Let yourself up if you don't want to be a damsel in distress!" she shouted, and Lachlan rolled his eyes. As he started to climb, Aine turned to Eyolf, who stood still next to her.

"I know you want to savor your wolf form, but we need to talk."

Eyolf looked up and whined, then changed back into his human form. He nodded his assent and waited for her to speak.

"My mother told me our bloodline was Royal and born with dark magic. My ancestors were the only ones strong enough to control the power, and it hasn't been seen in generations. It felt like a tsunami trying to escape, harder to keep it from rushing out than it was to push it further out. I can..." Aine paused to take a ragged breath. "It is hard to stop it from gushing out."

"Was there a question in there?" Eyolf looked sheepish, and Aine scowled.

"You knew? What else haven't you told me?" Aine crossed her arms and huffed. Eyolf laughed, and she huffed again.

"You look like your mother used to as a four-year-old when you do that," he said. "Now, don't be cross, Aine." Eyolf tipped her chin with his knuckle. "Your mother said that I was only to tell you when you were ready. You were so young when you took over the pack, and with the difficulties you've had with Rolan over the years, I didn't want him to find out if I told you. We have a lot to discuss."

Lachlan pulled himself over the edge of the pit and stood before them. Eyolf glared at the hunter as he put out his hand toward Eyolf to shake. Lachlan looked at his hand, then wiped it on his jeans.

"Am I late to the party?" He stood tall, muscles flexed, and Aine watched his chest heave from exertion after his climb. Lachlan put his hands in his pockets.

"You must be Eyolf," he continued. "Eloi told us you helped her escape."

"Indeed." Eyolf sniffed him and turned to Aine. "You really couldn't tell he was a hunter? Just look at him."

Aine's mouth dropped open, and she stammered, but no words came out.

Lachlan laughed and put his arm around her shoulder. "She didn't remember what she was—how was she supposed to remember not to hang around a hunter?"

Eyolf scowled at his arm, and she shifted, uneasy.

"I haven't been a hunter for a long time, old wolf," Lachlan said, sensing the tension.

Eyolf still watched Lachlan's arm around her and frowned at her next. "I see."

Aine shifted under Eyolf's gaze and walked towards the older wolf, away from Lachlan. Nyko had stood to the side while the two men scowled at each other.

"Where is Eloi, Nyko?" she asked.

The young shifter fidgeted. "Rolan wouldn't let her leave his sight. He influenced her, so I don't know if she will be the same. Looking back now, I can see I was being influenced by him along with the others. It can be hard to shake, especially if you're not aware." Nyko swallowed hard. "Don't get me wrong, I joined them willingly, but now what Rolan said doesn't even make sense." The boy's face fell, and he looked at the ground.

"Let's go find her." Lachlan strode towards Nyko, and the boy looked up into his face with awe. "Lead the way. I know what it is like to be controlled by the older warriors around you."

ONCE ELOI WAS free of Rolan's influence, thanks to her mother, she silently moved towards her bedroom door. Aine had taught her from a young age to move quietly. If Rolan believed he controlled her, he might not have locked her in this time.

Cautiously, Eloi turned the handle on her door, shocked when it slowly creaked open. Once she could slip through, she stopped and sniffed, poking her head through the gap. The girl looked around the home she had grown up in; it was silent and felt eerily empty. She could only remember the tension between her parents and their unhappiness there in the last few years.

Eloi wondered what her mom had seen in the spiteful man she called "Father." The girl had only ever seen him try to undermine her mother. Rolan constantly questioned Aine's decisions and caused her to doubt herself; he must have been different when he was younger.

The girl crept to her parent's bedroom and grabbed her mother's leadership dagger. It was rightfully hers, and Eloi would return it to her.

She had spotted it through the open bedroom door. The dagger had been in Aine and Eloi's family for generations and had become a symbol of their right to lead the pack. Rolan must have stolen it when he performed the Severance ritual on Aine to prove his right to lead. As the leader of the pack, Aine should be the one who had it, not Rolan.

Eloi wandered around the rest of the little house, but couldn't see anything else she wanted to take. She had spent her whole life growing up in their home, and she was sad she couldn't see anything else precious to her.

As she turned toward the door to leave, distracted by her melancholy, she didn't hear Rolan's approach. Eloi reached for the door as it opened, and she froze in shock as her father looked down on her. Rolan took one look at the dagger, his face dark with anger, and lunged for her.

Eloi ducked and leaped to her left to escape. As Rolan spun to catch her, his momentum faltered when she kicked out at his leg and caught his shin. She put the table in the center of the kitchen area between them and waited for him to make his next move.

"Why are you doing this, Eloi? You must know that I want the best for you and this pack. That is not cowering in the shadows—we must rule the humans. We deserve to rise above them and take what should be ours!" Rolan's hands banged on the table, making her jump.

"There must be another way! Why must we rule them? They haven't done anything to us!"

"They hunt us!"

"They can't hunt us if they don't know about us!"

"What about the hunters, Eloi? Shifters have been wiped out in Europe because of the O'Reilly clan. It's led by Lachlan's father."

Eloi recoiled. Lachlan had been so sweet and protective of her mom and her. There was no way he was still involved with the hunters.

Rolan used her moment of distraction to leap over the table at her. Out of pure instinct, Eloi moved to dodge him, but not fast enough.

Rolan fell towards her and landed hard. Eloi's breath left her body as his weight landed on top of her, and Rolan grunted. She could feel a warm, sticky substance spread over the hand and arm which held the dagger. With her other hand, she pushed Rolan off her and looked down at her blood-stained clothes.

Horror washed through her as she looked at the wound in Rolan's side. Gripping the knife harder, she backed toward the door. Rolan tried to stand, his breath labored, but he failed to get up. Eloi gasped and turned to sprint out the open door.

Mervan strode toward their hut, face puzzled, and he stopped when she ran in the opposite direction. The smell of the blood must have alerted him that something had happened to Rolan; he quickly entered the house.

Eloi's lungs burned as she ran across the village towards her mother as fast as she could. The smell of Rolan's blood stung her nose, and she stopped when she saw a bucket of water. She poured it over herself to rid herself of the blood.

The dagger in her hand felt heavy, and she started to feel sick. Eloi became dizzy, her vision swimming. Then, just before the dagger fell from her hand, another hand grabbed it from her. She opened her eyes and saw her mother in front of her.

Sorrow welled up, and Eloi burst into tears. She sobbed into her mother's shoulder as Aine held her tight and whispered that it would all be okay.

ROLAN GROANED as Mervan helped him to his feet, the pain in his side dissipating. Unfortunately, when he used dark magic for healing, it took a lot of energy.

"Where would she go?" Mervan fretted near the wall as he watched Rolan recover.

"To her mother. Is Aine secure?"

Mervan didn't say anything, and Rolan looked up sharply at his Second. "What?" he snapped.

"She managed to reconnect with the rest of the pack. She showed them what you did...those of us loyal to you didn't see it. She severed us. How could she do that without the ritual?" Mervan wrung his hands together, then shook them out. He swallowed before he spoke again.

"I could feel her in my head; it felt like she clawed my brain." He slapped his head and shook it.

"She can't do that; it isn't possible." Rolan watched his closest friend. "She must have used Eloi to reconnect with the pack, then used their combined power to disconnect you."

Now that Rolan tried, he realized he could no longer feel the pack. The feeling left a hollowness in his chest, and he rubbed the spot.

"There's more..." Mervan paused, and Rolan growled. "She sensed who was loyal to her, and she gifted them with control of the change. Many of the warriors have sided with her now, even older wolves who haven't shifted in years. They can all now change at will, without dark magic. I even saw Eyolf shift, and he should be far too old."

Rolan's vision blurred, and his jaw clenched so hard he thought his teeth would shatter. His fingertips tingled as claws emerged from his nail bed; he took a breath to control the shift and another to try to calm himself. How dare she? It must be some sort of manipulation or a false dream. Though he knew that no one could lie in dreams.

There was no way she was that powerful. Then again, if she were, and Eloi had the same power, then he could use it to create his own pack that could shift at will. It would take less energy than using dark magic. Aine would have to be killed, and Eloi would have to be influenced. He would have to dig deep to take Aine down—he would use everything to annihilate her. If only she had seen that he should have been the true leader. She could have joined him, and he could have used her power instead of Eloi's.

He would have to take control of his daughter. Then, Eloi could reconnect them to the pack.

"Put a call out to the others in the area. We will need support. It's time we brought the Aoibhans to heel." Rolan chuckled at his own pun.

Mervan didn't look so sure, but Rolan grinned. It was time to show this pack what a true leader should look like.

"WE NEED TO GATHER THE PACK." Aine still held Eloi close; she had felt her daughter's distress after she stabbed Rolan. Eloi had projected, and with Aine's power so close to the surface, she saw it happen.

Aine was connected to the Chosen pack members, and they could feel her calling as the group worked their way to the Temple. After being held in a cage, the meeting area looked more like an arena with the pit at its center. Aine was reluctant to go back there, but they needed to find Rolan.

Lachlan strode next to her but didn't put his arm around her as he had before. She hoped he understood that her relationship with the pack was fragile. The presence of a human hunter would be hard enough to explain without clear evidence that he meant more to her and Eloi. The pack would have felt how Lachlan and Aine's relationship had grown when she showed them what happened to her. But it would take a while for most to accept his presence.

As Aine approached the Temple, she was pleased to see a crowd had gathered and that many had answered her call. To be reconnected with the pack was a relief; the hollowness she had felt before now gone. Eloi had made her proud —the fact that she could already perform a reconnection showed that her strength and power would be immense. But

Aine couldn't think about that now. She took a deep breath and faced the pack that hadn't seen her in a month.

"Now that you are all aware of Rolan's deception, it is time to decide how we want to move forward. If any disagree with my leadership and methods, then speak up now." Aine's voice was firm as she stood still and looked out over her people. She noticed some of the younger warriors were missing, ones who didn't feel loyal when she extended her power.

"I do not want to force anyone to follow me. I've always done what I thought was for the best, what my parents taught me. I've realized recently that keeping us isolated from the rest of the world may not have been the best path. But trying to enslave humans is wrong. I feel we need to try and integrate with humans more, learn the new technologies and try to modernize our homes."

Aine looked out at the blank faces. She could feel the fear radiate off many of them. But they had only known one way.

"We should rule the humans, not join with them. You're a disgrace and have no right to lead this pack." Rolan's voice echoed around the Temple entrance; the crowd parted as he strode toward her.

There was no sign of the wound on his side from Eloi. Aine turned to look at her not-so-little girl; Eloi stood straight and stared her father down during his approach.

"And you do?" Aine clenched her fists and stood her ground. "My family has led and cared for this pack for generations. What right do you claim? My family took you in, this pack helped you thrive only for you to betray us all. Tell me, Rolan, who is your master? Who sent you to infiltrate us? You are too weak to be a true leader. And Eloi was next in line here, to claim my role. You had to poison me in cowardice instead of challenging me, as is the shifter way."

There were collective gasps among the pack members; most started to talk amongst themselves. Aine could feel their shock reverberate through her. It was almost too much. A buzz started in her ear, and she could feel her fury feed her power. Pain shot through her skull, and she closed her eyes.

Lachlan's shout was her only warning as Rolan charged towards her. He was a great warrior, but she had trained with her grandfather's men. The movement of his hips signaled his first move as he raised his arm to strike her.

Muscle memory graced Aine's movements as she stepped sideways and used Rolan's own momentum against him. She felt strength surge through her as he landed on the ground, and Aine pounced on his back to pin him there.

"You are too weak to lead. Who is pulling your strings, Rolan? You might not even be aware of it." Aine spoke through clenched teeth, not loudly enough for the rest of the pack to hear. "You disgust me."

LACHLAN WATCHED Aine disable Rolan in one move. He had not been close enough to reach her, but she heard his mental shout. The connection between them was strange; he could sense what she felt as she felt it, and her rising rage was palpable. As she crouched over Rolan, his arm twisted behind him, dark smoke began to curl around Aine. She looked like she was on fire, but Lachlan could see no flames. The older man, Eyolf, stood frozen next to him; the hairs on his arm stood on end. The old man's eyes were wide as they watched her.

Lachlan caught movement from the corner of his eye and saw dark shapes form toward the west of the settlement. Rolan started to laugh under Aine as he felt their approach.

"My supporters approach—those loyal to me are here to tear your precious pack apart, *my mate*." The venom in Rolan's voice and the words themselves made Lachlan feel sick.

A presence on the other side of Sumter caused his gaze to search the tree line there. A flash of metal made his heart stop, and he looked into the eyes of his cousin Girvan. He caught his cousin's glance and shook his head as he stepped to Aine's side.

"Aine, there are shifters in the forest. Rolan probably called them in for support. You need to instruct your pack and...." Lachlan paused before he spoke in his mind. He hoped she would hear him.

I haven't told you, but my family is in the area. My father wants me back, I turned him down. But my cousin is here. Your shifters are in danger. Leave Rolan. You can deal with him later.

Aine's face had started to shift, and claws emerged from her hands.

Your pack needs you, Aine. Your daughter needs you. Don't lose yourself now.

Lachlan hoped he got through to her. Slowly, Aine let Rolan go, and instructed two of her warriors to throw him in the pit. Lachlan laughed at the dark look on Rolan's face.

Aine turned to face Lachlan, and he smiled at her. A loud crack broke the air as the sound of a gun echoed through Sumter, and all hell broke loose.

20

Aine groaned as she picked herself up off the floor. Nyko had shifted mid-air when he collided with her and now laid whining next to her. She could see blood seeping from a rifle wound in his flank, but it didn't look serious.

"Get everyone into the Temple!" Aine shouted, loud enough for more than Nyko to hear. She reached out and gave everyone a mental nudge. She needed the warriors to protect the pack. The noise and fear pouring off her pack almost paralyzed her, but she pushed through and tried to make sense of the scene that unfolded before her.

Rolan's shifters, which had approached from the west, were engaged with what looked like human hunters from the east of Sumter. Aine watched the hunters in horror as they moved with graceful, practiced movements. The shifters coming to support Rolan were in human form and clearly untrained; the hunters easily overpowered them. As Aine watched them, she didn't recognize any of the shifters Rolan had called for. They seemed feral and fought with a viciousness that sickened her, and no regard for their own lives. Rolan would have many casualties before the day was over.

Some of Rolan's supporters shifted, displaying the same dark magic as Mervan. They moved ahead, and aggressively defended the others. Aine watched as one of the younger hunters was taken down by a pair of wolves. She already played the repercussions of this attack through her head, and knew the fallout would be catastrophic for her pack. She had to keep them out of the fight to prevent retaliation from the hunters.

They were trapped between two sides of a war; this was why she had always tried to keep her pack hidden. Aine surged into the action. She quickly gathered as many of the old and the very young as she could and shepherded them toward the Temple. It wouldn't protect them for long, but it would create a bottleneck and become easier to defend. There were secret tunnels out the back that the older pack members could use to escape with the younglings. Through the pack connection, she instructed the warriors to protect the entrance, though she could feel their urge to join the fight.

Aine looked for Eloi but couldn't see her among the crowd; she searched for Lachlan, who had also disappeared. They were alive and unhurt as far as she could tell, but she had other responsibilities.

Aine put herself between her pack and the two sides as she watched them tear into each other. She was aware that they were Lachlan's family, and horror coursed through her. As she watched, one hunter changed direction away from Rolan's shifters toward the Temple, where the Aoibhan pack desperately tried to find safety. He had similar features to Lachlan, his face older and spread with a cruel grin. Aine realized she had seen this man in Lachlan's memories—and he tortured shifters for fun. Anger boiled inside her, and blackness started to creep in on the edge of her vision. She could feel smoke and shadow crackling over her skin.

"So you're the whore that corrupted him," the hunter said. "Not that there was much to corrupt. Our Lachlan was always weak. Never did have what it takes to be a hunter."

"He is not weak, Finn. It takes extreme strength to overcome an oppressive family." Aine moved forward and firmly placed herself between him and her pack.

Surprise shot across Finn's face when he heard his name.

"I've seen your torture methods, those of a bully who has no power. If a defenseless creature isn't tied down for you to cut, then you are useless."

Aine could feel her rage spiral and reveled in the power which coursed through her. A voice in her head told her to rein it in, but she ignored it. As Finn finally stood in front of her, he gave no warning before swinging an ax toward her head. Aine easily dodged and twisted toward him to land a punch to his exposed back. Finn bent over, winded from the blow to his kidney.

"You have some skill, it seems—less like the untrained mutts of Europe." Finn's grin was wicked as he drew a dagger and adjusted his stance to account for both weapons.

It took all Aine's skill to outmatch the large man and maintain enough contact with her pack to tell if they needed her help. A battle raged around them among Rolan's shifters and the hunters. Sweat stung her eyes, and her muscles started to ache as she met Finn blow for blow. Without a weapon, she would not beat him, and if she shifted, he would have the advantage. Her experience and dexterity would help her more in her human form—that was the way her grandfather had trained her. Aine's newly discovered power gave her a surge of energy, and her attack had renewed vigor.

Finn found it hard to keep up; the fatigue showed in his strained eyes. Aine put in a quick move to disarm his ax, which was flung to the side and left harmless. With labored breath, Finn stared at her, unable to believe he hadn't killed her yet. The glance over her shoulder was the only warning Aine had before the sound of a gun rent the air.

Aine's duck saved her from death, but she felt a pain in her shoulder, blood blossomed over her shirt. She felt the power surge inside her and desperately tried to hold on. Pain overwhelmed her control. Darkness exploded from her as she screamed out and flung the hunters backward. A sickening crack sounded, and she saw Finn flung against the Temple walls.

Lachlan watched, mouth open as his family of hunters poured into Sumter from the east. He hadn't seen his family for fifteen years, and now they were all before him. They quickly engaged Rolan's shifter supporters as they invaded from the west.

Aine had hit the floor with Nyko as a shot from his father fired in her direction. Lachlan glared at his family and immediately looked for Eloi. She had been standing next to him when the fight broke out. To his dismay, she was no longer by his side. Lachlan wildly looked for her; his heart had stopped, and it hurt to breathe. He would never forgive himself if anything happened to either of his girls. Meanwhile, Aine had directed her pack toward the cave entrance, where she had stood earlier.

A cry to his left made him turn to see Eloi being carried

by Rolan, away from the fight. Without thought, Lachlan moved; he slid under the strike of a shifter and grabbed a discarded dagger in one movement as he maneuvered back to his feet. A well-aimed throw would stop Rolan, but Lachlan didn't want to risk a sudden movement from his fleeing form that might cause it to hit Eloi.

Lachlan dodged another shifter as he sprinted after Aine's daughter. He gained on Rolan, who slowed and breathed hard. He would do everything in his power to protect her. Rolan glanced over his shoulder, eyes wide, when he saw the large Irishman in pursuit. Lachlan braced when Eloi was thrown at him. He easily caught her and slowly laid her on the ground.

"Go find your mother—she needs your help getting the others to safety."

Eloi blinked and shook her head as Lachlan pulled her to her feet. Bits of leaf and dirt clung to her hair, and she reminded him of Aine when she had first crashed into his life.

Lachlan smiled at the young girl and gripped her shoulder gently. "Need a second?"

"My head is fuzzy." Eloi shook it again and stumbled as she moved forwards. "I'll be alright."

Movement caught Lachlan's eye, and he gracefully stepped in front of Eloi as Rolan charged towards them. Eloi turned and ran towards the Temple as Lachlan turned to face her father. Rolan's eyes glowed, and his claws had started to extend. Lachlan surged forward to meet him and struck out as he and the wolf collided. Lachlan rolled to a standing position and turned to look at Rolan sprawled on the ground. There was no sign of the injury Eloi had told them about. Lachlan frowned as Rolan easily rose from the ground to growl at him.

"Filthy human, I can't wait until we enslave you all!"

"Humans will never be subdued, Rolan. There are too many of us, and I know extensively of the trained hunters. You and your small support group do not stand a chance."

Rolan laughed hard as Lachlan spoke. "This is not all of us. The Faction has been gathering for centuries. There are too many of us now to stop. The time of humans is over, and shifters will take their rightful place."

Lachlan blocked and dodged as Rolan struck out at him. The other man's moves were violent and uncontrolled. Lachlan hated to kill for no reason, but the safety of the pack in this area and the threat against humans was enough that he wouldn't feel any guilt. The warm hilt of the dagger in his hand and the ease at which he fell into his fighting moves centered Lachlan. He would enjoy this fight. He made his move, and Rolan could barely keep up with his unrelenting attack.

Lachlan flowed with power and lethal grace as he fought Rolan; in comparison, he could see Rolan tire and falter as the fight went on. Both men aimed to kill the other. Lachlan dodged a blow that would have taken his head off if his head had still been there. He ducked and moved in close to Rolan, which limited his enemy's advantage with his partial shift. Other than Aine, Lachlan had only ever seen a shifter complete a change. Never had he seen a shifter use a partial shift as an advantage in a fight.

Lachlan felt pain up his left side as Rolan sliced through his defense. Rolan's moves were desperate but effective. Lachlan sprang backward, away from another slicing claw; when Rolan overbalanced, Lachlan saw his chance. He swung himself around behind Rolan and took his head between his hands.

In an efficient, move, Rolan's neck cracked, and he fell to the floor.

Lachlan breathed heavily as he stood over Rolan's body, the wolf's lifeless eyes stared toward the sky and a dark shadow seeping into the ground as Rolan became fully human.

Lachlan felt the tension leave his body, and he looked up to assess the fight around him. Sorrow filled him when he saw the fallen hunters, whose only mistake was following his father. The hunter ranks had grown since Lachlan left; he didn't recognize many of the fallen. They were all young, mixed in among the bodies of Rolan's shifters. Both sides had taken heavy losses. Lachlan hoped Aine had managed to keep her pack out of it.

When Rolan fell, it broke his control over his supporters, and they started to flee. He saw hunters chase them down and execute them without mercy. He cringed as he watched a younger hunter slice across the throat of a shifter who had displayed no fighting skills.

Turning, he looked for Aine and Eloi. His heart stopped as he saw Aine standing between the Temple entrance and a group of men. Black smoke extended from her body and covered the entrance. Blood poured down her front, and she placed herself between Lachlan's father, who stood at the front of the group of hunters, and her pack. Fear lanced through him as he realized what she faced.

AINE COULD BARELY HOLD the power which surged and fought for control within her. Sweat ran down her back, and blood seeped out of the bullet wound as she kept the barrier in place behind her. She had never known such things were possible and had thrown up the shield out of pure instinct but was grateful her pack was safe. Finally, the fighting had died down, Rolan's supporters turned to flee, and the hunters gained the upper hand. Once the fight was over, they turned toward her pack. The group of hunters in front of her approached with caution, weapons drawn, looks of violence in their eyes. Angry over their fallen comrades. Aine faced a large man who could only be Lachlan's father.

"Leave this place, or I will be forced to take action. We did not fight you, that was another pack, and you have dealt with them. We had no part in this." Aine watched the blank face of the man before her. His cold eyes burned into her while he stalked toward her. Aine started to feel claustrophobic as the men encircled her and crept forward. They all saw the powerful blast from her and recovered quickly from any shock. She struck out with her power when one hunter got too close. They kept their distance then, but Aine wasn't sure how much longer she could hold back another surge.

"We will not leave until every shifter is dead! You kidnapped one son, and you've killed the other!"

Aine could feel the rage and sorrow radiate off the man. Her power always allowed her to feel her pack, but since her memory loss, she had been able to feel humans as well.

"I didn't kill your son, and Lachlan wasn't taken by my pack. There is more to this than you understand." Aine strained as the power rolled through her. It felt like she balanced on the edge of a knife. One push and her power would lash out—Aine worried that it would kill everyone around her.

She almost cried in relief when she felt Lachlan's presence coming up behind her. His rough hands gently gripped her shoulders, and she leaned back into him.

"I saw you throw him into that wall, and Lachlan was

taken by force by your pack members. I have a witness!" Liam's hand gestured towards Girvan, who stared between his uncle and Lachlan.

"We were both taken by a renegade shifter in this pack. The renegade and his followers have been dealt with. You aggressively attacked a superior pack that tried to defend without causing harm. I see a gunshot wound on Aine, the Pack Leader. Did you expect her to allow you to kill her and her pack? Do not expect to be spared when you start a fight against a stronger opponent." Liam's face reddened as Lachlan spoke, and Lachlan bent his head closer to Aine's.

"I don't know if I can hold it much longer," Aine whispered under her breath. "I didn't know what would happen when my anger took control...Lachlan, your brother...." She watched as Lachlan's gaze fell on the broken body of his older brother, Finn.

"Is he dead?" Lachlan's voice held no emotion. His face was blank, and his hands were steady on her shoulders.

"I don't know." Aine's eyes stung, but she refused to cry. "We need to get them to leave. I don't want to kill your family, Lachlan, but if it comes down to them or us...I will always choose my daughter and my pack." Her voice was tight with emotion, but she wouldn't show the group of hunters in front of her any weakness. She took a steadying breath.

"I nominate Lachlan O'Reilly to act as mediator on behalf of the Aoibhan pack," Aine spoke loudly and watched the confusion on the hunters' faces.

LACHLAN'S STOMACH jolted when Aine made her pronouncement. The weight of the task ahead pressed on him. But he could see the strain in Aine's face as she held onto a power he could never understand. Shadows poured from her and leaked toward the hunters.

First, Lachlan walked over to Finn. His brother hadn't moved during his exchange with Aine. He checked for a pulse and found it, weak and thready, but there.

"Finn is alive, select two warriors to retrieve him." Lachlan's voice was clear, and he held back any sign of emotion. His father would be proud. He was no longer the young man who cowered under his father's authority. Turning, he faced the man who had once controlled his life. Both men held blank expressions.

"Speak." Liam's voice was rough and deep.

"Aine is the most powerful shifter I have ever met. She has just gifted many of her warriors with the ability to shift outside of the moon's cycle. They are also a pack that has been trained as warriors and are proficient with protecting themselves. You do not see a woman protecting her pack here; you see a woman holding back an immense power. And a group of warriors that would annihilate you if she let down that barrier. If you push this, you will be destroyed. They will not be taken down as easily as the wild shifters you just defeated."

Lachlan wasn't bluffing. When Aine had connected with him, she had shown him the history of her people and their vigorous training. Rolan's moves had been wild and vicious, but he had still been well-trained in this pack.

The silence was deafening between the group of hunters and Aine after he spoke. A gust of wind ran through the area, and Liam shifted to face his warriors. Lachlan knew his father was in a difficult position; if he backed down now, it would be a sign of weakness. But if he pushed forward, his entire family could be destroyed.

The two warriors assigned to carry Finn had brought him over to Liam, who knelt and felt for a pulse. Once satisfied, he stood.

"No shifter should be allowed to live!" Liam roared, "They are a disgrace and unnatural. How can you stomach being around them?"

"How are they unnatural? If they have been born into the world, then they are part of it. I agree with our ancestors that shifters that kill innocents must be dealt with. But you have perverted our laws into hunting them into extinction for no reason!" Lachlan paused and gestured toward the Temple cave. "These shifters here held themselves back from the fight. They have not harmed humans. What is your justification for attacking them now?"

Liam's brow furrowed as he looked towards the cave. "It is only a matter of time until they start attacking humans."

"They have lived in secrecy for generations. Why would they attack humans now? No person is born evil. You've seen hunters who turned bloodthirsty and killed humans. We've had to hunt them too. It's not us versus them, Pa; why can't you see that? Not all shifters are evil. Most live in peace. Why are you focusing on this pack when there is another out there, intent on enslaving humanity? Focus on them!"

"They are part of that pack!" Liam argued.

"No, they were infiltrated by that pack; there's a difference. If we are to defeat the renegades, then we will need to fight alongside the wolves who oppose them." Lachlan watched the emotions on his father's face as he digested this information. Liam sighed before he spoke.

"We cannot fight with shifters, we must fight against them." Liam's voice was quiet as he considered his position. "You have given me much to think about. In return for allowing us to retrieve my son, we will leave, but you must accompany us, Lachlan. You're needed in this family, a man of your skills is required in the coming war." Liam frowned when Lachlan didn't answer.

"Son?" Liam walked towards Lachlan, who considered taking a step back but stood his ground. He would not be intimidated by Liam O'Reilly.

"If what you say is true and there is another group that seeks to enslave humans, we need to squash this Faction before they gain a footing in our war. We need you. I've let you be all this time, but we don't have fighters of your caliber or men with your strength of character." Liam looked uncomfortable as he continued. As he drew close, Liam put a hand on his son's shoulder, and Lachlan had to control his flinch.

"We need you."

"Did you ever consider that your ruthless actions have driven survivors into the Faction?" Lachlan scoffed. Of course, his father knew. Lachlan couldn't feel the normal manipulation behind his father's words. But from what he had seen, what his father said was true. There was an uprising, and there would be a war. He would need the hunters as allies in the future.

"I will be in touch. I will only work with you if you consider working with shifters. I know there are other hunters open to it." Lachlan turned from his family as Liam opened his mouth to speak again, then he shut it and looked toward the hunters.

Lachlan walked towards Aine. She stood tall and rigid with black shadow and smoke curled around her. Lachlan turned to stand beside her and faced down his family. His father didn't speak again, as the hunters gathered their injured and dead. The anger had drained from them, and many looked confused by the words Lachlan had spoken.

Those who had been killed by Rolan's supporters would be mourned, and he hoped his father wouldn't hold it against the Aoibhan. Aine had held them back in the cave to protect both sides and prevent more bloodshed. He loved her more at that moment; it would have been easy for her to let go of her control and destroy anyone who was a threat.

Once the hunters left, Lachlan turned to embrace Aine. He could feel her tremble in his arms and kissed her forehead. He could smell salt and blood on her skin.

"You need to let go, Aine, and let them out of the cave. Everyone is safe." Lachlan stroked her hair, and she shook less. The blackness which surrounded them slowly drew itself back into her. Lachlan watched the strain on her face and looked on in fascination as the black smoke melted away and the pack stared out from the Temple entrance. A line of warriors stood ready if they were needed.

"It's over." Despite the weariness he felt from her, Aine's voice was strong and clear. "Let's get everyone in their homes. Warriors, organize a watch in case we have any more unwelcome visitors. We will meet tomorrow."

Eloi ran from the cave and hurled her arms around her mother. Aine gripped her daughter tightly as the pack spread out around them.

21

———

A ine spent the next morning with her pack. She walked among them, talking to all. She learned how each member felt and helped any she could to repair the village and return their home to what it had been.

Eyolf seemed like a different man to Aine now that he could shift again, he appeared a decade younger. She approached her old mentor and smiled at him. Eyolf grinned in return and pulled her in for a bear hug. They stood outside his small house. Ivy and moss grew along the walls and roof, giving it a hidden and abandoned look—it had always felt homey to Aine.

"I know you prefer to be proper as Pack Leader, but I've missed you, youngling."

"I'm not so young anymore." Aine pulled back. "Now quit stalling, I know you have information for me, and I think it is time I hear it."

Eyolf sighed wearily and opened the door. His home was cozy with little furniture but paintings on every wall. His mate, Dawn, had loved to paint, but it had been hard for them to come by materials. Aine's mother had always made sure when she sent out her scouts to the human world for supplies that they had always brought something back for Dawn.

Aine took a seat at the table in the kitchen and suddenly wished Lachlan were there. Eyolf was uneasy around the hunter, and Aine didn't blame him after they'd avoided humans for generations. So Lachlan had stayed with Eloi, who seemed to have formed an attachment to him. Aine hoped they bonded and that Eloi wasn't too traumatized by Rolan's actions. She sighed as she thought about her ex-mate.

In the eyes of her pack, their mate bond had been severed with his death. Rolan's body had been left by his supporters. Aine swallowed tightly. Rolan had betrayed her in the end, but she mourned the boy she had fallen in love with. He must have been good once, or she was a fool who had been manipulated from the start. Nevertheless, she couldn't bear to not bury him and would have a small ceremony. It was more than he deserved, but it felt right.

Aine shook her head to clear it and looked at Eyolf, who had taken the seat across from her. She could see sympathy in his eyes and quickly looked away. It was better than pity, but she didn't want to see either right now.

"Let's get back to what my mother told you," she said.

Eyolf nodded and took her hand. He squeezed once before he began.

"You know you're from a long line of Royal shifters and about the prophecy. You are a descendant of the original Aoibhan family. Our pack is mostly made up of those adopted by your bloodline, but not descendants. This is because your bloodline finds it hard to breed and rarely has more than one offspring."

Aine's heart squeezed as she remembered the difficulties her mother had while pregnant with her younger brother. Aine had been told that her family line could only have one offspring. It came as a surprise when her mother fell pregnant again, but that was probably why her mother hadn't survived. Pain ripped through her as she realized her mother must have known it was unlikely either of them would live.

"The original Aoibhan had the ability to shift at will. But what you don't know is that they had unheard-of mental powers, allowing them to communicate more easily with their pack. Other packs do not communicate as we do, Aine. Our pack is rare."

Eyolf stood from his chair and walked over to a cupboard in the kitchen. He took out an ornate leather book; it looked old and had beautiful detail on the cover.

"Everything you need to know is in here. What your mother never told you and what your bloodline kept secret is that you have a second side to your power, a side you have now discovered."

"The darkness." Aine pulled the book toward her and ran her fingers over the embossment on the cover. "It's like a storm inside me. It takes effort to keep it under control and stop it from gushing out."

"Your mother didn't tell me of such power. The way she described it,...it's not supposed to be as strong as yours unless a talisman is used to bring it forth."

"A talisman?" Aine tilted her head and thought back. Her chest tightened. "Describe it to me."

"What? A talisman? There is a drawing in the book." Eyolf took the book back and leafed through it. Finally, he stopped toward the center and passed it back to Aine.

She gasped, hand over her mouth. On the page in front

of her was a drawing depicting Lachlan's medallion. Aine quickly read the passage, and her stomach sank.

"According to this, the talismans were used to bring forth potential and power in the original shifter families. The power was then used to protect shifters, but when one family used the power to try and seize control of the founding families, the others fought together. This destroyed many of the families and reduced numbers to near extinction." Aine's shoulders sagged as she read on.

"The talisman places those touched by it into a dream state for up to several days. Once awake, the shifter will begin to show immense power and abilities. This will allow them to reach their full potential. Most won't survive the transition, but the chosen few will need to be trained by the matriarch of the family and the knowledge passed down through each generation. It is imperative the shifter practices good control.' Eyolf..." Aine paused. "This is Lachlan's medallion."

Eyolf frowned at her. "What do you mean?"

"Lachlan has this medallion." Aine sounded wary to her own ears. "When Eloi escaped, and I felt her attacked by Rolan, I still didn't really remember anything. I knew Eloi was important to me, and I started to lose control. It's the first time I shifted in front of Lachlan."

Eyolf watched with no emotions on his face. Aine could feel anger come from him when he realized where she was going with this. His hands were in his lap, and he didn't fidget. Aine let the silence stretch, and Eyolf waited patiently.

"I don't remember much, but Lachlan told me he begged me to calm down. I didn't know he knew anything about shifters, but I was so panicked about Eloi. I had felt like part of me was missing but didn't remember I had a daughter. I can't believe I couldn't remember her." Aine put her head in her hands and took a deep, shaky breath. Tears threatened to fall, and her chest felt tight. She felt Eyolf's hand on her shoulder as he shifted closer.

"Aine, it's a miracle you ever got your memory back. The Severance process is designed to give a pack member a fresh start. There is no intention of recovery. The fact that you were still connected to Eloi and could see her dreams and memories just shows how much you love her. Don't feel guilty for something out of your control."

Aine looked up at her old mentor with a weak smile. "Thanks, but I just can't help it. I know logically I had no control over what happened to me, but I'll still blame myself. I could have hurt Lachlan, too, and he had only ever helped me. I guess he could handle himself, though."

Eyolf scowled, and Aine laughed at the dark look in his eyes. "I'm guessing you don't approve?"

"He is a hunter, Aine, a European one. They have a reputation for being vicious and cruel, and now you mention a medallion? What does that have to do with the dark power?"

Aine sighed. "When I lost control, Lachlan tried to pin me down. I've seen scratches on his arms, but in my fully shifted form, I don't think he would have been able to hold me back. Instead, he touched me with his medallion." She paused again, her fingers skimmed her forehead where Lachlan had placed the medallion. She watched as Eyolf processed what she had said, then she pointed at the talisman in the book.

"It's identical. I think Lachlan has accidentally 'released my potential,' according to this book."

Eyolf frowned, then his eyes widened. "Oh, dear."

Aine laughed at the understatement, then paused.

"What will happen if I have no training?" Ice gripped her heart. Would she have to leave her pack to keep them safe?

"I don't know, but we will work this out together." Eyolf smiled. "You are the strongest and most stubborn shifter I have ever met. If anyone can master this and control it, it's you."

Aine returned his smile, some of the tightness in her chest loosening, and she thought about everyone she had to support her. But she couldn't continue to endanger them. When she had walked amongst her pack earlier that day, she felt their relief that she hadn't abandoned them. Some were cautious of her, and she could feel pain from those that lost family to Rolan and his cause.

"Eyolf, I'm going to have to leave for a while, I don't want to implode and harm my pack if I can't learn to control this. You will lead the pack while I learn to control this darkness. Lachlan and I will return to his house. I don't think I can be the leader this pack needs—I let Rolan fool me, and it nearly tore this pack apart."

Eyolf stammered a denial, but Aine held up her hand.

"No objections. This pack deserves better, and I will just end up making them a target. With Rolan gone, the danger will pass. Especially if we aren't here. If anyone realizes that Eloi could have the same power as me, they will go after her as well. I need to protect her, keep her away from all this for a while." Aine rose from her chair; the wood creaked in protest at the movement, and Eyolf stared at the ground.

"I think you're making a mistake, Aine," he said. "They need your protection, now more than ever. You will be stronger around your own kind. The book will only help so far. I have a theory that the original families formed packs with other shifters to help stabilize their power. You will need your pack to share the burden."

"How can they trust me again after this? I can feel that everyone is loyal to me again, but I can also feel mistrust. I don't think…" Aine swallowed, her throat tight, "I don't think I'm worthy of their trust, and I don't blame them. The pack will never accept Lachlan, even if I am connected to him now."

Eyolf's face flashed briefly with surprise before he controlled his features. He sighed and stood to hug her.

"I will miss you, youngling. But please don't stay away too long. Will you stay with the hunter?"

"Yes. I know you don't like him, but I love him. Eyolf, I can connect with him—I didn't think that was possible with humans. I need to know what we have, and I can't do that here. You've seen how he is with Eloi. They trust each other. My family must come first."

Aine turned to leave. She could feel the sadness coming from Eyolf and hoped he would understand. She knew she was being selfish, but she needed to prioritize Eloi after all that had happened.

22

Lachlan watched Eloi as she went through another drill. He had spent the morning with her and shown her some of his fight drills. They taught muscle memory and helped with dexterity and strength. The girl was a fast learner; she picked up his techniques and took criticism well. Lachlan wondered whether he could encourage other younglings to join in.

He had adopted the name Aine used for the children and smiled as he thought of her and their morning recovery. He coughed and shifted to a more comfortable position, hoping the evidence of what he'd been thinking about wasn't too noticeable.

The younglings watched from across the meeting area clearing. They had put the pit between themselves and the scary hunter, but he could see they were curious. He had tried to encourage some to join in, but an older shifter woman had yelled at them and told them to get back to their lessons. Eloi ignored her and said she was too big for lessons now.

Lachlan watched in fascination as the older shifter and

Eloi stared at each other. He could feel the tension between them and the hairs on his arms lifted; he could almost feel static in the air during the exchange. Yet, surprisingly, the older woman backed down, lowered her gaze, and nodded once meekly before she left Eloi with Lachlan.

Since the fight yesterday, the pack had kept their distance. Lachlan didn't blame them. He came from a long line of hunters who had massacred shifters nearly to extinction; he was only surprised they hadn't tried to throw him down the pit to rot.

Eloi finished her sequence and looked to him eagerly. Her smile was so like her mother's. His heart ached at the thought that he had been alone a few weeks ago and now had two incredible women in his life.

"Brilliant, you've improved with each circuit. I'll make a warrior of you yet!" Lachlan couldn't help the pride he felt as Eloi started the sequence again. He felt Aine approaching; since she had connected with him while they were captured, he could sense her presence and emotions. It was a weird feeling, one which would take a while to get used to.

"I wish she would listen to me like that." Aine laughed as she came near. When they weren't alone, she kept her distance. Lachlan imagined it was difficult for her as Pack Leader to be objective. He would have to be content just being close to her.

"Give it time, the novelty will wear off, and she will start ignoring me too." Lachlan could feel Aine's hesitation and uncertainty as he spoke.

"You want us to stay in your life then?"

Lachlan's head snapped to Aine.

"Of course. If you can accept what I am, then I want to help you. Being by your side feels right." Lachlan longed to touch her but could feel the eyes of the younglings burning into the back of his head.

Aine's sigh and small smile eased his tight chest. "I'm glad. I need to address the pack, but after that, we can go."

"Go?" Lachlan turned to face her. She stared off into the distance, and her face betrayed no emotion.

"I can't stay here, Lachlan, with this darkness in me. It's dangerous. I can barely control it, and I need somewhere to do that away from here. I won't endanger the town. We can go to the lake, and I can practice there. I should really take Eloi and do this alone, but I'm too selfish. I need your strength." Aine still wouldn't look at him, and he could feel a faint sense of unease in their bond.

He slowly took Aine's hand and turned her to face him. "We are in this together," he said. "Nothing will change that. I won't abandon you." Lachlan smiled as his hand reached to brush his thumb across the single tear that rolled down her cheek. He looked up to see Eyolf at the edge of the area; the old man looked thoughtful.

He took a step back from Aine, not wanting to make any of the pack uncomfortable. They still stood firm on the "no relationships with humans" boundary.

Eyolf strode toward them both, his brow scrunched and his mouth tight. "I need to speak with both of you, and you, Eloi. This involves you too." He quickly turned to walk out of the meeting area. Aine's mouth twitched with amusement as Eloi stopped the sequence she had been working on.

"Already giving out orders," Aine chuckled. She took Eloi's hand briefly before the girl let it go and ran after Eyolf. "Teenagers," her mother huffed.

Lachlan smiled and took the hand Eloi had rejected. They turned toward the direction Eloi and Eyolf had gone and walked after them. "Let's find out what he wants."

EYOLF FIDGETED as he waited for Aine and Lachlan to approach. He had led them to a rough clearing outside the village. The sun attempted to penetrate the thick leaves and dappled the floor in golden spots.

Aine had never seen Eyolf look so nervous. "More information you've kept from me then?" She swallowed her disappointment. She had thought the old shifter was done keeping secrets.

"I had to be sure." Eyolf swallowed hard and held Eloi close to his side. "The original families didn't mate with other wolves. Instead, to increase their power and the chance of successfully bearing children, they only mated their true mates. In most cases, their true mates were humans."

Aine gasped and held her hand to her chest. Lachlan shifted but didn't speak.

"They mated humans?"

"For some reason, your bloodline has always struggled with fertility. As a result, it is very rare to bear more than one child. This you know."

Aine thought of her mother again. Her mother knew the chances of her survival were slim but refused to terminate the pregnancy. She always said there was still a chance they would both survive, that their ancestors had more than one child. She felt the pain creep into her as she thought of Arwen. Aine had long ago accepted that Eloi would be her only child.

"I believe that it was a way for nature to balance the power the original families had. If procreation had been easy, then the world would be overrun with powerful shifters. So when you told me you could connect with Lachlan, I had to check to be sure. He is your true mate, Aine. It's why you've been drawn together so easily and why you can connect. In time, he will be able to connect with the pack. I know that true mates are unheard of in this day and age, and I find it hilarious that I have to tell you what you are to each other." Eyolf smiled.

Aine's head swam. Lachlan was meant to be hers, and she was meant to be his. Looking back, she felt the pull and recognition on the day they first met. But she hadn't remembered what she was until later. She might have recognized the signs if she had her memory. She shook her head and beamed at Lachlan. They could have children together. She looked at Eloi, who grinned at her.

"I think that means you can keep him," Eloi laughed, tears running down her face.

"We still have to leave for a while." Aine felt cold as she spoke. "This doesn't change that I need to be able to control my power. Eloi, this will also be something you have to fight in the future as well." She wouldn't tell Eloi about the medallion until she was ready. At least she would have the choice not to take on the power in the future.

Eyolf frowned and sighed. "I thought you might say that, but now at least, I'm not keeping anything from you." He walked away as she pulled Eloi and then Lachlan into a hug.

Aine could feel the connection to the two most important people in her life, and she held onto it with everything she had. She would overcome the pull of the darkness. She had to.

AINE AND ELOI followed Lachlan into his house. She had told the pack that she had to leave, to train herself. But that she would be back, despite their unease she felt it was the right thing to do. Aine looked around the place that had become her home with Lachlan. The furniture in the lounge had seen better days. Aine heard Lachlan sigh with relief as he strode through to the kitchen. Eloi stepped closer to her and wrapped her arms around her mother's waist. Aine kissed the girl's forehead and held her close as they looked at the destruction from when Rolan searched the house.

"It won't take long to tidy up," Eloi said. "I'll go and grab a garbage bag."

Aine smiled at her daughter. She felt guilty that she had taken her from the only home she'd ever known, but it felt right to stay separate from the pack. If they needed her, they could come and find her, but it would be safer for everyone if she got a handle on the darkness at a distance. She could still feel the power rumble through her, occasionally trying to overwhelm her and boil over.

Eloi watched Aine as they started to put the lounge back together. Aine worried about her daughter; she had taken Rolan's death well and seemed to have attached herself to Lachlan, but she wasn't herself. More reserved and quiet than she used to be. She didn't blame her; the girl had been through a lot over the last month.

"Knock, knock!" Phil rapped on the open front door to the house. Lachlan had called him when they'd got back and asked Phil to bring over some food from the diner. As promised, Aine could smell the delectable burgers in the large bag Phil carried. The large man grinned at her. "I have to say, it's great to see ya all in one piece."

"Glad we are in one piece!" Lachlan's deep voice came from the kitchen before he strolled through to the hallway. He gripped Phil's arm, pulling the big man into a hug. "Thanks for having my back."

Phil looked bashful and held out the bag for Aine to take while he looked at his feet. "S'nothin'," he mumbled.

"Join us." Lachlan pulled Phil into the kitchen, where they all crowded around the small table. Aine didn't mind; it felt comfortable and homey. It was nice to relax and enjoy the moment. She bumped Eloi's side when she saw her pull her burger apart but not eat it.

"You need anything?" Aine whispered while Lachlan laughed at Phil's jokes.

"No," Eloi responded quietly. "I just can't help feel something is wrong. Like there's darkness approaching. This isn't over."

"Eloi." Aine paused. She put her hand on her daughter's arm. "If you need to talk about Rolan, then talk, it doesn't have to be me. Just don't keep anything bottled up inside; it doesn't help. You don't always have to be strong. It's okay to be overwhelmed."

Eloi smiled weakly. "I guess I'm just tired." She picked up her burger. "Can I take this downstairs? I can always finish it later."

Lachlan looked up as Eloi stood. "Of course you can. Need anything else? We should head into town tomorrow and grab you a few things." He smiled at her. "If you're both going to live here, then we need to deck your room out."

"I'll have to start making and selling a lot more furniture," Aine laughed. "How am I going to pay for all this? I can't use any of our funds; the pack will need it." She stood to take Eloi downstairs. The girl was being quiet, and she didn't want to leave her alone.

"I'm okay, Mom, honestly. I'm just tired."

"Well, I'm going to tuck you in. I know you're too old for it, but you'll always be my baby."

Eloi laughed, and Aine relaxed a little. She stroked Eloi's hair as the girl laid down on the bed; Aine pulled the sheets up over her. Once Eloi had drifted to sleep, Aine joined Phil and Lachlan in the kitchen. She looked at the two men who had helped her when she couldn't remember who she was.

"Thank you, both of you. I don't know where I'd be if you hadn't found me, Phil." Aine smiled at Lachlan. "I'm lucky to have you in my life." She took a seat and was about to speak again when she snapped her mouth shut. She could sense someone approach the house.

Lachlan tensed when Aine did, coiled and ready for action. She put her hand on his arm and concentrated. The presence was familiar and friendly; Aine was just surprised the pack had come to find her. It hadn't even been a day.

Nyko had his hand raised to knock on the door when she opened it. Aine's smile was amused as he looked confused; she stood back and gestured to the kitchen.

Nyko bowed his head before he stared around the house in wonder. The last time he was there, he had been too busy fighting. She thought about how fascinating it must be to look at the house and the different objects compared to their little town. It made her more determined to modernize once she had her dark magic under control.

Aine walked across the room to sit next to Lachlan; Nyko stood behind her, hands behind his back. He glanced towards Phil, who swallowed nervously as he watched the young shifter.

Lachlan lightly punched Phil on the arm and laughed. "He won't bite you."

Phil's head snapped towards Lachlan and back to Nyko. He looked horrified. Aine put a hand over her mouth to hide her laugh without success, and Nyko looked uncomfortable at the exchange but waited for Aine to let him know he could speak.

"I'm not Pack Leader right now, Nyko," she finally said. "You are a friend to us, and I trust you."

Nyko's shoulders sagged as he relaxed. "I'm sorry to bother you...I know you wanted to put some distance between the pack and Eloi. But Eyolf wanted you to know. Rolan's grave has been dug up, and his body is gone."

Aine felt the blood drain from her face and her cheeks tingled. Lachlan growled and banged the table, making Phil and Nyko jump.

"Fuck." Lachlan stood and started to pace. "I guess you think his supporters took him. What would they want with his body?"

"We don't know, but the pack is uneasy. Some have reported seeing Rolan alive. Eyolf wants you to reconsider leaving. He needs you."

"I can't leave you undefended." Aine was torn between the safety of her child and her responsibilities. She stood and walked over to the window, her back to everyone in the room. "I don't want to leave you, Lachlan, but the pack needs me. I think Eloi should stay with you."

"Aine, whatever we do—we do it together. I won't abandon you, or Eloi, or your pack."

"But the pack won't accept you."

"Give them time. What if we are mated? Eyolf said we are true mates. If we were mated in their eyes, then they may find it easier. We could go into town in the morning and get married. Or elope? Or perform any ceremony your pack will accept. You can't get rid of me that easy."

Aine's eyes stung, but she blinked away her tears. Lachlan was willing to completely commit to her and be part of the pack.

"You would have to leave." Her voice was quiet as she watched Lachlan's face.

"I can still make my pieces and bring my woodwork back here. I don't go into town that often anymore anyway. Anyone who wants an order can leave it with Phil." Lachlan looked at his friend, who had a resigned look on his face. "Don't worry, big guy, you won't get rid of me that easily."

Aine hugged Lachlan and looked up into his face. "I feel like I've known you all my life. I don't know what I'd do without you." She lightly kissed his lips.

LACHLAN STOOD before Eyolf at the head of the pack. Initially, they had been uneasy with the idea of living with a human among them. Eyolf held a meeting and explained the history behind Aine's bloodline. He revealed her power and that the original families mixed with humans. It took some time, but after working with the warriors for the past month, he earned their respect. For Aine, he would put in the effort.

"Nervous?" Eyolf wore a white tunic and white linen pants. Lachlan was now close with the old shifter. He explained his family history and helped with defense plans in case the hunters decided to attack again. He didn't expect his father would stay away for long.

"Nope," Lachlan lied. His fingers twitched, and he felt like he could run ten miles.

Eyolf laughed richly at the expression on Lachlan's face. Eloi appeared at the other side of the pack, and the crowd parted. She was wearing a yellow knee-length dress, her hair decorated with local flowers. Lachlan had never seen her so clean. Eloi was very much like a tomboy and loved to be out and about in the woods. Aine worried that she would endanger herself, but Lachlan tried to let her enjoy her independence. In a few years, he could imagine she would break a few hearts. Slowly the girl walked toward him, a huge grin on her face.

"Wait until you see her." Eloi winked as she gracefully walked off and stood to the side.

Lachlan took a deep breath and looked to where Eloi had entered the clearing. His heart stopped in his chest, and his stomach tightened. Aine entered on Nyko's arm; she had initially asked Eyolf, but he needed to perform the ceremony.

She looked breathtaking. Her hair was plaited into an elaborate hairstyle that swept up and kept her hair off her shoulders. White flowers were intricately woven into plaits. She wore a simple one-shoulder white gown, which looked inspired by Greek mythology. A golden armband glowed in the afternoon sun on her other arm. The smile on her face completed the stunning ensemble.

"I've never seen her look so happy," Eyolf whispered, his voice cracked as he spoke.

Aine walked towards Lachlan, and he felt like he was the luckiest man alive. His mouth was open, and he found it hard to swallow. Nyko kissed her on the cheek before he left to stand behind Eloi.

"Hi," Aine whispered once she stood before him.

"Hi." Lachlan's voice came out higher than usual, and he coughed to clear his throat. Aine giggled.

The ceremony was simple. Eyolf bound their hands, and they exchanged promises to support each other as equals. Lachlan would now become the first human Pack Leader in generations. The pack hadn't known about true mates, but once Eyolf explained the history and allowed the records to be unsealed they came around. As Aine's true mate, he would have the same authority as her. In the pack's eyes, he would be one of them.

"You shall from this point forward be truly mated and jointly responsible for the safety of the Aoibhan pack," Eyolf spoke.

Lachlan grinned. "Is this the part where I get to kiss the bride?"

Eyolf looked slightly confused. "Kiss her if you want but make it quick. I'm hungry."

Lachlan laughed and kissed Aine deeply. "Just wait till we are alone later," he whispered in her ear. She shivered, and he winked before they walked towards their pack to celebrate.

EPILOGUE

T he air felt damp, and Rolan could smell dirt and moss tickling his nose as he slowly came back to consciousness. His neck hurt as if he'd been lying awkwardly as he slept. His eyes opened, and he took in the cold, uninviting cave. The bed he was on was a cheap single bed but better than the floor. Rolan could feel the lumpy mattress beneath him; no wonder he had a pain shooting down his spine.

Slowly, he sat up, and dizziness caused a roll of nausea to spread through him. He closed his eyes again and took a deep breath. The air felt stale, and he couldn't smell any others nearby, but someone had been in here in the last hour.

The walls were rough, and Rolan felt like he was underground. It was a natural cave system that he didn't recognize. He opened his eyes slowly this time. The nausea wasn't gone but had gotten better. His bare feet scraped the frigid stone floor, and he used the bed for support as he tried to stand. A noise near the entrance of the area caught Rolan's attention.

"Ah, you're awake." Vernon, an old shifter with a sour

demeanor, sneered at him. "I wasn't sure we could bring you back with your injuries, but obviously, we got to you in time."

Rolan growled and shuddered as he remembered an ear-splitting crack that had recently reverberated through his head. He moved his neck from side to side, and the dull ache eased with each movement. An image of the Irish hunter formed in his head. The fight had been brutal, and he had underestimated the hunter's skill. He would not make that mistake again.

"Was I dead?" Rolan jolted as he realized what must have happened. He had heard of wolves coming back from the brink using dark magic, but to have this happen to him? Nausea returned, and he struggled not to collapse, vomiting on the floor.

"My, my. That isn't the first time I've had that reaction. Yes, Rolan, your failure caused your death." Vernon sneered again.

He probably doesn't have another expression, Rolan thought as he swayed.

"You need to rest and regain your strength. He wants to see you."

Rolan groaned. It would be better to get this over with. "Lead the way; I can see him now."

"You may want to change." Vernon nodded his head towards a clean set of clothes on the end of the bed. Mercifully, the vomit had missed.

Rolan changed quickly, or as quickly as he could. He stumbled a couple of times, with no help from Vernon, who dispassionately watched him struggle.

Rolan leaned heavily on the cave wall, the damp cold a shock to his skin before he followed Vernon out of the cave. The system they were in was a labyrinth used by the

Faction. They had been using hidden caves for centuries to hide their numbers and organize their rebellion against the humans. Rolan did not recognize this system; after several turns, his head started to throb, and he struggled to remember the way back to the room.

The latest tunnel they walked down suddenly opened into a large cavern. Several groups of shifters worked on various tasks. The groups mostly kept to themselves; they prepared food or worked on weapons toward the edges. At the far end, a large fire had been built for a kiln and heat. There was a natural chimney, and light flooded through an opening in the roof of the cave.

Rolan took another deep breath of fresh air as he stumbled across the cavern. He fell to his knees before what looked like a throne. The tall figure who leaned on one arm chuckled as his head touched the cave floor. Rolan looked up into the face of his mentor, the shifter who molded him from a young age to follow his ideals. Rolan had been entirely devoted to their cause since childhood.

"Master, I..." Rolan trailed off as he saw the sharp look in his mentor's eyes. There would be no excuses.

"I told you not to underestimate her, Rolan. The plan was never to kill Aine." The voice was deep, rich, and disapproving. "You only succeeded in weakening us. I nearly didn't bring you back, but you will be needed." As his mentor stood to approach him, Rolan flinched and looked back at the cave floor.

"I saw an opportunity to take the power that should have been mine, as it should have been yours. The hunter was an unexpected misfortune." Rolan ground his teeth as he thought of the hunter. He would not best him next time.

"What's done is done. We cannot change what has happened, but the hunter's intentions have been revealed.

We now know they are here and that they are aware of our activities. They no longer have the element of surprise."

"Whatever you need, master, it will be done."

"Good."

Rolan watched as the dark-haired shifter with deep green eyes turned to walk toward the kiln. "And Rolan, do not attempt to kill my daughter again. I have need of her."

Solus's eyes burned amber as he stared at Rolan until his gaze dropped to the floor.

CLAN WHELAN PUBLISHING (CWP)

CWP's mission is to help readers discover new or less known paranormal romance (PNR) and paranormal women's fiction (PWF) authors and books while assisting authors with the business side of getting their stories into the world.

If you are interested in supporting CWP's mission, join our Facebook reader group called Clan Whelan Publishing, become a part of our Street team. You can also sign up to CWP newsletter and, follow us on TikTok and Instagram.

ABOUT LIZ CAIN

Liz Cain started writing because she wanted to help a friend finish a story which deserved to be told. With Anne K. Whelan, The Royal Pack Trilogy came to life.

When she is not writing she is usually reading or playing video games with her friends online. She loves visiting the Lake District with her better half, wandering around Ambleside or Windemere.

<u>Liz Cain Books</u>

The Royal Pack
  Reborn
  Hunter

ABOUT ANNE K. WHELAN

Anne K. Whelan is a paranormal romance author. She loves creating and sharing stories. Anne knows life is all about stories: they impact lives and shape the world.

When she is not thinking or working a story, Anne hangs with Harry, Mal, Spiderman and Minnie Mouse. "Odd human being" they say "eats apples with salt and loves dried yogurt balls." Her amazing husband and awesome three little ones couldn't agree more.

Anne K. Whelan Books

The One Goddess
Katarina The One Goddess Book 1
Katarina The One Goddess Book 2
Katarina The One Goddess Book 3
Katarina The One Goddess Book 4

The Royal Pack
Reborn
Hunter

KATARINA - THE ONE GODDESS: CHAPTER 1

"Can you believe this is happening?"

Rose turned to face me as she smoothed her red dress down over her curvy hips. Her smile was wide, and her deep blue eyes were alight with joy. I couldn't help smiling, too, although I knew my grin didn't quite reach my eyes.

How could it? It might have been our graduation day, but this? This was very much *Rose's* day.

I glanced around her bedroom. I'd been in here a million times before, but I still felt as out of place as ever. The entire house was decorated with regal-looking furniture, all golds and deep reds, with paintings of family members hanging on the walls throughout. The first time I ever came here, I thought it looked more like a museum than a house. Rose's room was the only one that held a little bit of homey comfort, thanks to the big fluffy pillows on her four-poster bed, and soft purple walls with photos of friends tacked to them, with posters of her favorite bands in between.

I looked at Rose. She was out of my league as a friend. She and her family were Supes, middle-class humans—

although I always thought they genuinely believed they were Gods with the way they looked and acted. All airs and graces, and designer clothes. I still wasn't sure why Rose chose me to be her best friend out of everyone on the planet. I was an Underling, the lowest class of citizen on Cillion and the galaxy, for that matter.

For the most part, different classes stuck to their own, but Rose and I had been besties since we met at the beach when we were twelve years old. She had taken pity on me since I sat alone, drawing circles in the sand. The beach had always been my favorite place to go when I needed to think or needed time away from the tiny, claustrophobic house where I grew up. I didn't have siblings, and I wasn't that close to anyone from school. So, I'd spent a lot of my time on the beach. Rose had invited me to join her friends for a game of volleyball one day. From then on, we spent as much time together as we could. Despite our class differences, our friendship had always been solid enough.

"Kat? Hello?"

Rose's hand waved in front of my face, and I blinked a couple of times to bring myself back to the moment. *Graduation. Party. Right.* I shook my head. "Sorry. What did you say?"

She rolled her eyes. "I said, can you believe this is happening? That we've graduated from college and are about to start the next chapter of our lives?"

I couldn't. Although, her next chapter was about to be a whole hell of a lot more interesting than mine.

"I know." I forced another smile. "We're real grown-ups now."

Rose giggled, then she reached over to fix the brown curls that hung around my face, a slightly critical look in her eye as she played with my locks. She had taken great joy in doing my hair and makeup for the party that was already in full swing. The sound of dance music drifted up the stairs, but Rose informed me—as she always did—that we were supposed to be "fashionably late."

To be fair to her, she had done an excellent job on me. I almost looked as good as she did. Aside from the curly hair, she had enhanced my brown eyes with eyeliner and mascara. Rose somehow made my lips look fuller, too. I wasn't completely useless with makeup, but I was more your "basics" kind of girl. I left the complicated stuff to her, the same with our fashion sense. I could only afford casual clothes like jeans and t-shirts. That was what made Underlings so easy to spot. We had the most casual, sometimes worn-out clothing. Supes were much smarter, choosing to dress in ways that blended with the higher classes. Rose favored cute skirts and tops. I was way out of my comfort zone in the simple black dress I'd chosen for the evening, but I figured I could suck it up since it was a special occasion.

"Seems like only yesterday we were sitting around, discussing what we wanted to do with our lives, and now..." Rose let out a small squeal of joy, threw her arms wide, and spun in a circle. Her blonde hair fanned out around her like a bright, shiny halo. She looked like she was taking part in a musical and was about to burst into a cheesy song about how we had our whole lives in front of us. "Now we've done it!" She fixed her wide eyes on me again. "I'll be an interplanetary negotiator and travel like I always wanted."

I nodded while trying to fight the lump that formed in my throat.

Hold it together, girl. Everything will be okay.

"I'm happy for you, Rose. And I can't wait to hear about all of your adventures."

She squealed again while jumping up and down in place. "Oh, my God! I can't wait! Can you imagine what guys from other planets are like?"

Imagining was as close as I would ever get to a guy from another planet. Rules for Supes and Underlings were a million miles apart. I would never be allowed to leave Cillion, or even Osh, my city. Ever. The opportunities simply weren't there for me. While in high school, all Underlings were assigned jobs according to societal needs. One position for a whole lifetime. No promotions. No chance to advance. Honestly, I was one of the lucky ones. I'd been assigned to a position in catering, and that meant I'd been allowed two years of college for further education. Many Underlings didn't get that. Those assigned to stores, cleaning, or basic construction jobs, for example, went straight to work from high school. But even with the benefit of college and graduation, it wouldn't help me escape. I was stuck on Cillion while Rose would fly all across the galaxy, and eventually forget I ever existed.

A stabbing sensation pierced at my chest with the reminder and made tears spring to my eyes, which I quickly blinked away.

"I bet they're amazing." I kept my fake smile in place as I grabbed her hands for added effect and squeezed them.

"Maybe I can smuggle one back for you," Rose joked and winked. I chuckled for real this time.

"Maybe."

"Come on." Rose fixed my hair one more time then added, "Let's take a quick selfie, then go and party!"

She reached over to her bed to pick up her phone, then raised it in front of us and pulled me close to her side. I'd left my phone at home since, well, everyone I knew was at the party. What did I need it for? I wasn't a big photo taker. That was all Rose.

Rose and I pouted into the camera, and she took a few snaps.

"Ooh, hashtag hotties!" Rose exclaimed as we looked at the pictures. With another grin in my direction, she linked her arm through mine, her phone still in her other hand.

The music grew louder as we walked out of her room into the large hallway that opened out to a red-carpeted staircase.

We descended the stairs, and the sounds of excited chatter became louder as we walked through the crowded kitchen and outside into the back garden, where the party was happening. It was a warm summer evening as we wound our way through the revelers. The lively pop music pumped through us as we approached the area that had become the designated dance floor. The atmosphere buzzed, and everyone raised their hands to the sky as they sang along to the cheesy lyrics. Everybody was lit up from the glow of the garden lights.

When Rose's friends saw her, they all cheered and greeted her with hugs and kisses. I stepped back slightly and allowed her to have her moment.

God, she looked so happy. I heard snippets of people asking her questions about her plans, and a little more of my joyful façade chipped away with every answer.

Don't get me wrong. I was happy for her. I was thrilled my best friend had taken the first step on her career ladder, but it happened so easily. Her family's position made every-thing so simple for her. She had gone to a better school, had a higher class of education and acquaintances, and she chose her career path. A path that would see her traveling not just all over Cillion, but all over the galaxy.

Me? My future would be a nine-to-five job. Not exactly what I'd wanted for my life, but it would pay the bills. Unfortunately, that was all it would do. The truth was, had I been allowed to attend a school as good as the one Rose had gone to, I would have thrived. I read a lot of books, and I was pretty sure I could have gotten a job similar to Rose's if I had the opportunity.

But what would I get instead?

If I were lucky, maybe I would one day meet a nice fellow Underling man. We would marry and struggle to raise a couple of kids who would grow up to be in the same crappy position I was in.

I was in serious need of a drink.

I wound my way through the crowds and back to the kitchen. I knew Rose wouldn't miss me now since she was still busy telling her friends about her upcoming trip.

People milled about in Rose's trendy silver and black kitchen looking for drinks, while some stood around talking and laughing. I glanced around at the masses of empty cups and bottles strewn on the counters.

The only drinks available were beer from the fridge and a gigantic bowl of some kind of punch that someone could have tampered with. I was a wine girl, but as rich as Rose's family was, there was no way they would let a bunch of college grads nick their finest Merlot. I could rummaged around for my favorite non-alcoholic drink— sparkling water with cranberry juice—but I needed something stronger to get me through the evening. As I reached into the fridge for a cold beer, hands on my waist made me jump and spin around.

"Gotcha!"

My knees buckled slightly when I saw Lyle Simpson

standing in front of me with a wide grin, his hands still on my waist.

"Hey." I tried to control the breathiness in my voice.

Holy fuck was he gorgeous. Tall, thick dark hair I wanted to run my fingers through, and full lips that I longed to kiss. He usually wore super casual t-shirts, but he wore a light blue button-down shirt tonight. My fingers itched to unbutton it for him and slip my hands inside.

Hmm, if this was the Underling I got to marry, maybe life wouldn't be so bad after all.

I had known Lyle for years. We grew up on the same street and went to the same school. Although nothing had ever happened between us, we had gotten closer over the past few months. We studied together and spent more time hanging out once our exams were over. I hoped this party would be the beginning of something. Rose didn't know many of my friends, but she said I could invite some to her party so I wouldn't feel left out and lonely when she talked to other people. She also added I could only bring "respectable" people—I rolled my eyes at that comment. She could be such a snob sometimes. I asked a couple of my classmates to come, but Lyle was the only one I'd seen so far.

I only needed one chance with him, and for him to look at me as more than a friend. This had to be it.

"Where have you been hiding?" I tried to get my crap together, so he didn't think I was acting like an idiot. That was difficult with those big blue eyes watching me and his hands still on my waist.

That's gotta mean something, right?

He shrugged. "I don't know that many people, so I thought I'd stay in here for a while." He jerked his head to indicate a couple of our other school friends. "Ally and Jay kept me company, but I wanted to look for you. I thought you might wanna dance."

The idea of being up close to Lyle made me hot. I was glad I was still standing close to the open fridge to cool me down a little. I was about to tell him I wanted to dance with him when someone dragged me away.

"Kitty Kat!"

I rolled my eyes as I realized who took me away from the man of my dreams. I glanced back at Lyle apologetically, and he laughed. He mouthed, "I'll catch you later," and my heart sank a little as he disappeared out into the garden.

I pinned Keelan with a glare. "Your timing could not be worse."

He laughed as he twirled me around with him. The scent of beer coming from him was subtle, but it was there. He wasn't drunk, though. Keelan Murphy was always like this. Silly, loud, and always in the freaking way. Like Lyle, Keelan and I had been friends—kind of—for a long time. We got along sometimes, but mostly I found him annoying. However, we talked about all kinds of stuff and never wished harm on each other.

"Katarina." Keelan bashed into the dining room table as he spoke, then twirled us into a different room. One where there were fewer people, which was lucky since we must have looked ridiculous. "You look amazing tonight."

He let go of me to rub the back of his leg and winced. I lightly slapped his arm. "We've known each other since we were in diapers. For the love of all the Gods on Cillion, call me Kat. You know I hate my full name. I hate Kitty Kat, too. So, stop it."

Keelan's smirk made me want to slap him again, but I couldn't help laughing after a moment. His shoulder-length blond hair was in disarray from our fast waltz around the house, and his red t-shirt was crumpled. He looked like he had fallen out of a washing machine after a fast spin cycle.

"I'm sorry, but seriously, you have to set your sights somewhere other than Lyle. I'm only trying to save you from getting your heart broken."

My eyes narrowed a little. "Why would I get my heart broken?"

"Because..." Keelan slung his arm around my shoulder. "As beautiful as you are, he isn't into you." I stared at him, waiting for him to elaborate on how he reached that conclusion. "You've seen the girls he's dated. Always blonde. Always curvy and..." he paused and looked me up and down. "That's not you."

Keelan wasn't pointing out anything I didn't already know. I had a slim frame with a kind of straight up and down figure. My curves were extremely minimal, and I hated it. I always was envious of Rose's more womanly physique, especially her D-cup boobs. Mine were barely a B-cup, like two fried eggs on an ironing board.

"What do looks have to do with anything?" My hand went to my hip as I stared Keelan down. "Maybe Lyle might want to try something different for once."

I knew I was wasting my breath. That wasn't to say I thought all guys were shallow. But with Lyle, I was pretty sure appearance was important to him—arm candy to show off to his buddies. While I thought I had a pretty enough face, I wasn't sure I cut it in terms of what he found attractive.

Keelan gave me a soft smile, a kind he'd never given me before. I couldn't quite read it at first, but when he turned to me and placed his hands on my waist, my heart raced, and not in a good way. It was the, *oh my God, please don't kiss me*, kind of way. I didn't have lots of experience in that area, but

I watched a lot of movies. I was sure what was going through his head.

"Erm…" I tried not to appear rude, but I wanted to widen the space between us. "Let's go outside. I need to find Rose."

Disappointment crossed Keelan's features, but he replaced it with another smile. "Okay. I wanted to dance anyway."

I relaxed when he let go of me. As we walked back through the kitchen, I grabbed a bottle of beer and quickly flipped off the lid with the bottle opener that had been left beside the fridge.

Despite Keelan's words, I couldn't help looking around for Lyle on my way back out to the garden. I wanted to prove Keelan wrong. Unfortunately, Lyle was nowhere in sight. There were too many people.

Once we were outside, Keelan left me and dove into the crowd of people dancing and singing. I breathed a sigh of relief.

I still wasn't sure exactly what had happened with him. Maybe he was drunker than I thought because he never looked at me like that before. He never called me beautiful, either. That or Rose had done such an excellent job with my appearance that he suddenly looked at me in a different light. Except, I didn't want Keelan to look at me like that. He was a decent-looking guy, and a nice person, but I didn't have *those* feelings for him. He was more like an irritating brother than someone I wanted to kiss.

Some graduation day, huh? This was supposed to be the start of the rest of my life, and yet, all I could think about was everything I would never have. With a roll of my eyes at my melancholy, I downed half of my beer then headed down toward the drunken masses with my eyes cast downward.

Thud.

I wasn't sure the person I crashed into, or I had been walking fast enough for the kind of impact we had. I stumbled back from it, trying to regain my balance when a hand caught mine and pulled me back upright.

My gaze followed the strong-looking hand up to an equally strong-looking arm, to broad shoulders covered with a dark green shirt. I slowly moved my eyes higher and gasped at the sight that greeted me.

A pair of piercing, golden eyes stared back at me.

Made in the USA
Middletown, DE
01 December 2022